MAYBE I'LL CALL ANNA

Maybe I'll Call Anna

By

William Browning Spencer

THE PERMANENT PRESS
Sag Harbor, New York 11963

This book
is dedicated to
Max Gartenberg

Library of Congress Number: 89-62518

International Standard Book Number: 1-57962-054-X

Library of Congress Cataloging-in-Publication Data

Spencer, William Browning, 1946—
    Maybe I'll Call Anna / William Browning Spencer.
    1. Title
PS3569.P458M39 1990

813'.54—dc20

Manufactured in the United States of America
First paperback edition February 1999

THE PERMANENT PRESS
Noyac Road
Sag Harbor, NY 11963

Part 1

David Livingston

August 1966

1

Garamond was on call for the E.R. that night. He was wearing a green scrub suit, and he hadn't shaved in a couple of days. Garamond was in his late twenties and much taken with his own romantic image: scruffy, world-weary saver of lives. When I came in Garamond was arguing with Invisible Vaughan (thus named because he was never to be found when needed, could walk across crowded rooms without being seen). Vaughan was the resident psychologist, a fastidious man with a naked face, large glasses, and an eerie deadness of manner, as though all the crazies that passed through the emergency room had sucked the vitality from him.

Garamond was shouting, and Vaughan, arms folded, was squinting darkly. "Don't fuck with a Ph.D. in psychology," Vaughan's squint said.

They were arguing about admitting a patient. I didn't want to hear about it, so I went across the hall and cleaned up from the last shift. I put a bunch of hemostats and scalpels in the autoclave. Then I walked into minor surgery.

She was sitting on the gurney, and the plastic tubing from an i.v. dangled next to her. A piece of white adhesive fluttered from the crook of her left arm. She wore a grey dress, the kind of dress that girls wore a lot in the sixties when we were all giving simplicity a run for its money. She smiled at me and said, "Hello." She was incredibly pretty, with clear dark eyes and long brown hair, young

1

and achingly bright.

She seemed composed, her hands folded in her lap, a good child in a folktale.

"Hi," I said.

She smiled. "Are you another doctor?"

"Actually, I'm a brain surgeon," I said. "I moonlight as an orderly though. Brains all day long. You get sick of them, you know? Who needs brains? Give me good looks any day. So how are you doing?"

I couldn't make out what she said at first, because she was looking at the floor, speaking softly, with a faintly flirtatious manner which, I later learned, was simply Anna's manner in the presence of men, a reflex, a physical tic. I had her repeat it.

"OD'ed," she said. She looked up and smiled grandly. "Bad dope. A girl can't be too careful. Doc says I can go but I better be careful. I told him: 'You bet!'"

She jumped off the gurney, a perky jump for an overdose victim. She put on a pair of wooden sandals, then turned and picked up a record album that was lying on the sheet. It was the latest Beatles' album, *Revolver.* Another incongruous touch, but I had come to accept a certain amount of surrealism working in an emergency room. She walked out of the room and down the hall, clutching the record in front of her. I followed her.

Dr. Garamond must have seen her striding purposefully for the lobby. He ran out from behind the admitting desk shouting, "Miss Shockley! Miss Shockley!" He put an arm around her shoulder and steered her back toward minor surgery. I followed. "We are thinking of admitting you," Garamond said.

Anna rolled her eyes toward the ceiling. "Dr. Vaughan said I could go. He said I was fine."

"He's rethought that," Garamond said, smiling painfully. "We think a little time in the hospital, just to sort things out, wouldn't hurt."

One of the nurses hollered for me, and I had to leave. A drunk under the inventive spell of alcohol had managed to cut his hand on an escalator. I got him into a cubicle, washed his hand in PhisoHex, and listened to a gush of invective against someone named Melanie.

2

An intern named Culver came in, sewed the drunk up, and I went to see how Garamond was faring with Anna. He was sitting in minor surgery alone; his hands were on his knees and his head was lowered. He didn't look on top of things.

I walked back to the lobby, pushed the doors open, and walked outside. It was August, a hot, black night. North Carolina had been invaded by a million crane flies, big, leggy insects desperate for human companionship, and I swatted them away and lit a cigarette. Anna, disconnecting from shadows, walked over to me and said, "I don't know what his problem is. Is this hospital so hard up for patients that they gotta take anybody who sneezes in a draft?"

"A drug overdose isn't exactly the common cold," I said.

"You got another one of those cigarettes?"

I handed her a cigarette which she held in her mouth waiting for a light. Thrusting the cigarette toward the flame, she looked a bratty thirteen. She blew smoke and she smiled again, an odd, sly smile. "Larry has always got stuff, drugs, you know. Chemicals are Larry's thing. I'm not a chemical person myself. I was bored and stupid, which happens sometimes. It's not a lifestyle or anything. I don't have to be checked in for observation."

"Who's Larry?"

"This guy I live with."

I didn't like Larry, instantly. Where was he anyway? Anna's taxi arrived and she patted my shoulder as though reassuring me and said, "See you around." I watched her get into the taxi. Then I went back inside.

The E.R. got busy after that. Two teenagers had driven off the road and the car had taken a couple of flops. They looked in worse shape than they were: a couple of broken ribs and some facial cuts that bled the way facial cuts will—with great bravado. I finally had time to look at Anna's admission record.

She'd been brought in by someone named Robert Kalso. The name sounded familiar, but I couldn't place it.

Anna's address was given as 502 Morley Avenue. Her full name was Anna Holmes Shockley and she was eighteen. She had, by her own admission, taken a lot of downers. "Handfuls!" the admissions clerk had quoted, the exclamation point tall with disapproval.

3

Robert Kalso lived at the same residence. He had found her in a groggy, incoherent state. Anna had volunteered the information about the drugs, and Kalso had become worried and driven her to the emergency room. Garamond had pumped her stomach, got the old electrolyte balance back up to snuff, and—grudgingly—set her free with an appointment to see Dr. Coleman, the psychiatrist on call that night. Invisible Vaughan hadn't found any reason to keep her, and Garamond had failed to talk her into voluntarily committing herself. The bird had flown.

I finished reading the report, smoked a cigarette, and wondered who Anna Shockley was and whether or not she had intended to kill herself. I could see her very clearly in my mind; she had a kind of fragility that was disturbing, that immediately sent a ghostly sense of loss echoing through me.

Nothing was going on in the emergency room. It was three in the morning. I went back to the nurses' station and tried to read a paperback novel whose hero was yet another Holden Caulfied clone. I couldn't concentrate. The girl, Anna, had made an impression on me that seemed unwarranted by our brief encounter. I didn't approve of Garamond's concern, which I felt was elicited not by any desire to help a fellow human being but by the wondrous, doomed shout of Anna's beauty. I didn't approve because I felt the same way, and I knew what kind of an altruist I was. I was, in fact, already in love with Anna. I knew nothing about her except that she was pretty. I didn't approve of the way men were treating her.

I didn't approve of Larry's drugged indifference and I didn't approve of Garamond's feverish solicitude.

The girl had put me in a bad mood; somehow her extraordinary beauty had wrenched me out of my routines. I felt faintly queasy, always a sure, lovesick sign.

I went home that morning and sat amid the clutter of the two-room garage apartment that I was renting on a week-to-week basis, and I studied the painting which I had tentatively titled *Presentiment of Rain*, which was beginning to feel all wrong. Finally I settled in to work on the canvas, bringing out some detail in the shadows, working mechanically, unemotionally. I stopped work after two steady hours. I lay down on my cot and slept, a sleep of thin, grey dreams. The telephone rang and I fished the receiver out of the glare and confusion.

"You're mad, Livingston. You can't go on like this; it will finish you. Haven't you had enough of the world's squalor and clamor? Come back to academia, my boy. Come back to the sweet, monastic silences, the late-night arguments on aesthetics, the blonde girls in their colored smocks, reeking faintly of turpentine, so serious, so sweet . . . . "

I hung up. Ray called back, of course, and I told him to come over later on—I looked at my watch—about two. I found that I was awake, however, with no chance of returning to sleep, so I fixed myself some eggs and put a pot of coffee on. An hour later I drove by 502 Morley Avenue because I didn't have anything else to do and I was curious. I was also, I suppose, a romantic, a term I grow less comfortable with as the years go by. Now it seems to suggest schizophrenics fixated on movie stars, but then it was a prouder thing, an acknowledgment of the great strength in dreams, life's infinite possibility.

502 Morley Avenue turned out to be a large white, three-story Victorian house on a corner lot. The grass was in need of mowing; grasshoppers whirred across the lawn. In the driveway a sleek, waxed Mustang, resplendent in sky blue and chrome, looked incongruously peppy in the tall weeds. There was a sign in the yard, handmade, announcing boldly: ROOM FOR RENT! Always a sucker for the declamatory, I went in and rented a room.

I thought I'd just take a look at the room. I had been meaning to move. The room, located at the top of the house, was lit by a skylight. I couldn't believe my good fortune. It was a painter's dream; the light was a bountiful, golden harvest. At that moment, I honestly forgot Anna's presence in the house. I simply marveled at my good fortune. The person who had brought me up the stairs to this perfect studio was a skinny teenager named Hank, shirtless and shoeless, wearing a pair of immense khaki-colored shorts. Hank told me that the owner of the house was Robert Kalso and that I would have to talk to him about renting the room. I said I'd come back later and left. I went back to the garage apartment, getting there just as Ray was pulling up to the curb.

2

"You are getting sicker, Livingston," Ray said. "Quitting college to work in the emergency room of Cameron Hospital is one thing, but renting rooms in the houses of suicidal chicks is another, darker pocket. I worry about you, Livingston. I wish I had more friends, so I wouldn't have to hang out with you. But I just don't know that damned many people. It's a shame."

I went to the refrigerator and got us both another beer. "I haven't actually rented the place yet," I said. "But it's great. The light is perfect."

Ray scowled and gulped beer. Ray had a haggard, wild-assed cowboy look that he cultivated: big ragged mustache, snarled hair. He was a methodical painter of realistic egg temperas, one of the few students at Newburg College whose work I sincerely admired. He was living with a very sweet Oriental girl named Holly. Since I had left the school, Ray and Holly were about the only people I still saw.

"I figure I can move on Thursday," I said. "Will you help?"

Ray looked disgusted. "Sure," he said.

I talked to Robert Kalso later that day on the phone. "My name is David Livingston," I said. "I was in your house today looking at the room for rent. I'm interested in renting it."

"Great," he said. He had a jovial salesman's voice. "You got a job?"

I told him I did and prepared to elaborate, but he interrupted. "Then move on in," he said. "We'll be looking forward to seeing you." He hung up.

3

That's how I came to live in the Villa. One of the vast transient population that passed through Kalso's house had named it the Villa, and the name had stuck. The name appealed to Kalso's quirky sense of humor. "I will meet you back at the Villa," he would say, pulling on imaginary gloves. Robert Kalso always appeared to be engaged in some sort of self-parody, some complicated, private joke.

He was a thin, red-headed homosexual and the son of Albert Kalso, a wealthy, prominent citizen of Newburg. I liked Kalso instantly. He was a professional photographer who took elegant, sepia-toned photographs of reedy girls in white. I was very impressed by these photos, more so, perhaps, because they sold for amazing sums in New York. I assumed Kalso was in his mid-forties, but there was no way of reckoning his age. His role at the Villa was less landlord, more master of ceremonies, renegade scoutmaster. "We are all riffraff here," he would say, drinking a glass of wine. "A threadbare, orphaned lot. But we are a democracy, God love us! We aren't a bunch of heartless, cold-blooded communists!"

Ray brought his pickup around on Thursday and helped me move. The sun seemed almost violent that day, and I was sweating in a pair of cutoff jeans and a t-shirt. Hank, the skinny kid who had shown me the room, came out on the porch with a quiet, round-faced girl named Gretchen. They helped carry stuff up to my room. In passing, I saw several denizens of the house: a pale, bearded kid who lay on the living room floor with earphones on, jiggling to mainlined music; a scowling, beer-bellied blond guy with a mustache; and a pretty girl with short, curly black hair. A variety of unidentifiable noises suggested the presence of teeming masses. This proved to be the case, and I never identified all the residents. I still hadn't met my landlord, who was downtown at his studio.

At noon, we stopped for awhile and Hank and Gretchen sat on the porch with us, smiling and eating bowls of brown rice and vegetables. They were a cheerful, delicate pair, absolutely comfortable in each other's company. Their type seems to have thinned considerably since the sixties when they flourished, roaming the earth in brightly colored flocks, taking vitamins, sharing insights and dope, getting clear, mating with an almost passionless goodwill.

Ray had baloney sandwiches and beer stashed in a cooler. We ate the sandwiches and drank the beer, and Anna came out on the porch and said, "Hi." She didn't seem surprised to see me, and when I told her I had rented the room, she nodded her head. I offered her a beer and she took it. She sat cross-legged on the porch

7

in a pale blue dress and smoked cigarettes and said nothing else. The heat of noonday made silence a fitting, proper response, and I felt a sense of well-being, of having, by some innate cleverness, revitalized my flagging sense of purpose, rededicated myself to Art and Genius.

The blond boy came out on the porch. He wore jeans, cowboy boots, and a vest over a dirty yellow t-shirt. He had a shiny, fleshy face and blue eyes.

"Let's go," he said, and Anna stood up and followed him through the tall grass to the gleaming Mustang. He had opened his door and was about to get in when she said something to him and he stopped. He looked up at us, looked back at Anna. He said something, and I could see Anna react, harden somehow. Larry—for I was sure that's who it was—said something else, and Anna glowered. I studied Larry. He was the kind of guy who had played football in high school, probably gotten a lot of mileage from the sport, had a few privileged years to indulge his arrogance. He had put on weight since then, put on bitterness. This present argument, I guessed, was an old one or a variation of an old one. It had that replay feel to it. Anna stood still, shoulders slightly raised, frowning.

Then, almost casually, Larry's hand shot out and collided with Anna's cheek. She spun backwards, gracefully pirouetting in the hot afternoon. Larry wrenched open the door of the Mustang, jumped inside, gunned the engine into life, and squealed out of the driveway. Anna was quickly on her feet and walking back to the house. I ran across the porch in time to see her face and the red, quarter-sized mark on her cheek. She walked past me and into the house. I didn't follow her.

We got the last of my meager furniture moved into the room and I went out to the pickup truck with Ray to thank him for helping. "You come and see Holly and me," he said. He squinted toward the house. "Anna," he said. He looked at me and shook his head. "This is gonna be a goddam mess, you know that? You have no sense at all, Livingston. Not a lick."

He shook his head again and got in his truck and drove away. I sensed some disgust in my friend, the kind of close-friend disgust that is sincere and unsettling. I figured he must have seen Anna's

8

face when she came back on the porch after being knocked down; he must have seen the smile, so sure, so full of winning. I was a little unsettled myself.

4

"I'd fuck her," Skip said. Skip was the skinny kid I had seen listening to music the day I arrived. He had shiny, putty-colored flesh and a scruffy mottled beard. He nodded his head when he talked, words tumbling out over a yellow, aggressive grin. No one else at the Villa listened to Skip, having learned long ago that Skip never said anything a person would wish to log in his memory. Right now he was talking about Anna, and I was ignoring him, having already determined that he knew nothing about her except that she was pretty.

Skip would pop in on me at any hour of the day. He was, supposedly, attending Newburg College, but I had never seen him crack a book. He considered himself a fellow artist, since he painted surreal canvases of hands reaching through brick walls to fondle nude female buttocks of legendary, wet dream proportions.

"I'd fuck her," Skip repeated. "I'd slide her little panties off and get down on that little honey pot and I would tongue it slowly, ease them white thighs apart ... " I didn't like to imagine Skip having sex with anything human, but I wasn't particularly offended since Skip and Anna in tandem were beyond my imaginative powers. I even liked Skip some. I had an affection for him because he was such a tremendously bad painter.

While he talked, I cleaned off my brushes and thought about Anna, Skip instantly fading into the shadow of that thought.

I had been at the Villa for one week, and I had talked to Anna six times: twice in the living room, twice on the porch, once in the kitchen, and once—briefly, but countable—on the stairs. Anna was always around, generally barefoot in summery shifts or sun-faded jeans, and I could have talked to her more, but I was determined not to let this obsession with a suicidal child make me miserable. So I resolved to avoid her, a resolve which only heightened the sweaty, heart-palpitating nature of the inevitable encounters.

I would often see Anna out on the porch drinking beer and smoking cigarettes (she didn't smoke pot because she said it made her paranoid). She read paperback gothics and odd little books with titles like *The Nature of Divine Laughter*, books written by someone named Father Walker, a local guru and ex-high school teacher who ran a commune just outside of Newburg in the mountains. Hank and Gretchen, those children of light, were true believers in Father Walker and his commune (called simply The Home) and they had seeded the house with little blue, yellow and orange books. The message seemed to take root in Anna, who, I quickly discovered, had a weakness for the exotic and otherworldly. Anna told me about Father Walker's message and his followers who were called Dancers of the Divine Logic or, for the sake of brevity, simply Dancers.

"We each have a Dance," Anna told me. "John Walker teaches how to hear the music of your Dance, how to move to it. He teaches Listening." She must have noted a certain skepticism in my expression, because she frowned and said, "I'm not selling anything. You don't have to believe in anything. Larry doesn't believe in anything, and he's strong that way. I know I'm not strong. I keep believing things."

Larry was often gone on mysterious errands. Anna rarely went with him during the day, although she always accompanied him at night when, I assume, they plunged into the social whirl. During the day she would sit on the porch with a sulky little kitten named Wooster—a gift from Larry—or she would sprawl on the living room sofa listening to records. She was crazy about the Beatles and would sing along to songs like "Help" and "Yesterday" with a small, clear voice that faithfully rendered every inflection.

Anna liked to talk, and would go on cheerfully about reincarnation, astral planes, television shows, movies, books she had read. She didn't talk about herself or about her past, and all I knew about her was that her parents lived in a small town out west and she had bolted (her word) when she was fifteen.

She did tell me one thing which suggested that her past was not a pleasant one. I don't know exactly how the conversation arose, but she said, "That's what Henry always said."

I asked her who Henry was and she told me that he was an

10

uncle. Then, in her breezy fashion, she added, "He started screwing me when I was eleven years old. We'd sneak off to this funky little shed with a mattress that smelled like dog piss. Said he'd kill me if I told anyone." Anna laughed then, surprising me. "I wasn't going to tell anyone. I loved Henry. Old Henry, he was mean, but he was strong, you know. He was a strong old son of a bitch."

As time went by I realized that Anna loved that word: strong. It was her finest compliment.

Anna's relationship with Larry was more complicated than I had hoped. My few encounters with Larry had been unpleasant. He seemed to actively dislike me, and I would have disliked him even if he hadn't been with Anna. Despite his illegal calling, he had a chubby self-righteousness, the air of a TV evangelist doing God's work.

And Anna loved him. They fought constantly, often violently, but they made up just as mercurially. This wasn't a relationship slowly disintegrating. This *was* the relationship, and it satisfied something inside Anna, an addiction to attention that asked only for intensity.

"Yes sir, I'd fuck her," Skip said again, and I put the brushes away and walked down the stairs, leaving Skip to his humid dreams. Wallpaper was peeling in the hallway, hanging in long, kelp-like strips. The Villa was in a state of comfortable decay. I knocked on Kalso's door, but he wasn't in, as I determined by pushing the door and peering inside.

Kalso's room was decorated in the same sepias that characterized his photographs, a pastel island in a house given to the garish styles of the sixties: quivering, primary colors, batik wall hangings, lava lamps and a variety of homemade art.

I wanted to pay Kalso the rent, but I wasn't worried about it if he wasn't. I went outside, into the August sun, and got in my car. I drove over to Romner Psychiatric Institute to have lunch with Diane.

She was waiting for me when I got there, and we drove to a restaurant where a lot of lawyers were eating lunch. We managed to get a table in the back, and Diane told me: "We are all going to

11

hear Saul play at *HaveAnother*'s. I want you to bring your friends Ray and Holly so I can meet them."

"Hey, that's great," I said, although I could have done without seeing Saul.

Diane Larson was the pretty, dark-haired girl I had seen that first day. I had talked to her that same evening when I had come downstairs and found her fixing a sandwich in the kitchen. We discovered that we both worked in hospitals and we were soon talking like old friends, comfortable in each other's presence.

We drank a lot of beer that night and Diane told me about herself. She was a social worker at Romner Psychiatric Institute, had just gotten the job, and was hell-bent to help people. I abandoned the cynicism of youth for the moment in deference to Diane's fierce determination to do good. She was excited about Romner, which was a shiny new psychiatric and neurological facility, a private institution but with a lot of funded money for welfare programs.

Diane had rich parents in Boston, something of an embarrassment to her, and she was tragically, illfatedly, in love with an asshole. Her boyfriend, Saul Weber, lived with her at the Villa. He was an arrogant, swarthy guy who wore headbands and jackets with fringe on them and had a limp desperado mustache and the yellow paranoid eyes of a man who will ingest any chemical substance that will alter his psyche—for better or worse, it makes no difference.

Diane told me about Saul that first night, and when I actually met him the next day, the contrast between Diane's glowing reports and the reality was irreconcilable. For a moment I wondered if there might not be two Sauls, but then I saw the look in Diane's eyes, and I knew, alas, that this was *the* Saul.

I had mentioned Anna that night, too. I had said something noncommittal like, "That Anna's a pretty girl."

Diane had said, "Gorgeous. Stay away from her. She's not well, you know. She has severe emotional problems." I didn't say anything. I suppose I could have said that I met her in a hospital where she had dropped by to have her stomach pumped, but I didn't. I was offended at the suggestion that anything was wrong with Anna.

At the end of that first night, Diane and I were friends. That fast. I suppose we both realized, intuitively, that we weren't destined to be lovers and so could be friends without preamble. Our obsessions were elsewhere.

The lunch wasn't as good as it could have been, because Diane talked about Saul with a blind enthusiasm that cried out for correction, and I had to content myself with nodding my head and eating a stale tuna salad sandwich.

Before dropping her back at work, I had agreed to go to *Have-Another*'s to hear Saul and his band play. I could switch shifts with Leon; he owed me one anyway. Anna was going too, but that wasn't incentive since Larry was also going. I expected an ordeal, but I was doing it for Diane.

The evening fulfilled my worst expectations. And then some.

5

HaveAnother's was the kind of bar that you would start hating just about the time that you were too drunk to successfully leave it. And we were all pretty drunk. Everyone was lurching around with brown paper bags, buying mixers at the bar. Saul's band, called Boilermaker, cranked out one lackluster cover after another, including a horrendous rendition of "I Can't Get No Satisfaction" in which Saul, singing lead, ignored the wry tone for sheer self-pity, sweat flying out of his forehead, eyes bulging as various chemicals hissed in his brain.

The room was thick with smoke, and the dance floor was slippery with beer, kids falling down, kids groping each other, larger groups of kids watching the gropers with envy and disgust. Ray and Holly, at least, seemed to be having a good time, holding hands and smiling. They were always happy together, brazenly so, I thought.

I was about to comment on this thoughtlessness when Skip and Saul and Diane came back to the table. The band was taking a break, and Saul looked like a man who had taken the opportunity to send new chemical messages deep into his cerebral cortex. Diane

13

looked happy but nervous.

Skip sat down next to me and gulped from his beer. "Beer really makes a guy piss," he said. "Tell you this joke, okay? There was this guy and he went into the john at a bar and there was this guy in there pouring a beer down the toilet and the other guy says, 'Hey, what are you doing that for?' and the first guy says, 'Avoiding the middleman!'" Skip laughed and slapped the table. Drinking made his face shinier with the glow of malnutrition. Suddenly he looked up and waved.

Larry and Anna steered over to the table. Anna looked angry and Larry looked pleased with himself, costumed in a silver vest and wearing a cowboy hat. They sat down and Anna said, "I want to go home."

Larry smiled in front of him, a sleepy smile that happened to be directed at me. "Wanting don't make as much noise as farting," he said. Skip, sitting next to me, burst into wet laughter. Larry turned to Anna and added, in a benign and regal tone, "I just got an appointment that I gotta keep, and then we'll go."

"I gotta go now," Anna said. "This place gives me the creeps."

"We ain't leaving now," Larry said. He reached over and caught her wrist. Anna was smoking a cigarette, stuck in the corner of her mouth, eyes squinted away from the smoke. She reached up with her free hand, took the cigarette out of her mouth and blew the smoke up toward the ceiling and said, "Let go of me, Larry."

Larry smiled wider, goggled his eyes in mock terror.

Anna jammed the burning cigarette into the back of Larry's hand, shoving with a vicious little twist. Larry roared, and the table flew up into the air, along with my beer and a number of other glasses and bottles.

Anna was out the door with Larry close behind her, screaming, "You fucking bitch! You fucking bitch!" We all followed them outside.

HaveAnother's was providentially located out in the woods where it wouldn't disturb a more civilized element. There was a lake where drunks could piss at frogs and push each other into the water. There were woods where, in good weather, sudden romances could be instantly consummated. It was a college student's idea of heaven.

Larry ran around shouting Anna's name and the rest of us drank beer and watched Larry. Larry, who wasn't entirely sober himself, slipped on a muddy spot and went down with a curse. When he got back up, he must have decided that enough of his dignity was already gone. He stalked back into the bar. Slowly, in twos and threes, the crowd followed him. I went down to the lake and took a piss and was just zipping up my fly when Anna laughed behind me.

I turned and she said, "I guess I showed that fucker, didn't I? I guess he'll know I'm not joking next time."

I shook my head. "I expect he'll beat you into rubbish the next time he sees you."

Anna sighed. "Yeah. He'll have to do that. The son of a bitch."

I drove Anna home. I went into the kitchen for a beer and Anna went to bed. The Villa was quiet. The folks were still out cavorting, and Kalso was in New York. The only noise was the soft susurration of cockroach feet.

I sat at the kitchen table and drank three beers. I didn't need them. They weren't absolutely necessary. I could have gotten along without them. But they were a comfort.

I heard a car pull up, saw its lights glaze the kitchen window. I recognized the sound of Larry's heavy boots. He came into the kitchen where the unkind light made his face look puffier than usual. He sank down into a kitchen chair with a big sigh.

He pushed his cowboy hat back and looked at me. "Well, pardner, I see you brought the little filly home. I want to thank you for your concern."

I thought Larry might get ugly. I had no idea what I would do if he did, but I wasn't frightened of him. I disliked him too much to fear him, if that makes any sense.

He leaned forward, resting his elbows on the table. "Let me tell you something. You probably think I'm a bastard. Sweet little Anna. Cute little button-nose Anna. Honey-assed Anna with a body that don't quit. You ever fuck a snake?" Larry burst out laughing. His hat actually flew off. His hair was sweated down over his forehead, thinning. He looked older than when I had first seen him.

He stopped laughing. "What I'm trying to tell you is you don't know shit about Anna and me. We belong together. I'm going up there right now, and I'm gonna be just as sweet as syrup. I ain't gonna say a word about tonight's little misunderstanding. I'm just gonna forgive and forget. Girl uses me for an ashtray, what the hell, too many drinks, that's all. I ain't one to hold a grudge. I'm gonna let it go. And you know what?"

I didn't say anything.

"Hey, come on now, ask me what."

"What?"

"Anna ain't gonna be happy till I hit her."

I stood up and started to leave the kitchen. I wasn't interested in Larry and his concern for Anna's welfare.

Larry grabbed my shoulder. He surprised me with a sudden burst of rage. He brought his face up close to mine and spoke in a trembling, hoarse voice. "Listen, you high and mighty motherfucker. I am telling you a truth that could save your life. You come waltzing in here with some notion of rescuing the fairy princess from the dragon. Well, it ain't that way, and if you want to leave with your educated balls intact, don't start that bullshit with Anna. Hell, she'll draw you in. You ain't the first prince charming on a fucking horse. She'll say, 'Oh that sorry Larry done me wrong!' Then she will whack your balls off, buddy. Believe me. She enjoys it."

Larry backed off, shook off the last of the rage. He seemed, suddenly, a little sheepish. "Hell, I'm telling you for your own good."

"I appreciate your concern," I said. I left the kitchen, went up to my room and looked at my latest painting and was struck by its pretentiousness. I wondered why I thought I was an artist and inhaled a great gout of drunken self-pity and fell asleep.

6

Somewhere in November of that year, Newburg got a rare dose of snow and freezing rain and everyone rushed outside, discovered the treacherous properties of ice, and broke something: an arm, a leg, a hip. The emergency room was in turmoil, and I was exhausted by the time I got off work.

I just wanted to sleep, but when I walked into the kitchen I found Anna, crying. She had been crying for some time, obviously. Her nose was running and her eyes were red. She was wearing a pale green terrycloth bathrobe and slippers with big yellow roses blooming on them and she was rocking a kitten in her arms. The kitten was obviously dead, its head pathetically skewed, mouth open. I reached down and tried to take the kitten from her. She looked up and glared at me. I said, "Let me have Wooster, Anna," and her mouth fell open and she moaned. "Woooooooster," and she let me take the kitten from her, following it with dazed eyes as though it were floating toward the moon. I wrapped the kitten in a towel and placed it in a shoebox I found in the hall closet.

I came back to the kitchen and fixed Anna a cup of coffee. Anna brushed her hair out of her face. Her face was blotchy, her lower lip was swollen and her hair was in snarls. While the coffee perked, Anna opened the newspaper and stared at the funnies.

When I put the steamy cup in front of her, she looked up. Her eyes glittered with tears. But when she spoke, her voice was under control. "Do you think cats have souls?" she asked.

"I don't know, Anna."

"You couldn't have a real heaven without cats," she said.

"Maybe not," I said.

"We'll have to bury Wooster. We'll have to read something over him. Something from the Bible, maybe. No, I'm going to read that St. Francis prayer. St. Francis would have liked Wooster."

I agreed that St. Francis and Wooster would have hit it off. I went looking for a shovel and Anna went up to her room to find the poem. We met back in the kitchen and marched outside.

The sun had come out, melting the snow, and Anna stood over the muddy patch near the oak tree as I dug the hole and laid Wooster to rest. Then, in a quavering voice, she read the St. Francis prayer from a wooden plaque. She was wearing a great woolly sweater, jeans, boots, and a blue ski cap for the ceremony, and she looked as young and full of divinity as a choirboy at Easter.

She read the prayer:

"Lord, make me a channel of thy peace—that where

17

there is hatred, I may bring love—that where there
is wrong, I may bring the spirit of forgiveness—that
where there is discord, I may bring harmony—that
where there is error, I may bring truth—that where
there is doubt, I may bring faith—that where there
are shadows, I may bring light—that where there is
sadness, I may bring joy. Lord, grant that I may
seek rather to comfort than to be comforted—to
understand, than to be understood—to love, than to
be loved. For it is by self-forgetting that one finds.
It is by forgiving that one is forgiven. It is by dying
that one awakens to Eternal Life. Amen."

When Anna finished reading the prayer, she turned to me and
said, "I am not going to let that sonofabitch get away with this."
"What?"
"I'm not going to let that fucker kill Wooster and get away with
it. I can take care of myself. He didn't have to go for the kitten. He
threw Wooster across the room. Big bullshit he-man. He killed
Wooster."
"Leave him," I said. I felt dizzy and sick out there in the cold
sunlight. I had had a long night, and I was unprepared for the
sudden irrational rage that engulfed me. I turned and walked back
toward the porch. "You should leave him," I mumbled.
I went inside the house and was halfway up the stairs when
Anna came in through the door and said, "You can't just leave a guy
like Larry. A fucker like that won't just let you leave."
"You don't want to leave," I said.
"How do you know what I want? When did you become such a
fucking expert?"
I continued walking up the stairs. "You're right," I muttered. "I
don't know anything."
"Well, you don't!" she shouted after me.
I went into my room and lay down on my cot and plunged into
sleep. It was late in the afternoon when I awoke and went
downstairs. Anna and Larry were on the sofa in the living room,
locked in a steamy embrace, your basic resolution of a lovers'

quarrel. I wasn't particularly surprised. I felt oddly disoriented, however. I felt that there was something in my life I had to resolve, some mystery I had to unravel. This was urgent business; some profound decision was demanded of me. There was a six-pack of beer in the refrigerator and I carried it back up to my room, sat on the cot and drank the beers.

I didn't go to work that night, but sometime during the evening I left—noting that the sofa was now empty—and walked to a nearby grocery store and bought a couple more six-packs, and even later on that evening, I resolved to leave the Villa entirely, maybe leave the area, go to California. I wasn't sure about California, however, since I remembered Diane calling California "lobotomy country."

Thinking of Diane, I decided to go talk to her, so I got up, carrying the last of the beer, and walked down the hall to her room. It was late, maybe two in the morning, and I woke her up. Saul wasn't around, his band was playing in Charlotte that week. I said, "Hi," and beamed my best smile and Diane wanted to know what the hell I wanted, and, reeling in the hall, I explained about my tentative decision to go to California and what did she think?

"I think you are drunk," she said. "And I don't know if I want to talk to a drunk."

"You are very pretty," I said. Which was true. She had curly black hair and fine, grey intelligent eyes. She was wearing a blue t-shirt and baggy sweatpants and her frown was a sleepy, just-wakened frown, tousled and full of secret dreams. "Very pretty," I repeated.

"Actually, I'm sure I don't want to talk to you right now," she said.

But she let me in and we talked about some things, like Anna, and Diane agreed that maybe I should leave the Villa, which hurt my feelings since that would also mean that I would be leaving Diane, my friend. Diane talked about Saul and how Saul had this problem with being faithful, but Saul was painfully honest, and that helped. Then she talked about Saul's gentle side, his almost lyrical tenderness; fairly disgusting stuff, but I listened. Later on, I asked her to sleep with me, and that's when she threw me out, but that was okay since the erotic overture had been impractical.

I went back to my room and fell asleep with a sense of accomplishment which the morning revealed to be spurious.

7

I stayed at the Villa, and I began to work seriously on my paintings. I didn't know if they were any good or not, but I felt that I was no longer simply intimidated by technical concerns. I had left college to escape what I felt was an academic fussiness, and I was trying to paint with some emotion, with some sense of life.

I worked hard. There is nothing like unrequited love for priming the creative pump, and I finished twenty-two paintings that winter. That was a lot, since I painted in a painstaking manner, layering paint, trying for a kind of translucence that would send the onlooker searching for metaphysical answers—with real hope of finding them. I painted realistic objects and scenes, intent on profound revelation. I was certainly grandiose in my dreams of what art, and mine in particular, could do. I always believed in art's transforming power, and I still do, although I sometimes feel as though I'm worshipping in an empty church.

Anna got in the habit of coming up to my room during the day. She would watch me paint, read her miniature metaphysical books, and doze on the dusty, sheet-covered sofa. She would sometimes leap out of sleep, shivering and scared, lost for the moment. "I'm a magnet for bad dreams," she said. "I draw them into my head." Looking at the winter skies, she would wax philosophical. "I always feel like I'm missing my life," she said one day. "Do you ever get that feeling?"

"Everybody gets that feeling," I said.

"Yeah. Maybe." Anna hugged herself. "I wouldn't mind dying if it would answer questions. But I'm afraid of dying most of the time, because it might be more confusing than living."

Anna thought long, convoluted thoughts, and, lying on the sofa, she would speak them at the rafters. I didn't know what she believed, and what she didn't believe, what she was merely trying out, launching into speech.

"I like your paintings," she said. "But they are sad paintings."

"Sad?"

"Well, maybe not sad. They just aren't hopeful. There aren't any people in your paintings, you know."

"There are enough people in the world. No need to fabricate more people."

Anna stood up and walked to a painting of the suburbs, houses with pink roofs that rose like the backs of dinosaurs foundering in a murky twilight tar pit.

"This is my favorite," she said. "It makes my mind fly."

"I'd like to give it to you," I said.

"David! Really?"

"Sure."

She hugged me.

"It's a wonderful present," she said. She was genuinely excited, and she took the painting and ran out of the room. Later she came back and had me come downstairs to look at where she had hung it over her dresser.

Larry's gonna love that, I thought, smiling around the cluttered room.

Ray wanted me to enter a juried show in Charlotte, and I let him submit some slides of a few paintings, but I wasn't enthusiastic about the proposition. In any event, the slides impressed no one, and they were returned with a polite letter of rejection. I wasn't surprised. My paintings didn't photograph well; they turned muddy and dowdy. My favorite aunt, Helen, was the same way. A beautiful woman, but put her in front of the camera and you would capture a stocky, sullen female with a formidable jaw, squinting into the sun in a rage. My father, on the other hand, photographed beautifully. The camera failed to reveal his self-serving soul.

Christmas came, and I got a Christmas card from my father with a check for five hundred dollars. I gave Anna a little necklace with a scrimshaw pendant. She was delighted and the next day gave me a present, the collected works of Father Walker, spiritual leader of the Dancers of Divine Logic. I expressed delight, and *was* delighted—Anna had given me a present.

I rarely saw my landlord, often going weeks without catching more than a glimpse of him. I would leave the rent check under his door on the first of the month, and he would cash it in a week or two. Then, two days after Christmas, when I was experiencing the usual holiday isolation blues, Robert Kalso visited my room. It was around four in the afternoon and Kalso was wearing an olive drab army jacket and blue, billowing pajama bottoms. His feet were bare and he was holding a bottle of wine.

"If you are busy, say so," he began. "Throw me out. If the muse is wearing her slinkies and breathing heavy, heave me out. I am an artist myself, and I understand that you can't drop the muse when her blood is up and expect to find her waiting patiently under the covers when you come back. So say the word and I'll leave."

I assured him that I was finished painting. He produced two wine glasses and poured us each a glass of wine. "Ostensibly, I'm here to invite you to the Villa's New Year's party. Actually, as a resident of the Villa, you don't need this invitation, but I know your type, pathologically sensitive, and you might not venture out of your room if you thought for a moment you weren't invited. It will be a costume party, but you needn't costume yourself if you are not so inclined. I have proclaimed it a costume party because some of my friends, alas, are always in costume, and this way they are less apt to look out of place. Anyway, I hope it will be fun, and I would like you to come if you can."

I told him I would be delighted to come if I were not working, but that the hospital would probably require my services that night.

"In any event," Kalso continued, "I've actually come to look at your paintings. The invitation was a transparent excuse for gaining entrance. I have known, of course, that you painted, but I confess I didn't have much curiosity about that. Frankly, I suspected that you might be another unfortunate fan of Dali's, like poor Skip, a sort of Grandma Moses on drugs. But you gave Anna a painting, and she showed it to me, and . . . " Kalso shrugged. "I thought I would like to see some other work by you. Do you mind?"

He was already up and prowling around the canvases in his bare feet and ballooning pants, evoking images of Charlie Chaplin in a highbrow skit, and I did mind, but I didn't tell him so. He took a long time looking at them, saying nothing, which I found yet more irritating as I began to imagine some comment being formulated, some summing up of my winter's work that, complimentary or derogatory, would be monstrously off-base and condescending. But when he returned to his chair, he only nodded and said, "You are a serious painter. Do you have an agent?" I told him I didn't. He nodded his head and poured another glass of wine for each of us. "It is almost impossible to make a living as a fine artist," he said, and I felt I was about to hear a lecture I had heard before, but he continued, "but I believe you can do it. You have genius and you have luck."

I raised my eyebrows. I wasn't taking exception with the genius, just the luck. Kalso, to his credit, recognized the gesture for what it was and nodded his head violently. "Yes, luck. You've met me. I'm going to be your agent."

As it turned out, I didn't have to work on New Year's Eve, having worked Christmas Eve and Christmas Day. I didn't think about the party until I heard it in full roar, and I didn't feel much like celebrating, so I stayed in my room doing some rough sketches for a large canvas, an abandoned warehouse that I had photographed earlier in the year. The photos were undramatic, but they helped remind me of the day, what the light had been doing, a certain ominous, alien feel, and I was trying to draw that and failing. Anna came into the room and sat down.

"Who are you supposed to be?" I asked.

Anna laughed. "Dracula," she said. "What do you think?" She was wearing a top hat and a black cape and her face was covered with pancake makeup. Her lips were bright red and two Halloween wax incisors increased a slight overbite. She stood up, turned around and sat down on the sofa again. "Well?"

"That's not who I would have guessed."

"Who would you have guessed? No, forget it."

"I would have guessed Bugs Bunny as a funeral director."

Anna laughed and I joined her, feeling suddenly light-hearted and witty. I could never avoid the echo effect of Anna's laughter; it always resonated within me even when there was nothing to laugh about. She was a virulent infection, in her brightness and in her darkness.

"There's too many people downstairs," Anna said. "And some of them are real weird. New York fags. Creepy stuff."

"'Creepy stuff?' says Dracula?" I asked, goggling my eyes. "Pot calling the kettle creepy."

Anna slid off the sofa and onto the floor. "Are you happy, David?"

"Huh?"

"Are you happy?"

"I love you and I ain't got you," I said. "You belong to an underworld drug magnate. Of course I'm not happy, under the circumstances."

I was seeing more of Anna by then, and my declarations of love, having met with derision, had evolved into clownish, self-depre-cating set-pieces. I wasn't happy with that evolution; it seemed to settle passion's hash for all time, but at least there was warmth between us now, friendship. I didn't want to be her friend. I wanted to be her lover, and sometimes I would go into sulks when she was around. In Anna's presence, I was capable of mood swings to match her own.

"No, really," Anna repeated, "are you happy?"

"Come away with me and I will be happy."

"Maybe I will," Anna said. "If that's all it would take to make you happy. You're sweet, you know."

I decided to kiss her then. New Year's brings out a horror of oblivion in me, with its terrible retrospective. She let me. She touched my cheek with her hand, and then she stood up and said, "I've got to go now. But everything will work out, you'll see."

I didn't know what she was talking about, but I doubted that anything would work out. Later on that night, I ventured down to the party. Kalso was dressed as a circus ringmaster, and he winked at me as I passed him. The house was jammed with people, most of whom I didn't know. I saw Diane, perched beside her man, who was supposed to be a sultan or something and who was leaning over a waterpipe making obscene sucking noises. Anna and Larry were engaged in a loud shouting match out back, their cloudy breath exploding over them. I could see Anna had had too much to drink—

we all had too much to drink that winter—and she was staggering slightly. She turned and ran off toward the woods that bordered the Villa in the back, running with a ragged windmilling of arms, and Larry chased after her into the cold, brittle black of 1967. I snatched the better part of a bottle of Gilbey's gin from an end table—with no remorse for the man whose hangover would be lessened by its theft—and went back upstairs to engage in some serious self-pity.

8

Somewhere around the middle of January, I met a pretty, extremely healthy girl named Samantha at a party Ray and Holly threw. Sam was one of those women doomed to find and nurture men at their most maudlin and self-involved. She found me, and she moved in with me, and she moved out again in the spring. I would like to do her justice; she was a wonderful person. I just can't remember that much about her. I do remember that she sang plaintive folk songs of the incest and murder variety while accompanying herself with the ukulele. It wasn't as bad as you might think. And she wrote poetry. And she seemed to live solely on brown rice and a kind of cardboard sold in health food stores, part of a religion which I never got straight although she explained it several times. I should remember some intimate and magical things, but I don't.

I remember that Anna glowered at me during this period. Anna didn't like Sam and was openly rude to her. Anna felt deprived of my company and it pissed her off.

"She's not your type," Anna told me when she got me alone.

Sam and I lasted until the middle of May, and I think that was a good time in my life, a peaceful time.

I was pleased with myself. I liked to think I was free of Anna. I wasn't, and when Sam left, leaving me with a poem of bittersweet farewell that began, "From yearning for night to dreaming of dawn, even lovers arrive at goodby," it wasn't long before Anna was once again ruling my moods.

Then, one morning in June around ten o'clock, Anna woke me up. "I need your help," she said. She was upset, shaky. Could I drive her downtown? I said I could. I had gotten around forty-five minutes of sleep, but Anna's genuine need brought me awake, alert.

As soon as we were in the car, Anna's sense of urgency evaporated. She leaned back, popped open a can of beer, and smiled at what was, certainly, a fine spring day. "You are a good friend," she said.

"Fine," I said. "What was the emergency?"

"I'm glad you got rid of Joan. I didn't trust her. She was too heavy, you know." Anna delighted in calling Sam Joan (short for Joan Baez). I had never found it particularly funny.

"I didn't get rid of her," I said. "She left."

"Hey, don't get all hot about it. She left—like the dinosaurs when they detected a chill in the air." Anna laughed wildly. She was delighted with the analogy. I, on the other hand, was growing more disenchanted with the whole adventure.

"Where are we going?"

"Hey, come on. Don't get all sulky."

I drove in silence. She leaned over and kissed my ear. "Here," she shouted. "Pull over here."

Following Anna's directions, I had brought us to the seedier side of Newburg, a land of scruffy dogs, trailer parks, and shedlike bars with neon signs advertising beer.

I pulled to the curb in front of a small brown house with tall, yellow grass and bald patches of dirt in the yard. This was balmy June, and everything was green, all the bright, hopeful shades of spring, but this lot was anticipating August, already burnt-out and weary. A skinny girl with lifeless brown hair and acne stood on the porch, regarding us with suspicion. She went inside the house without saying anything.

"It's okay," Anna said, and her reassurance awakened the first real spark of fear. *What's okay?* A grey dog with sharp, rat-like features came around the side of the house and growled at us. Anna went up and knocked on the door.

The door was opened by a big, bearded guy. He had one of those immense, Southern stomachs, belligerent stomachs, and meaty arms covered with curly black hair. "Hey little girl," he said, and he smiled at Anna. "Who's your friend?" And he glared at me.

"This is David," said Anna. "He's okay. This is Grant, David." Grant stared at me and I smiled. "Hi," I said.

"Come on in." He stepped out of the way, and we walked into a room only slightly larger than Grant. It contained the skinny girl and a child in diapers. The child was chewing on a candy wrapper. The candy, something chocolate, liberally bathed her pasty body.

I sat down on a sofa surrounded by trash. Someone had got to the sofa, and slashed the tweedy brown fabric with a knife. A yellow, desiccated sponge stuff leaked from the arms. "This is Loraine," Anna said, introducing the girl. I nodded and smiled. I don't think I said anything. I was still having trouble with the trash. I couldn't imagine such an accumulation of McDonald's sacks, Kentucky Fried Chicken buckets, crushed beer cans and empty soda bottles occurring by accident. There was something theatrical about the squalor—as if I were in some skit about garbage. The girl was watching a game show on a small TV, and she turned to me and said, "I don't know how they do it. I don't know how they can know all those things. I said to Grant, 'It's fixed.' What do you think?"

I said I didn't know, and she nodded and looked triumphantly at Grant, as though I had sided with her. He glared at me, sensing a troublemaker.

Anna reached into her purse and began hauling out plastic vials of pills—blue pills, steely black pills, two-tone pastel pills. Grant knelt down and began picking up the pills, opening bottles, pouring the treasure in his broad hands. He smiled piratically.

Fear, which had been rising in a black tide, gave way to quiet rage. *Goddam you Anna!* I thought.

I seethed while the transaction was completed. I turned to the TV, trying to disassociate myself from the proceedings, and watched a fat woman study the relative whiteness of two blouses.

Grant had his drugs, and now he felt that some primitive social amenities should be observed. I declined a beer and watched Anna accept one and drink it and flirt with Grant.

"You're mad at me," Anna said when we were back in the car and driving away.

27

"Good guess," I said. I didn't want to talk about it. I was experiencing self-loathing of heroic proportions.

Anna sighed, the exhalation of a human being much maligned and misunderstood. "You aren't even going to ask me why this was such an emergency, are you?"

"No."

"I had to have the money. Larry is getting weirder all the time, and I need some money of my own."

"Sure."

"You don't know how bad things have been going. You haven't been noticing anything lately. Joan moved in, and that was it. Fuck the rest of the world."

"It's Sam, Anna. Not Joan. And you're not the rest of the world; you are just one spoiled girl, one small, selfish, crazy person."

"You don't have to get so goddam angry. It's amazing, really amazing to me how you can make a big deal out of everything. I mean, everything has got to mean something, right or wrong. You are touchy, is what you are, and I never know when you are going to get angry. I can't help it the way things are. I'm sorry it was such a fucking imposition. I won't ask for any favors anymore."

"No, don't," I said. I drove back to the Villa, and we both got out of the car without saying anything—Anna had now settled into her martyr's role—and I went up to my room to discover that four of my paintings, including the largest canvas, were missing. I found a note from Kalso saying he had taken the paintings to New York, but I felt too beat down and traumatized to seek revenge for this incredible presumption. Instead, I called Ray up and asked him if I could move in with him and Holly for a couple of days. He said that would be fine. I threw a few things in the car and drove away. I didn't see Anna when I left, which was good. I felt rotten—but oddly relieved.

9

I only stayed with Ray and Holly a few days, just long enough for Ray to sit me down and give me a lecture. "The thing is, Livingston, you ain't interested in real relationships, that's the thing. I don't know where that comes from, maybe your mother being put in that asylum. I know you feel she was taken away from you by a bunch of tight-assed relatives. I've heard your side of it, although your old man strikes me as a decent enough guy. I still think you ought to talk to a shrink about that stuff. Anyway, you're afraid of intimacy. So you get these relationships that aren't relationships at all; they are doomed fantasies."

I protested. Ray continued, "Yeah. What about Melissa? Another hysterical girl, and a murderous psychopath to boot."

"That's something of an exaggeration," I said.

"What about that time she tried to set you on fire when you were sleeping on the sofa? That goddam sofa reeked of lighter fluid."

Ray, like any good friend, had a keen memory for the telling detail.

"Melissa was volatile," I allowed.

Ray sighed. "Relationships are hard, but you have to have them with real people. You can't fixate on some lovely—and I'll admit you have an eye for authentic beauties—and ignore the person."

"I'm not," I said. "You're making me sound like a shallow guy, Ray. You aren't doing me justice."

Ray sighed again and went into the kitchen for another beer. He hollered back to me. "You ain't shallow. You are deep, my boy. Deeply sick and, as your friend, it is my duty to point that out. You are sicker than a dog full of dirt."

"I'd marry Holly in a second," I said. "I'd do that."

Holly came into the room on that note. "No such thing," she said. She smiled her perfect, Far East smile. "You don't settle down. You too quick for me."

I didn't feel quick (or fast, which may have been a sharper translation of Holly's thought). It was true that in college I had pursued several young women passionately, and I had been mistaken in my affections. But I was seeking true love, an eternal verity.

To a casual observer, it might have looked like a number of brief liaisons, but it was no such thing. It was a quest.

I was in love with Anna. My leaving had resolved nothing, and I worried about her; yearned for her. I would encounter her in my dreams in situations of dire peril. She would be hanging from the edge of a cliff, and I would arrive just in time to watch her plummet to an angry sea. Or I would catch a glimpse of her terrified face in the upstairs window of a burning house just before the whole tremulous structure crashed in flames.

I moved into another garage apartment and began painting full time, thanks to Kalso, who had miraculously managed to sell several of my paintings. I quit Cameron's emergency room the day after Kalso handed me a check for twenty-seven hundred dollars, payment for two of my paintings minus a modest ten percent. Since then, Kalso had sold several more paintings. My expenses were few. I declared myself a professional and bid goodby to the world of sick and injured people, who, in any event, I had come to regard as querulous bullies.

At one or two in the morning, the phone would ring. It would be Anna, awake, frightened of the night. Sometimes she would be wound up, talking a mile a minute. Sometimes she would be drunk, incoherent.

Anna talked about anything, everything. Anna talked about Father Walker and The Home. She had been out to the commune with Hank and Gretchen, and it had made a great impression. Father Walker was a strong man (her famous compliment again) and the Dancers were truly enlightened folk. She understood my reservations. A lot of religions were just bullshit. She told me that when she was thirteen she had attended a Sunday school class where the teacher had demonstrated the miracles of the Bible with card tricks. Anna had seen the teacher palm an ace, and the fraud had shaken her faith in Christianity.

"But I've got to believe something," Anna said. "It's my nature to believe things. Women are more like that than men, you know. We have to keep going on, so we are born to believe."

"I miss you, Anna," I said.

Anna said that her relationship with Larry was degenerating. That is what she said, and I was sure she was telling the truth. But degeneration seemed to be the relationship's fuel, a compost of the spirit in which they both thrived, and I didn't see the two of them breaking up in the near future. Anna hinted that she and Larry might split up, but such hints were, I think, a kind of payment in hope, something to sustain me while I listened to Anna's far-wandering, late-night chatter.

She didn't realize that she didn't have to lure me on with promises, that her late-night ramblings filled me with longing. I was, indeed, sicker than a dog full of dirt, stupefied with desire. Anna seemed terribly vulnerable, and her excitement and laughter, the by-products of alcoholic euphoria, made the circumstances of her life seem more appalling, more fatally set on a tragic course.

"Larry's getting weird," she would whisper (Anna liked to whisper her revelations; a whisper was her dramatic italics). She told how she had gone into the bathroom one day to find Larry sitting in the bathtub in water up to his armpits with a .38 revolver in his hand. Another time, she had found him in the closet.

"He was on something heavy, some kind of speed," Anna said. "He was all squeezed up, hugging himself, and it gave me the creeps. I mean, Larry is a big guy, but he looked small and dead. His eyes were tight closed, and his knees were pulled up to his chin, and he said, 'Close the door' in this dead voice, without opening his eyes or moving at all. It was fucking creepy, I tell you."

It sounded creepy. But I knew that Anna didn't intend to leave him. Indeed, she told her "creepy" Larry stories with real relish, delighting in them, anecdotes to cherish.

Diane dropped by to tell me that she and Saul were splitting up. Good for you, I told her. She came by two weeks later and said that she and Saul were back together again. Good for you, I told her. A friend should be supportive. I asked her how Anna was and Diane said, "Noisy. She and Larry are pretty noisy. I think you should stay clear of Anna. I don't like living in that house. I keep telling Saul we should move, but he doesn't want to move, says the rent is too good a deal."

"Saul wouldn't move," I said. "He loves Larry like a brother. Like a car loves gasoline. Like a cigarette loves a match. Like a swimming pool loves water. Like—"

"Okay, I get the point," Diane said. "Saul isn't doing the harder stuff anymore, you know."

"No, I didn't know that. What do you mean? He's not doing anything explosive, is that what you mean?"

Saul's drugging really wasn't a good subject to rib Diane on. She was a straight arrow herself—drank a few beers on the weekend and that was it—and she hated Saul's chemicals. But she blindly loved the guy, was desperate to absolve him from all wrong. Loving Saul was a formidable task, and I should have been charitable. I knew a thing or two about obsessions.

"I hate Larry," she volunteered.

"Me too," I said. "He's a hateable kind of guy."

Diane changed the subject. She talked about working at Romner Psychiatric. Some of the glow had worn off the job. Her good intentions had collided with apathetic fellow workers, schizophrenic young men who couldn't hold jobs, middle-aged women who thought they were Joan of Arc, the chronically depressed and the irreparably damaged. Because Diane was who she was—a serious, solid citizen possessed of an almost mystical well-meaning (call it decency for lack of a better word)—she got things accomplished in spite of the obstacles. She praised one fellow worker, a new staff member, Dr. Richard Parrish, for his dedication and attention to individual patients.

"Romner would be a tremendous hospital if it had more doctors like Dr. Parrish," she said.

I envied Dr. Parrish. Aside from Saul, who had slipped through on Diane's blind side, her approval was hard won. While I knew that Diane liked me, even loved me as a friend, I was also aware that she thought of me as a fairly frivolous specimen, someone inclined to loll in the sun with the radio turned up loud to drown the pained cries of importunate humanity.

There was some truth there. I was prepared to envy Dr. Parrish but not to emulate him. My social conscience wasn't large.

When Diane left, she turned and hugged me. "I like this place," she said. "It's healthier here; you're healthier. You can lead your own life here." I didn't like the assumption that I was leading someone else's elsewhere. I thought I had done a fairly good job of being my own person while at the Villa—despite Anna's powerful gravitational field.

After Diane's exit, I thought about the irritation her last words had inspired. I wasn't happy with her glib conviction that life away from Anna was better. It wasn't. I was lonely and I missed the Villa. I missed Anna. Diane could say I was well out of it, but she was still there. What did she know about being out of it? I was in exile.

I felt like an exile when I ate lunch with Kalso. The busy world seemed just off stage. He talked about New York. I was going to have to go to New York soon, he said. There were people I had to talk to. He had been telling them that I was a misanthropic dwarf who lived in a hovel, but that happy fiction would have to be destroyed in the near future. I didn't want to go to New York.

I felt like an exile when I met Skip in the Safeway. He had his arms filled with frozen pizzas, the staple of his life, and he walked outside with me into the heat.

"I flunked out of school," he told me with disbelief. "I can't believe it. The cocksuckers could have given me some warning. Instead—blam! My folks say no more money, and I've got to get a job, but I can't see myself working. I mean, I tried to squint up my eyes and maybe picture myself in a McDonald's hat or something, but I couldn't do it. Fucking work! Look, maybe you could talk to Kalso about selling some of my paintings in New York. I mentioned it to him, but he seemed preoccupied or something. I know he got you a good deal, and I was hoping maybe he could do the same for me."

I mumbled something about not seeing much of Kalso myself, and I left Skip standing there in his undershirt and ratty, threadbare jeans, looking dumfounded, a child hexed by evil magicians, turned tall and skinny, bearded and orphaned in an instant, his tricycle stolen, stranded in adult town.

Me too. I missed the Villa. Even Skip.

10

In the middle of July, on a day of terrible loveliness, Hank and Gretchen drove Anna and me out to The Home. It was Father John Walker's birthday, and therefore a big occasion. Anna was excited, more animated than I had seen her in weeks, so I went along, although I didn't relish the prospect of hundreds of people high on the spiritual emanations of an ex-high school teacher and practicing guru whose message (which I had gleaned from the books Anna had given me for Christmas) was, essentially, this: Everything's okay.

Walker had originally belonged to Eckankar, another group of astral traveling mystics, but he had had a revelation and started his own group. Cynic that I am, I have always assumed that the revelation went like this: "Astral plane business is a sweet deal. Maps to nirvana are selling like cheap dope at a Grateful Dead concert. Where can I pitch *my* tent?"

Anyway, the drive out of town to the farm where Walker and his followers lived was lovely. We drove through green, rolling hills. Yellow and white wildflowers made a shimmering pilgrimage across open meadows toward the promise of blue, benign mountains. Anna's brown eyes caught every gleam of lake, every majestic, rolling cloud. She was wearing a blue denim shirt and tan shorts. She was laughing and sun-washed, touching my arm as she talked, her words racing along, flirting. We sat in the back of the old Dodge while Hank drove, Gretchen at his side.

We lifted beers from the cooler at our feet.

"That Walker is no fool," I said. "Just getting to his place sets you up for some sort of spiritual enlightenment, a divine knockout punch."

Hank and Gretchen knew I was a doubter, and they were untroubled by my cynicism. I was standing in my own shadow, as far as they were concerned, and they would smile with the sweet tolerance of the saved, hoping I would come around. We drove over a bridge and I looked down at the wild, scrappy Yurman River, heaving and jumping, water in a hurry.

We turned onto a dirt road and rumbled along for several miles before turning onto a yet smaller road. Gravel pinged against the car as we bounced through a tunnel of trees and dusty shrubs. Then we lurched out into full sun again and stopped at a wooden gate where two teenagers with long hair and radiant countenances waved us on.

We parked the car in a field that had been roped off for that purpose and walked up to a big white farmhouse where Hank and

34

Gretchen and Anna began hugging people and were hugged in return. No one hugged me. I expect my aura shone with too cold a light. We all trooped down to a field and sat down on blankets in front of a wooden stage platform with a mike, a snaky tangle of electrical cords, and two monolithic grey p.a. speakers.

The afternoon continued to exhibit beautiful weather. Larger, whiter clouds rolled across a bluer sky. Various laid-back types got up on the stage. Most of the people were young. They talked of love and light. They sang folk songs and little homemade songs about joy, and the crowd sang with them. There were soft-voiced testimonials to The Home, to being lost and then discovered in the great, warm compass of God's care. Occasionally the speeches would grow too diffuse for me, the karmic references too obscure, and my mind would float off, but I wasn't overly irritated. I looked at Anna, and saw her face glowing with true-believer zeal as she leaned forward, hands flat on the ground.

Finally, the big moment arrived, and John Walker came on stage. I don't know what I had been expecting. He was a short, stocky man with close-cut hair. He was wearing a blue, short-sleeve shirt and white slacks, and his face had a scrubbed, affable shine, big smiling, faintly evangelistic. He began speaking quickly in a quiet voice. He thanked us all for coming, made a joke about the press being in attendance, said that he had promised he wouldn't perform any miracles that might embarrass a journalist—that got a laugh—and launched into a discussion of love that was an odd combination of pop psychology, down-home preaching, and mystical paradox.

He seemed a sincere, articulate man. I felt no vital urge to abandon my old life and come live on the commune. I found myself watching Anna. She was obviously much impressed. I had never seen her so excited. After the meeting, she went off with Hank and Gretchen, and I would catch glimpses of her in the distance talking to one group or another. I looked over once and saw that she was talking to John Walker himself, who was surrounded by a smiling entourage, a chosen group whose faces glowed with privilege.

When I looked again, Walker was gone and Anna was returning across the field, wending her way through blankets, attracting the

35

frank stares of young men.

On the drive back the sun sent out thick golden, last-call light, granting to trees and farmhouses and rusting cars a shimmering, triumphant reality. The light fell across Anna's enraptured face as she talked and laughed, and I knew that I was bereft of will in her presence, that the best I could hope for was some luck in keeping the extent of my powerlessness a secret from her.

It was dark when we pulled into the driveway at the Villa. I walked Anna to the door, and I turned and started toward my own car which was parked across the street.

"Hey!" Anna shouted, and she ran to me. "I don't feel like dealing with Larry. It's been too good a day, and I don't want to spoil it. We could drive around or something, what do you think?"

I said I thought that was a good idea.

I got some more beer at a 7-Eleven and we drove over to the ruins of the Sully Amusement Center, a failed shot at a highbrow Disneyland. Ralph Sully, a local entrepreneur, had felt that the world needed culturally uplifting amusement parks, so he had created one based on classical myths. The avid pleasure-seeker could ride the Ulysses roller coaster or cross the river Lethe in a paddle boat. The idea was to educate while entertaining. It was an idea that only attracted vandals. The park fell into almost instant disrepair, then burst into flames in the middle of its first summer, sinking into weedy, vine-snuggled abandonment. Now it seemed truer in spirit to the long-ago myths, filled with mysterious shapes, cyclopean corpses.

We sat in the shadowy moonglow in a ruined pavilion where the last of large, vandalized wooden pigs—remember Circe?—rooted, and Anna, sitting astride a blue boar, talked about Walker. The pale moonlight seemed to cover her with milky light, and I felt enchanted, fortunate.

"You think he's a phony, don't you?" she said. "Yeah, well, Larry does too. What you guys don't understand is that you are just reacting to what Walker calls 'soul disappointment.' He says that lots of times really spiritual people go for drugs and alcohol because they have quarreled with God. When Walker told me that, it explained a lot, because Larry is always angry. It's because he's fighting God. Probably, in a different reincarnation, he was close to God. Maybe Larry wanted something, wanted it too hard, and they fought over it. Walker says ... "

Anna talked about battles in the astral plane, the ways of God, and the ways of Larry in particular. Then she was talking about her parents, although I'm not sure what the transition was, some thought that careened her off into childhood.

She got surprisingly vehement, remembering. "Dad was this skinny, mean guy who was always after us kids to get Jesus. Dad was someone to duck. He was mostly sick. I remember him in bed, sitting up in his undershirt, coughing and smoking cigarettes and telling me what I couldn't do. 'Don't go talking to none of the Joneses,' he would say. 'They's trash.'

"He was a man with a lot of don'ts. Don't go playing with the cats, they was likely rabid. Don't go takin' too many baths, cause it's a sin. Don't watch television cause they can control your thoughts with the TV waves."

Anna frowned, still sitting on the wooden pig, and threw her empty beer can into the bushes. "That ignorant old man. He would have killed me with his ignorance if he could have. He hated the way I took to school. Ma, she was born to suffer, so she married a man who suited her. But I couldn't stand it. I've got three brothers and two sisters, and, to this day, there's not one of them can read. One's a preacher, too, makes a virtue out of not knowing the alphabet, gets that congregation nodding its head, amening away at the sin of reading."

Anna laughed, slid suddenly off her perch, and hugged me. "You're messing with trash," Anna said. She kissed me, taking me by surprise, her hot tongue pushing against my teeth, her arms encircling my neck.

I held her in the cooling night and kissed her hard in return, knowing that it was something other than me that inspired this physical exuberance.

We rolled around on the ground, picking up little pieces of twig and rotting leaf. I unbuttoned her shirt, willed it to disappear amid disorienting kisses and the incredulity that always accompanies sex. The whiteness of her naked flesh awoke me to my surroundings, and I muttered something about going to my apartment.

"Your apartment?" Anna said. "Oh, I know your kind. Gonna show me some paintings, I bet." Anna reached forward and deftly unzipped my fly. She took my hardness in her hands, ran a bawdy tongue over the shaft. "I ain't that kind of girl," she said, "to be eyeballing a bunch of paintings in a strange man's apartment." We sank down into the tall grass, Anna growling in my lap, all giggles and voluptuousness.

"You are all right, David," Anna said, as we lay naked, pebbled with mosquito bites, sweaty and sticky with bits of grass and sand.

We were still coupled, loosely, and although I was physically spent, the uncanny nakedness of Anna, the flare of her hips, the swell of her fine breasts, made me want to keep the moment forever, shelter it from time.

"I love you," I said, looking as far into her eyes as my soul could carry me.

"I love you too."

I took Anna back to my apartment. It was understood that she was leaving Larry, that our lovemaking had consummated that decision.

That's how I understood it.

I awoke to the steady blare of a car horn. We had made love again in the room, revived by showers and the luxury of sheets, then fallen into righteous sleep. Now the bed was empty, and Anna stood with her back to me, looking out the window. I got up and crossed the room as the car horn persisted, filling the night. I touched Anna's shoulder, the rough fabric of her shirt. She stiffened slightly. "That motherfucker," she said.

I looked down at the gleaming Mustang under the street light. Larry was staring up at the window, honking the horn. He was smiling and thumping the horn like it was a broken thing.

"Come back to bed," I said. "The neighbors and the cops won't let him honk that horn all night."

I touched Anna's arm and she jerked away. "That son of a bitch," she said. "Who does he think he is? Does he think he fucking owns me?"

"Come back to bed," I repeated, feeling a smallness in my voice, a scratchy late-night noise of defeat. I realized that Anna was dressed, that she wasn't coming back to bed. She turned away from the window and marched to the door.

"I'll be back," she said, and she was out the door, and I heard her tennis shoes thump down the wooden stairs. I waited. Perversely, I didn't go to the window. It was three in the morning. Then it was three fifteen, the long minutes filled with seam-splitting silence. Every now and then the silence would jump with the slam of a car door. Then the Mustang squealed away. I waited another fifteen minutes, and then I got up and looked out the window at the empty August street. A Volkswagen bug buzzed down the street at around five, but other than that, not much was happening.

Anna called that afternoon, but I wasn't in a conciliatory mood. We fought. It was the first fight of many. She came by that evening. "You are just like Larry," she said. "You want to own me too." We made love. She didn't stay that night, and I didn't protest.

11

Reluctantly, I allowed Holly and Ray to feed me dinner on an evening when the company of a doting married couple was a way of courting suicidal thoughts. Diane was there too. I drank a lot. At some point in the evening, I entered the kitchen to find Diane and Holly kissing. They were wrapped around each other, kissing with unseemly earnestness, and Ray was pulling the last of a six-pack from the refrigerator. We were all fairly drunk. Ray and I went back to his living room where we sat down on his sofa (a rotten sofa upholstered in fiberglass fabric that had tormented my flesh on more than one comatose night).

"Your kitchen has turned into a hotbed of lesbian activity," I said.

Ray shook his head. "Nope. As usual, you miss the point. Neither Holly nor Diane is queer."

"I've seen less impassioned fucks," I said.

"Yes, yes, that's just it," Ray said. He was drunker than I was (if memory serves) and he was pointing a sententious finger at me. "It's passion, of course. But it ain't sexual passion. That has always been your great confusion, my boy. You see all passion as sexual in nature. No, Holly and Diane are engaged in the passion of consolation. They are sharing their disappointment in men. That is a great bond women have."

Diane and Saul were split up again, so maybe Ray was right.

"How's Anna?" Ray asked. It had been six weeks—six stormy weeks—since Anna and I had become lovers.

"Same as ever," I said.

"I take it she couldn't make it tonight."

"You don't see her, do you?" I said.

Ray wasn't improving my mood. He was my best friend, but he had an uncanny ability to find a sore spot and thump it with a hammer, all the while displaying an expression of scientific interest.

"I read that people who don't keep appointments or are always late are exhibiting hostility," Ray said.

"I'm going to exhibit some hostility if you don't shut up," I said.

Diane and Holly came into the room holding hands. Holly went over to Ray and cuddled him while Diane sat on the sofa arm and absently patted my head in a gesture that I found immensely demeaning.

"Cut it out," I said.

Diane looked surprised, hurt. Then, quickly, her face turned all understanding, lighted with maternal insight. That did it. I had to get out of there. I left and drove absently around Newburg, then back to my apartment. The door was unlocked, and Anna was in bed, waiting.

"Don't turn the lights on," she said. "Just come here."

She reached for me and drew me into the bed. She was naked, and her body radiated heat. I scrambled out of my clothes, a shameless puppet to her will.

I hadn't been expecting her. I was never expecting her. Her presence, therefore, was always a surprise and a reward. Now I kissed her and tasted the salty taste of her, and cupped her exquisite breasts, and raced with her toward climax. In the bathroom, afterwards, I saw the blood smeared over my face and turned back into the room, snapping the light on. One of her eyes was glued shut, the lid turning purple, and blood dripped from her lip.

But she grinned. "I didn't want to spoil things," she said. "I thought we could fight about this after."

"What did he do?"

Anna shrugged. "Nothing special."

"You should put some ice on that bruise," I said, and I walked toward the refrigerator. Halfway to the refrigerator, I turned, sickened by the reasonableness in my voice, the resignation that I loved a girl who was, as a matter of course, going to get beaten up on a regular basis by a psychotic boyfriend.

I ran back to the bed, grabbed her by the shoulders, and shook her. "You are never going back to him!" I shouted. "Listen to me. You have to make a choice."

We screamed at each other. Anna prowled the room, naked and angry, shouting back.

The argument ended with Anna dressing in a rush and slamming out the door. Other arguments had ended that way. A pattern was emerging.

I fell asleep and was awakened the next morning by the ringing of the phone. I didn't immediately recognize the voice on the end of the line. It was Kalso, but his voice was uncharacteristically shrill.

"Larry's dead," he said.

I asked him how it had happened.

"Look," he said. "I want you to get over here right now. It's not Larry I'm worried about. It's Anna."

"What about Anna? Is she okay?"

"She's fine. Just get over here."

12

Diane was there when I got to the Villa. She was sitting on the sofa with Anna. Anna looked up when I came in but there was nothing in her eyes, no greeting.

"I killed him," Anna said. "I killed the motherfucker."

Kalso spoke: "Heroin overdose. Anna didn't have anything to do

41

with it. But she found him, and she's shaken up. We can't get her to go to the hospital, but I want you to get her out of here for awhile. The police are going to be back, and I don't think she should talk to them right now."

Anna was pale and still, sitting on the sofa with her hands in her lap. I sat down next to her, touched her shoulder. "It's okay," I said. "I'm sorry."

"I don't care who knows," Anna said.

Diane brought Anna a cup of coffee, and she drank it. Anna was wearing a bathrobe, and her hair fell over her face. She began to shiver, and Diane took her upstairs. When they came back down, Anna was wearing a yellow blouse and jeans, but she still looked and moved like a child who has been tugged into clothes while half asleep. Anna's face was puffy and alien, as though the shock had awakened a different person, now inhabiting her features. Her eyes and mouth were blurred by trauma, and her expression, unreadable really, could have been identified as an ill-tempered pout.

"Just get her out of here," Diane said. "Anywhere. Go."

I drove out of town. Skies were vertigo blue and I found myself heading toward the mountains, toward the commune.

Anna said, "It's okay. Larry wanted to die."

I looked at her. "You're upset," I said. "You didn't kill Larry."

"Larry will be glad to hear that," Anna said.

We drove in silence until Anna, spying a 7-Eleven, demanded that we stop and get some beer. I didn't argue. Back in the car, Anna popped the top on a Budweiser and said, "Larry didn't like needles. He took a lot of things, but mostly speed and downers, pills. He had this crazy attitude about prescription drugs. They were okay, stamp of approval from the AMA or something. He was as crazy about that stuff as Hank and Gretchen are about brown rice. Sometimes, listening to Larry, you'd think he was a health nut, just like Hank and Gretchen. He really believed in chemistry."

Anna was growing more animated with the alcohol; it always had a marked, instant effect, as though the taste alone shifted a psychic gear. "I hated that motherfucker," she said. "He got meaner all the time, and it was the drugs that were doing it, but the drugs *were* Larry, you know, so there wasn't any way of separating the two, of saying, 'He's an okay guy when he don't drug.' Hell, the fucker was always drugged. I got so I could tell what drugs he was taking by the kind of trouble he'd come looking for. He was really ugly last night."

We drove on through the beautiful mountains. I didn't want to say anything, and I thought perhaps that Anna would fall into one of her private silences. But she didn't.

"He didn't feel anything," she said. "He didn't even jump, didn't moan. So long, Larry." I glanced at her. Her face was wet with tears.

"Stop here," Anna said. "I want to walk down to the river." I pulled in before the bridge and we walked down to the broad, still-raging Yurman River. We had to scramble through chest-high bushes and negotiate a shadowy pine forest before arriving at the riverbank. Anna, who had been carrying the beer, sat down on a rock with a triumphant air and squinted at the sun.

She looked at me. "We can be together now," she said. "Larry's gone."

"Simple as that," I said.

Anna frowned. "No, it's not simple. I know that. Don't treat me like a child, David. You like to treat me like a child. But don't do it, please. You can say a lot of things about Larry, but he didn't treat me like a child."

She hadn't killed Larry. I knew that.

"I love you, Anna," I said.

She nodded her head, took a quick swallow of beer and said, "I did it for you."

Anna stared at the river and drank another beer and started to cry. I went over and put my arms around her and she rocked back and forth against me and said, "I hate it. I hate it. I hate it." It became a crazy chant, then lost coherence and she fell asleep in my arms. I didn't move, but held her against all ugly odds and my own willful hunger, and I held her through the afternoon and watched a crow scavenge in the stagnant pools, and I thought about stuff, much of it profound, and reached the foregone conclusion: Nothing mattered but Anna and me.

13

I drove Anna back to the Villa that night. She was tired and went straight to bed. Diane and I sat in the kitchen and talked. Diane said that the police had come again, but they didn't indicate that they would be back tomorrow. They seemed to know about Larry's drug habits. They weren't in mourning, and an o.d. wasn't suspicious considering Larry's history. Kalso, who had called the ambulance, had told them that he had found the body. Anna hadn't yet entered the picture. But she would. We agreed that the police would want to talk to Anna, since she was living with Larry. If nothing else, they'd want to know where she was that night.

"Do you think she killed him?" Diane asked in a rush.

"Of course not," I said.

"No," Diane agreed. "Why does she insist she did?"

That was a trickier question and I sidestepped it entirely. "You know," I said, "I wouldn't feel any differently about Anna if she had killed Larry. It would have been self-defense, really."

"I doubt the police would take that view."

But we overestimated their interest in a dead drug dealer. For the next couple of weeks, we waited for something to happen. Having a talent for paranoia, I assumed the quiet hid some Hitchcockian maneuvering on the part of formidable sleuths. Slowly, I realized that the cops had been glad to see the last of Larry, were uninterested in the precise nature of his demise, the nuance of circumstance. No one expressed the least interest in Anna's part in Larry's death. The coroner's inquest swiftly settled on accidental death by self-administered overdose.

I moved back into the Villa, back into the old studio room. I would have preferred for Anna to come live with me, but there was no extricating her from the room she had shared with Larry. Indeed, although we were still lovers, she would always leave at some point in the night to return to her own room.

This behavior, which I found exasperating, was a bountiful source of argument.

"I need my privacy," Anna said.

"I love you," I said.

Anna folded her arms and glared at me. "That's cheating," she said. Which was, of course, true.

14

"Don't do that!" I shouted, having resolved to say nothing, to close my eyes.

We were hurtling through absolute blackness on what I knew to be a country road, too narrow for two cars, too narrow for two fat men on bicycles, and Anna was laughing, the black air screaming through the car's open windows, the slippery smell of rain carrying a clean terror of its own.

Anna snapped the lights back on, and a stark, dripping wall of vegetation erupted in front of us. She spun the wheel and we swooped effortlessly downhill.

"Goddam it, Anna. I don't think it's funny," I said. My hands ached from clutching the dashboard.

Anna laughed. "Don't worry. I'm a good driver. I had a good teacher." Her eyes sparkled with concentration; her hair flew in the black wind.

I regretted teaching Anna to drive, but it had seemed like a good idea. It would be a step toward independence, away from the passive, passenger existence that had characterized her life. That was my thinking on the matter. Besides, fortuitously, she had a car. She now owned Larry's Mustang.

Larry's father had come down in the wake of his son's death. He was a thin, balding man whose manner suggested that his son had picked a particularly poor time to die. "My wife"—Larry's step-mother (his real mother was dead)—"just left me. And things ain't going well at the shop. I hope this can be cleared up quick enough." Larry's father, who urged everyone to call him Bud, cried considerably, was red-eyed every time I met him, but his tears seemed drawn from irritation as much as grief. "What am I supposed to do with this hot rod?" he asked Kalso. "I reckon I'll have to go about selling it. I can't see myself driving a hot rod."

45

By accident, I happened to be present during this conversation, and I was surprised when Kalso spoke up.

"I'd like to buy the car," Kalso said.

I couldn't see Bud driving the Mustang, it was true. But I couldn't see Kalso driving it either.

Bud's eyes had narrowed, transforming him into a sort of suspicious Airedale, and he said, "I'd have to think about it. I don't know much about cars, but it looks like it's in real fine shape, like it's been kept up."

"I'm sure we can work something out," Kalso said.

They did. And that night a euphoric Anna burst into my room to tell me that Kalso had given her a gift. Guess what?

I guessed. A sky-blue Mustang.

I was right.

I asked Kalso about it when I got him alone. "Expensive gift," I said.

He shrugged his shoulders. "I've gotten used to the car in the driveway. Besides, I am a sentimental fool. I take in boarders and acquire family. If Anna were a boy, she would inspire less noble advances. As it is, she inspires a mawkishness that appalls me. Let's not talk about this again."

So we didn't.

I taught Anna to drive, but she was fearless from the start, ready to rocket into traffic. I went with her to get her license. It was a proud day for her, and she wore a dress. She seemed nervous but capable, determined. The officer who gave her the test was much taken with her. And she did look beautiful, victorious in white when she came out of that austere building and raced down the steps, jumping into my arms, forcing me to take her full weight and swing her in the sunny air. After she had her license, she insisted on driving everywhere. And when I was busy she was often out flying down back-country roads, drinking beer.

"It's okay," she told me when I worried about it. "It's something I like to do. It's freedom. Freedom can't hurt me. I need freedom."

That late summer and fall brought me moments of intense

happiness. There is a temptation to haul out the photographs: Anna in a bathing suit, sitting stolidly in a wading pool holding an umbrella over her head, the shimmering arc of water from a garden hose descending like laughter around her; Anna eating a watermelon, mouth wide; Anna standing on a beach in a windbreaker, hair flying; Anna wrapped regally in blankets, looking up from a book, peering over giant, horn-rimmed glasses. The evidence of good times is overwhelming, undeniable. And I can never forget the glory of Anna naked, as she moved across the room. She would stand very straight, flat-footed, smoking a cigarette in the middle of the room. It was a picture I wanted to paint, but I never did, because the act of painting would have stolen from the simple act of being with her. She was not a graceful girl—clumsy, awkward, often self-conscious—but she was possessed of a magnificent femininity that transmuted everything she did, enclosed her in erotic intent. I was obsessed with her, and that obsession doesn't make me the most objective man available regarding Anna and her charms. But there is no doubt that Anna had a powerful, physical authority.

To say that my attraction to Anna was physical is to say more and less than the truth. Anna did not go unnoticed in any crowd. But her physical beauty had shaped her character more than beauty—always a powerful force—shapes most of us. She had a refugee air about her, as though still stunned by some calamity, a tornado, a terrible war, and I believe that the trauma, the storm behind her, was this piercing physical beauty. I loved Anna and I loved the victim within.

I suppose I thought of myself as a victim, too. That summer and fall were not carefree. We often argued, loud shouting matches that usually ended in Anna's roaring off in the Mustang. Arguments were a way of life with Anna. I wasn't exactly an innocent bystander myself. I was better than most at discovering betrayal and resentment. We argued and we made up. Anna enjoyed teary reunions. She recovered quickly, forgetting everything. I brooded, saying nothing. I found it palatable some days to think of myself as a man bludgeoned into an untenable relationship by the fatal hammer of sex. There is something to be said for believing that you have been deprived of volition, robbed by some force older than evolution. And some days—the bad ones—I would try to believe that I had been swept along against my will.

Those days when I would try to deny any responsibility in this relationship were the frightened days. By late September, there was no avoiding a cold reality: The mental and emotional tremors that haunted Anna were increasing in intensity and frequency.

I could no longer dismiss Anna's fitful behavior as emotional turbulence, the birthright of pretty girls.

We were drowsing in bed one night. It had been a chilly day, and the furnace had kicked on, filling the small upstairs room with thick heat. The lethargic aftermath of our fevered, desperate lovemaking, combined with the heat, made it hard to stay awake. I was aware that Anna had gotten out of bed and was prowling around the room. I heard things being knocked over, heard Anna sobbing, and I pushed myself out of sleep.

"Wooster," she was crying. "Wooster, come out." She was shivering, despite the heat, and I ran to her where she knelt by the side of the sofa. She didn't seem to recognize me at first, jumped and trembled. "Wooster is unhappy," she told me, with wide, unseeing eyes.

"He's here," she said. "I know he's here."

I reminded her that we had buried Wooster and she said, "I know that, David. It's why he's so unhappy. We had no right, no right to do that. No right!" She began shaking her head, repeating, "No right. No right!" I brought her back to bed and held her. She jumped away, would not be quieted, ran to the window and peered out. "The ground's so hard," she said. "So hard." I brought her back to the bed again, and this time she stayed. Finally, she slept, and in the morning, she said nothing about the incident.

I didn't ask about Wooster. I didn't want to look into the abyss. I just wanted Anna.

Diane said, "I know you don't want to talk about it, but we have to talk about it. Anna appears to be having schizophrenic episodes. This morning she told me that she had seen an angel. And that's not the first thing she's told me that's been really odd."

"Anna talks like that," I said, writhing on the sofa where Diane had directed me to sit while she had her say.

Diane shook her head. "If I know about this stuff, then you certainly know about it. You have got to stop denying that anything is wrong. It's immoral, really."

"Immoral? You been talking to angels too?" I asked.

"David, I think Anna should see Dr. Parrish. Just let him talk to her for an hour. If he gives her a clean bill of health, fine, but if not, he can help her."

"Anna's fine," I said.

"You know she isn't."

I was beginning to think that Diane's living at the Villa was a mixed blessing. Saul was gone for what appeared to be good. He had left for California (Diane's "lobotomy country"), taking the at-loose-ends Skip with him. While Diane's freedom from Saul was cause for celebration, she now had more time than was healthy to scrutinize Anna and me. What she saw altered her face subtly, superimposing a ghostly disapproval over her smiling, civilized features. She had to work at not saying things, and the need to say them had, as I knew it would, finally overpowered her.

I got up from the sofa, exit on my mind, "I'm worried about Anna. I know that Larry's death freaked her out, but I think we're working things out fine. Look, I'll be the first to holler if I think anything is really wrong."

Diane frowned at me. "Okay."

I disengaged, retreating to my room.

I was worried, and I don't know why I didn't grab at Diane's suggestion. Yes, I know why. The same reason a person who suspects cancer doesn't rush out for a biopsy.

But I was worried about Anna. Anna had told me about the angel, too. The angel had told Anna not to eat red meat. "If you eat red meat," the angel had said, "I will come back and kill you with a butcher's knife." Anna had been genuinely terrified.

But no more hoodlum angels spoke her name, and the days were quiet, and I painted, and Anna drove her car and lay on the sofa and watched me paint, and everything was normal enough.

The odd thing about this period is that, despite the emotional chaos, I was painting better than I ever had. I was young—I had just turned a portentous twenty-one in April—and while I felt ancient when talking to Anna (Kalso always referred to Anna as my "ward." "How's your ward getting on?" he would ask), I was becoming increasingly aware that I knew almost nothing.

Kalso had finally convinced me to fly up to New York with him, to see just who my benefactors were, and I had done it, grudgingly. I hadn't enjoyed the trip because I didn't like being away from Anna, and I was convinced that I would be exposed as a fraud. I had the arrogance of youth—and youth's self-consciousness.

The trip went well, but it didn't feel like an experience I wanted to repeat. Harold Brell, the gallery owner, was a small, elegant man in a three-piece suit. His face was deeply tanned, his hair was cloudy white, and he had blue, searching eyes. He seemed extremely comfortable in the city of New York (he told me he had been born in Munich). He assured me I would be rich and famous. He suggested I move up to New York and when my refusal was immediate he laughed and said, "Not for you, of course. Too much here. I agree. Excitement, but nothing to think about, no serenity, I think." He had clapped me on the shoulder. "The recluse, you."

I look at the paintings I painted back then, and I don't feel the need to apologize for them. They are better than they should be. I was very lucky. Had I chosen a direction that demanded more emotional maturity, I would have failed. But I settled for hymns to the surface, shiny wonders. It was when I looked deeper, stretching the limits of my emotional integrity, that I failed. That's why, after that first self-satisfied leap to success, there was a dark, floundering period when I thought I might never paint again. Having failed to struggle as a young artist, I struggled as an older one.

But that is getting ahead of the story.

On the first day of October Anna returned from a day at the commune with Hank and Gretchen. She often spent the day out at the farm, and since I was painting all day long (an awesomely selfish business), I could hardly object to her pursuing her own spiritual destiny. I liked to think that she was drawn by the comradeship and the clear bracing weather. I liked, actually, to think about it as little as possible. On this afternoon, Anna was particularly flushed and excited. Guru Walker had told Anna that she had, in a former life, been sold into slavery and prostitution by her parents. This was in eighteenth-century England. Her father had owned a pub, and times were rough.

I told Anna that that was an old fortune-telling tale, a common lie to titillate elderly women who wanted, desperately, to believe that excitement had once visited their drab lives.

I may have gone on at too great a length. I hated the balmy, effortless believing of reincarnationists, astral travelers, transcendentalists. I was in the middle of a sentence when Anna screamed, shoved me backwards, and ran into the house. I ran after her, but she slammed the door to her room and refused to let me in. I apologized through the door and went away. I assumed that the usual time would elapse in our ritual quarrel, that all would be forgiven by evening. I was complacent on that point, I suppose, for I remember going back to painting and rapidly settling into the rhythm of work. I forgot what time it was, and when I glanced at my watch I was surprised to find it was after ten. I had assumed that, somewhere in the course of the evening, Anna would have come in, and I would have apologized, and she would—with some initial resistance—have accepted the apology.

I went and knocked on her door, and a slurred voice told me to go away. This happened sometimes. Anna's drinking could throw the whole ritual out of whack. I shrugged and resolved not to talk to her until the next day.

The next day was overcast and chilly. I awoke later than usual and went downstairs. Anna wasn't anywhere around, so I went upstairs and knocked on her door. No one answered, but I thought I heard a voice, so I entered. Anna was sitting up in bed reading out loud. She was reading from one of Walker's self-published books, a small blue paperback titled *The Road Home* which I had once opened and perused. The book contained sentences like: "Imperfection is man's physical reaction to perceived death. Imperfection consists of this and nothing more: believing the lie of imperfection." Heavy stuff, really, the midnight revelations of college sophomores in chemically-altered states of mind. I never understood how the Hanks and Gretchens—lilies of the field folk—could wade through this stuff. But they did.

The room was dark except for a small bedside lamp that bathed Anna in yellow light. She had on an old blue flannel nightgown decorated with roses and cigarette burns. She was wearing her glasses, which always made her appear younger and slightly incredulous, and was reading aloud in a monotone.

"Anna," I said. She read on. "Anna?"

I went over to the bed and touched her shoulder.

"Get out of here," she said. "You are the Shadow Principle. Maker of Darkness."

"Anna."

Anna turned away from me and read on. Now she read at an even faster clip, like a priest in a cheap vampire flick, keeping the undead at bay with a barrage of holy words. I felt another wild diatribe bubbling up within me, another cult-debunking lecture, so I left quickly.

But I was worried now, really scared. There was always a breathless, scattered look to Anna just before a fit, and that panicky feeling had been very much in evidence, a black spirit of hysteria. When Diane came home from work in the afternoon, I asked her to look in on Anna. Diane's face, when she returned, was not hopeful.

"I think we should get her to a hospital."

"I thought you might say that," I said.

Diane took my hand and patted it. "David, hospitals help people; Anna needs help."

"Yeah," I said. Diane had picked an unfortunate phrase. Since I was a kid, "needs help" had been a euphemism for insane, a phrase always on the lips of my father and my father's immense clan of relatives who had nothing much to do, in the narrow town of my birth, but be solicitous and overbearing. My mother had "needed help" and she had gotten it with a vengeance.

I got up and went upstairs. Anna was sleeping, and I didn't want to wake her. The book lay by her hand. I picked it up and put it next to her on the night table. Then I turned off the light and went back to the studio.

I couldn't sleep that night, and I felt unusually cold, as though the autumn had crawled into my bones, worked a change toward winter there. And so I was awake when I heard the door open and I heard Anna's quiet tread, and I started to sit up just as the room erupted in a single, mind-numbing thunderclap, a red shriek in my ears and eyes. I was cuffed off the mattress by a powerful blow. I tried to stand, but I felt lopsided, baffled. My shoulder began to throb as I knelt against the window sill. I heard shouts. The room light blazed on, and Anna, wearing a flannel nightgown, blinked owl-like and unseeing. Kalso came running in and took Larry's gun from her hand.

I had wondered what had become of that gun. The police hadn't found any gun. "Well, there it is," I thought.

I noticed then that I was bleeding.

"Anna?" I said. "Are you okay?"

Anna was definitely not okay. She stood in the center of the room moving her lips soundlessly.

I started to cry. I felt...what did I feel? Defeat, I think.

15

I had always been able to charm Clara Newcomb, the night shift head nurse. A long-running routine had evolved in our working relationship. I maintained that Clara, who was the mother of three teenagers and happily married, was a wild, pot-smoking hedonist who lived to party. She maintained that I was feeble-minded, that a rich uncle had bribed the hospital's director. How else would I have obtained the cushy job of orderly, a job so obviously beyond my mental abilities? I tried to charm her that night with the old jokes, the old routines, but she wasn't buying it.

"You don't walk into an emergency room with a gunshot wound and walk out again without it being reported," she told me. "I'm sorry, but that's the law."

"Clara, I'm okay. I'm pretty sure I'm okay, anyway. I tell you what. I'll make a deal. If you'll page Gill, and if he'll come down here and take a look at me in an unofficial capacity, and if he says I'm okay, then we'll forget I even walked in the door."

Clara shook her head sadly. She wore silver-rimmed glasses and wore her hair pulled back so tightly it sucked her cheeks in, made her eyes bulge. This was all in a vain attempt to wrest authority from an impossibly benign, maternal countenance. "No," she said. "I can't do that."

"Yes you can. This was an accident. But Anna's not well, and the last thing she needs is a lot of police milling around. They've got her over at Romner Psychiatric right now. Diane rang up a doctor she knows over there, and he admitted her. I just think she doesn't need a lot of noise over nothing. I think." I stopped talking; the words just came to an end somehow.

I didn't know what I thought, but I wasn't able to talk about Anna yet, that was clear. Clara said, "Okay. I'll get Gill down here."

I assured her that I would be fine. I had made my own cursory examination of the wound. A bathroom mirror revealed a two-inch-long furrow racing up my right shoulder, an inch to the right of my collarbone. I had been in the act of sitting up when Anna fired, and if she had moved her hand slightly to the right, the bullet would, just as smoothly, have entered under my chin and skidded unceremoniously into my brain, causing all manner of confusion. As things stood, the bullet must have gone on to smack against the wall behind me.

That was my diagnosis, anyway, and Dr. Gill Andrews confirmed it as he stitched me up. "Yeah, she didn't draw a good bead on you." Gill had listened to my story of an accident, the classic didn't-know-the-gun-was-loaded story, and his matter-of-fact acceptance, a series of thoughtful nods, turned the tide with Clara. The police went unnotified, my visit unlogged. Gill was a young resident, five or six years older than I was, a lanky, long-haired guy who didn't take himself too seriously. We were good friends, having discovered a number of shared enthusiasms (like P.G. Wodehouse and Bob Dylan) in late-night conversations in the E.R.. I'd had him over to the Villa a couple of times. He had briefly met Anna, although his sole comment had been raised eyebrows and the exclamation, "My God, what a beautiful girl." I didn't like the lifted eyebrows; they seemed to suggest that he had pictured me with someone less stunning. But then, I was always defensive about me and Anna together, always expecting some dissenting voice to shriek, "This union must be sundered. It is against Nature and all the gods!"

Gill sewed me up and then asked me what I intended to do. I realized, quickly enough, that he hadn't bought my story.

"You are looking rotten," he said.

"Thanks."

Gill leaned forward. He had a long face with a large, beaked nose, a handy countenance for interrogations. "You look rotten," he repeated. "All your freckles are faded out, and you have a general swampy, underground look to you."

"*Swampy?* Is that a medical term?"

Gill nodded. "Worse than that. It's the truth." I laughed.

"You want to talk about this stuff?" he asked.

I told him I didn't, and he nodded his head. "Yeah, well, you aren't dead. Maybe I should get Vaughan to lock you up while your luck is holding."

"Thank you," I said. "I appreciate your concern. I've had a rough night, no doubt about it. But I'm okay now, honest."

Gill said, "If they release your girlfriend tomorrow, what are you going to do? If some underpaid and overworked social worker says, 'Take three Librium a day and see us on alternate Tuesdays at six' what are you going to do? Look, I'm asking because I'm your friend, remember? I don't think that gun went off by accident, at least not the way you describe it, and I don't think your friends dropped her at Romner Psychiatric just because the trauma of almost killing you temporarily unhinged her. I would just like to know what you intend to do. You don't look too swift, and I'm really not at all sure that you should be walking the streets."

"Thanks for the vote of confidence," I said. I watched Gill's mouth clamp shut in recognition of my unreasonableness. He shrugged his shoulders and stood up.

"Okay," he said. "If you feel like talking later, give me a ring."

I thanked him again and left.

When I returned to the Villa, Diane was up waiting for me. She told me that Anna had been admitted without incident, that everyone at Romner had been kind and efficient. Dr. Richard Parrish himself was going to interview her in the morning, and right now she was sedated.

"How is she?" I asked.

"She's okay," Diane said. I stared at her. "I don't know how she is, really. Just because I work at Romner doesn't mean I know what's wrong with Anna. I'm vocational rehab, you know. I'm not a psychiatrist."

"Did she say anything?" I asked. "When you were driving her over there, did she say anything?"

"No. Yes. She was in shock. She wasn't making any sense, ranting all that mystical bullshit."

"Did she say anything about me?"

Diane looked weary. Those quick, grey eyes had dulled, and the lateness of the hour brought me a vision of her ten years hence, still pretty but braver, more determined.

Apparently she hadn't heard me. I repeated. "Did she say anything about me?" Diane looked up, clearly exasperated.

"Jesus, David. Jesus."

"Well?"

Diane shook her head sadly. "As a matter of fact, she did. She said, 'Tell David I love him.'"

I smiled. I hadn't intended to, but I could feel an idiot smile stretch across my face. I don't know what that smile looked like, but Diane's eyes widened. "Goddam it, David!" she screamed, and before I could say anything she had jumped off the sofa and raced up the stairs.

I went upstairs to my own room. I could smell the fiery smell of the gun's discharge, and I began to feel faint. I walked downstairs, knees trembling, and drank two beers, sitting in the soupy yellow kitchen light.

I felt better after the beers, and I lay on the mattress and thought of Anna's words. "Tell David I love him." *Maybe everything will be all right*, I thought. Why not? Well, why not?

16

Dr. Richard Parrish saw Anna the next day, in the morning, and Diane called me from the Institute to say that they were keeping

Anna for observation.

The second day that Anna spent at Romner Psychiatric Institute, my life was altered by a letter in the mail. It was a letter that a lot of people were receiving back then. The United States Army requested my presence.

I saw Anna once before I left. We met in the dayroom of one of the wards. The room was bright and clean with a television, sofas, a ping-pong table in one corner. Two grim-faced patients were slowly bouncing a ping-pong ball back and forth as though it were a task they were being graded on. I watched them, waiting for Anna to come into the room. I gave them a "D." On the walls there were paintings by patients, and inspirational poems, poems about the goodness of life and God. I studied a pencil drawing that someone had obviously labored over for weeks, erasing, redrawing. The drawing was titled, "Jesus and His Dog," and sure enough there was Jesus with a dog on a leash. The dog had a halo. The unknown artist had worked hard on Jesus' smile, erasing and redrawing until the paper was translucent, but the smile still wasn't right. Jesus had the cheesy smile of a born huckster.

Anna came into the room, and she looked good. She smiled and ran to me and hugged me. "Get me out of here," she said, and laughed. I asked how she was doing, and she said it was okay really, that she got on well with crazy people, and that Diane was going to help her get a job. Everybody in group agreed that she ought to have a job, some independence. She had been letting other people run her life for too long, just floating from parents, to Larry...just floating. She said that Dr. Richard Parrish was a great man, a man who could tell what she was thinking before she thought it.

I told her I was going into the army. I hadn't known how to tell her. I had feared that this revelation would trigger some new emotional breakdown, but Diane had advised me to go ahead. If Anna was going to react badly, it was just as well that she do it now, while she was around folks equipped to handle such outbursts.

Anna said it was too bad. The fucking army! She asked if there was any way I could get out of it, and I said that the time for getting out of it was past, that I was stuck now. She commiserated with my bad fortune, told me to write, said she would miss me. We didn't talk about her shooting me. We both understood that that was a part of her illness, an unhappy, pathological twitch. I left thinking that she looked good, better than she had in months, happier. She was even wearing makeup. She had taken my leaving well, too. That had gone much better than I expected. I hated her a little.

I went to Charlotte, North Carolina, where I was inducted, then a bunch of us were flown down to Fort Benning, Georgia, for basic training. One of the guys in our group was appointed temporary platoon leader for the duration of the trip. Moments earlier, he had been regaling us with a dirty story; now he was transformed into an authority figure. He seemed to change physically, his face blooming with new corpulence and anxiety. A whining tone entered his voice. "All right you guys. We gotta be at gate thirty-two at eighteen hundred hours." *Eighteen hundred hours?* He began to walk with a funny, officious waddle and complained when we lagged behind. "This is serious business," he shouted.

I didn't like the army. I didn't like the flat, squat buildings and the unblinking solemnity of things. It was not a place for anyone with a sense of the absurd. Sand Hill was aptly named, and leaping awake at four in the cold November mornings was a depressing business. I was surrounded by fierce, frightened children. I had other things to do, and the army had picked a bad moment to tap me on the shoulder.

My attitude was bad. I got a summary court martial for refusing to obey orders. "Cut it out," the lone colonel warned me from behind his desk. It wasn't much of a court martial.

I was transferred out of my original platoon and into another platoon. The members of this second platoon were in the army because they chose it over reform school, and they were a contentious, brawling bunch. They were informed that their new member, David Livingston, wasn't playing the game properly, and that his failure to shape up would adversely affect the whole platoon. So shape him up, boys.

This is sound psychology, and the army way. Peer pressure is powerful stuff. But the plan failed. It would have succeeded with your ordinary lot of good citizens. It probably would have succeeded in the first platoon, all of whom were eager to fare well in their new career. But the army had forgotten that this particular platoon had an authority problem. These kids had entered the army when asked, "You want to do some time back in juvenile detention or you want to enlist and help out Uncle Sam?" Their dedication was not absolute, and the largest of the lot, a red-headed Irish boy who sang, "Duke of Earl" with real power, came over to me and said, "I like your attitude. Any of these gimps try to give you a hard time, you let me know, and I will personally straighten them out. I'll jump flat in their shit."

I thanked him for his concern. Word got around. My bad behavior went uncorrected by my peers.

Refusing to fire a rifle, refusing a wide variety of orders that stuck me as unreasonable or foolish, I received a general court martial. This was fancier: more colonels, a court stenographer. I was sentenced to the Fort Benning stockade.

The stockade wasn't the hellhole of rumor. No one tried to knife me or rape me. The place was largely stocked with AWOLs, just frightened kids who had run away several times and were now sitting behind bars waiting to go back to their companies or receive undesirable discharges and go home. I wasn't uncomfortable. Like many people I have since encountered, the army taught me to hone certain skills of invisibility. I became adept at dodging work. There was a fenced-in compound where we inmates chopped wood and hosed down olive-drab automobiles. I lay in bed for hours reading *Remembrance of Things Past* which I had discovered in the prison library. I don't know what that tiny little library was doing with Proust. I read Proust's convoluted, sickbed sentences until I suffered my own derangement of time, until reality shivered in parenthetical expressions and fine delineations of meaning. I remember looking up from the novel to listen to an argument. The argument was about the location of Africa. Three of the five arguers maintained that Africa was in Texas. A fourth said that Africa was somewhere in South America. The fifth person maintained that Africa was "a big motherfucking place" across the ocean, but he was a lone voice crying in the wilderness.

I got letters from Ray and Holly that adopted a cheerful, newsy quality, totally alien to the real Ray and Holly. I wrote back saying that whoever was pretending to be Ray and Holly cut it out and let the real Ray and Holly write. I'm not sure they knew what to make of that, but, saints, they continued to write me. Diane wrote, talked about work at great length and then apologized for talking about it. She wrote that ex-boyfriend Saul had staged a whirlwind conversion, giving up drugs for Christian Science, marrying a solemn, thin woman named Cynthia Downs who, like so many people, had briefly resided at the Villa.

Kalso wrote, keeping me abreast of my career. He told me that my stock had risen considerably with my incarceration, that it had been a brilliant move in a business where personal style counted for so much. Not only was I a brilliant painter, he wrote, but I had a tremendous flair for self-dramatization.

He had sold a still life of mine called *Mud Lamps* for a little over fifteen thousand to a private collector who was interested in purchasing additional works.

And Anna wrote. Her letters were surprisingly articulate. I know that "surprising" sounds condescending, but I was surprised. I had always known that Anna was intelligent, but her intelligence didn't seem to glow white hot in the area of personal communication. She could never quite say what she intended to say, and she was aware of this. It frustrated her and she withdrew, saying nothing at all.

"I woke up this morning and I thought of you," she wrote. "I thought so clearly of you that the whole room dimmed and I myself dimmed so that, all morning, I felt unreal and was confused when customers came into the store and spoke to me. I was amazed that they could see me, that I wasn't a ghost from being sick with wanting and missing you."

Anna's letters made me ill with longing. And they made me ecstatic. I had always doubted that she loved me with the same fevered intensity that I loved her (one of the oldest kinds of accounting in the world) and I suspected that I had always been a convenient lover. And yet, now, she was writing me ardent, eloquent love letters.

She had gotten a job as a cashier in a drugstore, and the novelty and adventure of actually going to a job every day, talking to a variety of people, getting a paycheck, delighted her.

She continued to go to an outpatient therapy group that was run by Dr. Parrish. She complained about various members of the group: Jennie who talked too much and a creep named Bobby who was too off-the-wall, scary, and paranoid to be in group anyway.

Anna's letters created a wrenching desire to see her. I had moments of doubt too, when I thought that maybe it would be like Anna to write love letters from a safe distance, that the ability to fashion such sentences would be reason enough for their existence, but I killed such thoughts with disgust. They didn't do justice to the girl I loved. I attributed such negativity to my surroundings, to the general all-male cynicism (dark-faced, long-boned Terry, lying on his bunk and saying, "My old lady probably pumping some dude right this minute, shouting, 'Slam it in, Henry!' and that's okay. Long as she mark her calendar for old Terry's release and don't forget that date. Now old David here, he don't think his woman fret none 'bout her pussy. Maybe, like when she's taking a bath, she might rub some soap on it and think of him is all. Yessir, that be about the most she would do. Sheeeeit, man, you living on Mars if you don't think she putting out this very second.").

I didn't know how long I was going to be in the stockade. I had celebrated Christmas in the stockade; now routine had drained time of any meaning and the end of April was approaching. I didn't like to go out into the compound because the warming of the days, the quick, rain-filled skies, spoke too many changes. I felt left behind, abandoned in the springtime celebration. Had I exhibited some willingness to return to my company and be a soldier, I would already have been back there. But the stockade suited me as well as anything in the army, and I stayed there while they decided how long they would let me stew before discharging me. During those months of waiting, Anna's letters sustained me.

Then Anna's letters took an odd, disconcerting turn. With uncharacteristic coyness, she wrote, "You know I would never do anything to hurt you"—this from the woman who had tried to blow me away with a .38—"but for a long time now I have been feeling differently about 'us.' Well, it isn't so much that. I still love you. I've been feeling differently about someone else. I guess you know what that means. He is a great person, a fine person, and I don't think we can ever be together. Circumstances won't permit it. But I would be lying if I didn't tell you about this."

Circumstances won't permit it? I decided that Anna had been reading too many gothic romances. Her talent for self-dramatization was immense, but I hated this new twist. I would have preferred her lying. I began to dread her letters. They were the weirdest mixture of candor and reticence. I wrote her angry letters which I destroyed for fear I would never hear from her again if I sent them. I wrote her reasonable, tolerant letters asking for more information, and these letters I also destroyed, because I didn't want to know anything about this mystery man, this sage, gentle character. I was satisfied with my own image of him. I imagined him as a smug, self-satisfied lecher with a glib smile, good looking in a manner which, while initially attractive, quickly palls. The cleft in the chin begins to look like an aberration, and that expression in the eyes, originally so winsome, is correctly identified: self-pity, vanity, low cunning.

Anna, no fool, would soon sour of this prince. I would get out of this goddam stockade where the army had hurled me, and I would set things right. I was making some money. We would move out of Newburg, go somewhere on the coast. Nags Head maybe, where the salt air healed, where the steadfast sun and the rolling ocean reaffirmed the essential goodness of life.

Anna could get a job working at one of the local shops. I would paint. In the evenings we would walk along the beach, and everything would be okay.

"What would you say if I told you I was getting married?" Anna wrote. "I know you would be happy for me. It's too early to tell you anything about it, and I shouldn't even be writing this, but I had to tell someone, and you are my best friend, as I hope you know."

How out of touch could she be? I wondered. I read her wildly irritating, hurtful, oblivious letter. She prattled on about how happy she was, what a miracle had occurred in her life, and how surprised and shocked some people would be when the marriage was announced.

I lay in my bed, listening to the din of stockade life, voices shouting, the dismal, chill sound of metal bars sliding, the hollow prison echoes, the blare of a distant television. I was amazed at how I hurt, as though I had been physically beaten.

I was not surprised, of course. Anna was acting in character, and I knew that.

A week after Anna's good news, the army decided they were done with me; the paperwork was complete, and I was released. It was the twenty-second day of June.

Two privates in a jeep drove me to the edge of Columbus and dropped me by the side of the road. "Don't say we gotta hand deliver this motherfucker, now does it? Don't say nothing about no bus station. This here is Columbus." It was a bright, windy day, and I didn't mind standing by the side of the road in my PX jeans and oversized shirt. The whine of the trucks racing down the highway struck me as the sound of freedom itself, filled me with joy. I wasn't thinking of the troubled future; I was enjoying my freedom. The day soured, however. My first encounter with the civilian world was a knobby-faced man with yellow teeth who waved me into his big Buick and immediately asked me if I knew of any hot spots in Columbus and did I have a girlfriend and did I let her suck my cock, and as far as he was concerned, any kind of sex was good sex and . . . I asked him to let me out and discovered that I was only three blocks from the bus station.

I got a ticket in Newburg and bought a bottle of wine and ate a cold turkey sandwich which sank like suicide in my stomach. On the bus I drank the wine and watched scruffy shacks race by. Gusts of wind shook the bus—which seemed more insubstantial than the buses I remembered—and I dozed off and woke in darkness and studied my face in the black mirror of the window. They had cut most of my hair off right before I left, and I had never become reconciled to this startled, naked-faced child with over-large ears and an unseemly youthfulness that resided in his too-full mouth. I looked too fragile to live, lost in my ill-fitting exile's shirt.

I was going back to Newburg to see Anna. My father had written, asking me to come home, but I wasn't up to his solicitude. No telling what he might do in my best interests. I wasn't strong enough for his protection, or the sullen righteousness of my big brother Johnny who would make it clear that my failures were the echo of bad genes—our mother's much lamented delicacy.

I had to see Anna, but I didn't want to think about it. I couldn't think about Anna without immediately walking into anxious country, peril on peril. I spent the last hours of the bus trip mentally avoiding dark alleys.

It was four in the morning when I arrived in Newburg, and I was dirty and semi-drunk, exhausted, a stale, lurching wreck who reeked of cigarettes and wine. I drank a cup of coffee in an all-night diner and then got a cab to a motel where I staggered into bed and passed out... the hero home.

I woke around noon, showered and shaved, and went out and forced myself to eat a breakfast of ham and eggs. I was going to need my strength for the confrontation with Anna.

I took a bus across town and walked the half-dozen suburban blocks from Hanover Street to the Villa, which looked as it always looked, ravaged but friendly, good-humoredly hanging in as the windows buckled and the concrete steps split open. I hadn't told anyone I was coming. No one knew I had been set free. Anna's shiny Mustang was still parked at the curb. I might have only been gone a day. I had a hangover, and the sky was dirty, growling, working up a storm. I felt awkward, sick on freewill. I wanted to turn and walk away, but I had this great faith in the inevitability of the moment, so I went up to the door, almost knocked, didn't. I pushed open the door, always unlocked, and entered.

Diane, in the best theatrical manner, stopped dead still on the stairway, opened her mouth and actually put a hand to her heart.

I don't know why I hadn't thought of it earlier, but now, vividly, I realized the possibilities of my unannounced presence. Sure, I had expected some kind of drama, some argument with Anna, who would fail to play her part, fail to recognize the spirit of reunion. We would fight, certainly, about her new infatuation, this mystery charisma man. But I hadn't—characteristically—thought of Anna as other than alone, waiting to play out the drama. Now I realized that Anna might be upstairs with a man. Might? She almost certainly was. Diane's expression said as much.

Diane ran down the stairs and threw her arms around me. Anna was sleeping with someone. He was upstairs right now. I could run from the house. Diane was shaking in my arms, sobbing.

"How awful for you," she was saying. "God, how awful."

Yes. That bitch.

Diane took me into the living room and sat me down on the sofa. "Is Anna here?" I asked.

Diane, wet-faced, hair glued to her temples, stared at me. She shook her head, a physical rearranging of assumptions. "No," she said, very slowly. "Anna isn't here. You don't know what's happened, do you?"

She looked at me, and I saw something coming to the surface of those solemn eyes, and I watched it coming, as a swimmer in the ocean might look down and behold a dark shadow growing rapidly larger, more ominous, and I knew that Diane was going to say something that would alter my life and I couldn't stop her and then she said it.

"Anna's dead," she said.

Part 2

Richard Parrish

1

Richard Parrish loved fine things, beautiful things. His mother, Grace, was beautiful, with blonde hair and a smoky, elegant voice. His father, Richard Senior, was bearded and powerful, a big man who fancied dark suits, a man too imposing and methodical to be considered simply fat. He towered over young Richard and spoke to the boy in the booming voice of an oracle.

At eight, young Richard was already well aware that he was a privileged child. His parents never relented in telling him how fortunate he was.

"I like beautiful things around me, honey," Grace would tell him. "That's why I brought you down from heaven. You are mommy's little angel."

They lived in Winston-Salem, North Carolina, in a big white house with a maid and a cook.

There were rooms in the house that Richard could not go in. Those rooms were too delicate and beautiful to withstand the presence of a small boy. But Richard would risk parental displeasure and enter those rooms to gaze at the rich, autumnal carpets, the luster of polished woods, the sparkling, cut-glass figures behind cabinet doors.

Sometimes, on the weekends, they would get in the big dark car and drive out into the countryside. They would pack a picnic lunch and sit primly on the blanket and study the imperial sky. Richard Senior would speak in a deep, pontifical voice. He was a man of many opinions: about the war, about poverty, about God. Richard was too young to follow his father's words, but the sense he got from them was that ugly people had brought their ugliness on themselves by their own laziness and dishonesty.

Sometimes, on these trips, they would encounter ugliness: dirty farm shacks, roadside families in rags. Years later Richard remembered the girl with something wrong with her face, as though her mouth had been slashed with a knife, and the boy with the crooked arm. He remembered, mostly, the look on his mother's face, a look of pain.

"I can't abide ugliness," she had said in the car. "I don't have the constitution for it."

Richard and his parents had been driving back from one of their outings when they had stopped at a roadside stand to buy apples. The boy had come right up to Richard and said, "That's some car your folks got. You must be right rich." Richard hadn't said anything, of course, and meanwhile his mother was being escorted quickly back to the car by Richard Senior, having met the girl with the twisted face.

"Buy some apples from the poor creatures," Grace instructed. Richard Senior got back out of the car and bought a bushel. A mile down the road, Grace had him put the apples out. "I know it's foolish," she said. "But I don't want them in the car."

Young Richard looked out the window and thought about the boy. He wondered if the ugliness had come on the boy suddenly, if the arm had twisted up into a useless claw as the result of some particularly foul deed, or if it had happened slowly, the accumulation of years of laziness and wrongdoing. What struck Richard as most astonishing was the boy's attitude. He didn't seem the least ashamed of his infirmity. What kind of parents must a boy like that have, to not feel any shame at all?

All the way home, Richard was grateful that he had the parents he had and that he lived in a beautiful house.

This gratitude was still in him when he killed Edgar, almost six months later. Edgar was a sleek and haughty Persian cat, so black that he seemed to draw light into him. He had large yellow eyes and a regal bearing. Grace loved Edgar, would carry him around the house with her or sit on the sofa petting him.

Then Edgar got hit by a car and had to be taken to the vet. He returned to the Parrish household missing a portion of one leg and with a large bald spot on his hindquarters, a spot that refused to grow new hair. The car had smacked the dignity out of Edgar, and he hopped around, mewing hoarsely, following Grace around the house.

Richard could see that look in his mother's eyes. It was the same haunted and unhappy look that he had seen that day at the roadside stand.

Edgar was lying in the sun on the porch, sleeping. The bright pink knob of his truncated leg jutted out oddly. His fur—no longer groomed by Grace—was a muddy tangle.

Richard swung the axe with all his might, and with one blow he severed the cat's head. Its body spasmed and a vast quantity of blood gushed forth. Richard had to hose off the porch after he had removed the body and buried it in a nearby vacant lot.

His parents were gone for the afternoon, and he had cleaned up before they returned. He felt good. He had done the right thing.

Grace confirmed that days later, when, at the dinner table, she confessed that she was glad Edgar had run away. The accident, she said, had ruined him.

Richard found he loved the secret of it. He wrote the secret down on a piece of ruled paper. "I killed Edgar." And he folded the piece of paper up and carried it with him in his shirt pocket where it exuded a sort of warmth, the heat of secrets.

One morning when Richard was thirteen, he blinked his sleepy eyes at the bathroom mirror and raised his hand and touched a great, red knob of swollen flesh over his right eyebrow. It was the grandaddy of pimples, a ghastly ballooning of his forehead, and it sickened him, made him want to faint.

Then, as he thought about it, fear invaded him. He couldn't go downstairs where Grace was waiting at the breakfast table, waiting to take him in her arms and say, "How is Mommy's morning glory?"

That look would come into her eyes.

He squeezed the pimple but it didn't burst. Instead, it seemed to swell, to gain new ground on his pale forehead as he worried it. He heard his father's voice downstairs. He began to feel desperate.

He hurried out of the bathroom and found his penknife in a drawer and went back to the mirror. He ran hot water on the knife blade to kill whatever germs might lurk there (Richard Senior had some grim tales to tell about germs), and then, ignoring the cold, clenched fist of his stomach, he cut the swelling with his knife. It hurt. Blood oozed out, and yellow pus. A kind of anger overwhelmed him, and he worked the knife deeper, feeling an odd dislocation of self. His skin jumped under the burrowing knife.

The pain was fierce, but the pain angered him too. He wasn't going to back off because of the pain.

He was going to slash the ugliness away; destroy the stupid bubble in his flesh. The eyebrow now seemed to conspire in the ugliness, and he gave his attention to that area as well.

He didn't even realize he was screaming until his father was standing at the door. Grace stood right behind Richard Senior, and the both of them had that look in their eyes.

"Richard!" Grace screamed. "My God!"

Richard Parrish had the words to explain, but they wouldn't come out. He saw his reflection in the mirror, his forehead a scrawled mass of blood and tattered flesh. He swooned, his fingers sliding down the blood-splattered sink.

They never did ask him to explain, and that was good, because the words were gone. His face healed okay. In six months there was just the smallest nick in his eyebrow. He was still beautiful, still welcomed in Grace's arms.

But Richard knew that the ugliness had simply retreated. It was waiting to boil up. In the morning, he would hurry to look in the mirror, and he would rejoice to find his face unblemished. But it was there, waiting, and he knew it, and the knowledge made him feel helpless and angry.

2

Richard's father was a man of strong opinions. "The boy has been over-mothered," he told Grace. "He'll become odd, perhaps a sexual deviant, if you go on coddling him so."

"Nonsense," Grace said. "He'll grow up just like you, breaking hearts and maidenheads with his good looks."

While Richard Senior had done no such thing, he was flattered, and so, for the moment, silenced. But the notion had taken hold of him: some firm, manly guidance was required for his son. Not content with lectures, Parrish Senior felt compelled to instruct his son by example.

"Self-control is everything," Parrish Senior said. This particular conversation was held at the dinner table while Grace maintained a rapt silence, playing the part of a second pupil, but brighter and more attentive than her son. Parrish Senior was wearing a tie and a white shirt, and smiling, leaning back in his chair. "You can't let others know what you think, what you feel. People are on the lookout for weakness; that's a heritage we have from the jungle. Some have called me cynical, but I'm not. I'm just aware of the way things are."

"Yes Father," Richard said.

"We're going for a walk," his father had said, and he had lit a cigar and pushed the screen door open. Father and son walked out into a fading summer twilight. "You think your old man doesn't know what he is talking about, Richard. You think I'm just an old fool, I suppose." Richard thought no such thing. He thought that his father was dangerous and brilliant. He didn't say this, of course. He didn't say anything, for he knew that these lectures were, essentially, monologues and he could be in real trouble if he said anything. "The old man knows what he is talking about," Parrish Senior said. He wasn't old, not much over forty, and Richard's mother was thirty-eight then (this was when Richard was fourteen) but Parrish Senior liked to think of himself as wise and weary.

They walked down a street of maples and the smell of cut grass was in the air and his father put an arm on Richard's shoulder.

71

"What say we walk on over to the warehouse?"

The night was fine, and people were sitting on their porches or walking along the sidewalks. Parrish Senior nodded to those he knew, adding a smile to the nod when the person was of sufficient importance, a doctor, a banker, a successful businessman.

Richard wished he were back in the house with Grace.

A thin, grey light leaked through the dusty windows of the warehouse, and Richard's father hummed tunelessly and fiddled with a set of keys, finally pushing the door open. "Don't get down here often enough," he said. "If you are running a business, you can't afford to ignore a part of it, or the whole thing will tumble down." The door creaked open on this sentiment and father and son walked into a gloomy, glue-smelling world of shadowy barrels and spiderwork machinery. "Be right back," Parrish said, and he hurried up a rickety flight of stairs and closed the door to the loft office. Richard waited in the semi-darkness, and a strange, frenzied scratching made him turn and stare into the gloom. A large Doberman emerged from the darkness. The dog, somewhat smaller than a pony, was slipping on the concrete floor in its haste to reach Richard. It wasn't barking, but a deep, evil vibration, a lunatic-wielding-a-chain-saw sound, came from its throat. The dog was black with small, glittering eyes. Richard's heart flopped and he turned and ran for the door. He had to turn again before he reached the door; the beast was coming too fast. Richard turned and backed up as the Doberman stopped in front of him and barked wildly.

"Hiller," Richard said. "Good Hiller." Fear had released this pocket of information. His father had referred to the dog before. "Just let some nigger try to break in," his father had said. "Old Hiller is death on niggers."

"Good Hiller," Richard repeated, but the dog was ducking its small head, growling again. Richard backed up slowly and something metallic rolled under his foot and he stooped slowly, saying, "HillerHillergoodHiller," and picked up a length of metal pipe and continued to back up. The dog started jumping up and down, as though it recognized this declaration of war, and Richard reached the door. He turned the handle. The door was locked. He remembered now. He remembered his father fumbling with the keys—*locking the door*. "Good Hiller," he muttered, and the fear was coming out of him like steam, hissing in his ears. He heard his father's voice and looked up. His father was leaning against the railing and speaking quietly, a lecture, of course. "Self-control, Richard. Dog or man, it's the same. You can't show fear. Dog or man don't respect you if you show fear. They'll both go for you if they suspect weakness."

"Father," Richard said. "Please."

"Just show Hiller who's boss. Just shout him on about his business, just—"

The dog was jumping and twisting around, confused now. It lunged, and Richard threw up his arms and fell backwards, head thumping against the concrete, body screaming with hysterical messages. The dog was on him; it smelled bad, like a dumpster on a hot day. Spittle flew from its mouth. The creature had a terrible, fanatic's strength, as though its bones were steel beneath the smooth black hide. Richard tried to push it away, but his hands thumped futilely against its furious body. It meant to kill him. "Hey!" Parrish Senior shouted, and he raced down the stairs. Richard was screaming, and the metal pipe rolled across the concrete. Parrish kicked the dog. Hiller yelped, skidded sideways and raced off. Parrish helped his son to his feet. "All right, now," he said, patting his son's shoulder. "Let's get on out of here." He reached in his pocket for the keys and unlocked the door.

On the way back home, Parrish elaborated on the necessity of self-control. Richard said nothing. "Well, no harm done and you've learned a valuable lesson," his father said.

Richard went up to his room and took off his pants. He studied his bloody thigh and washed the blood off with a sponge, watched it well back up, and rinsed it again. Finally the bleeding stopped but he still didn't like to look at the black pits in his flesh that sank to a hideous depth. Looking at the wound made him feel odd, weightless and insubstantial, as though he could easily and without warning fall into pieces, bloom with dark holes, sprout death like an old potato under the kitchen sink.

The next two weeks were hell. Richard had heard the schoolyard tales of rabies. These stories were particularly gruesome, having gotten mixed, somehow, with stories of werewolves and the undead. At night, he lay in bed waiting to go mad, body and mind both knotting into cruel contortions. Sometimes, breathing in shallow gasps, he was convinced the disease had him. Then it would go away and he would lie there thinking about his father, thinking, actually, about his father's back as his father unlocked the door to the warehouse and let him out. Those were bad weeks and that's when he began keeping the diary. His first sentence was: "I hate my father, and I wish he were dead." The first pages, written in a desperate flurry, were later transferred to notebooks, organized.

The diary became Richard's religion, his confessional. It helped to keep the ugliness away. He began to write in it every day, and he was superstitious about missing a day. Here he didn't have to be in control; here he was safe.

The diary was survival.

One day he wrote, "The old man's dying. Hooray!"

Richard was there when one of the doctors explained to Grace how the cancer had spread, virulently, though the lymph system. It made Richard feel itchy inside, thinking about it, and he wanted to run from the room—where he was invisible to the adults in any event—and he thought of the cancer as busy ants, hollowing his father. There was an operation, and then a second operation. The second operation did something to his father, but no one, not even Grace, remarked on it. After the first operation, Richard Parrish Senior complained and roared. After the second, the old man (really old now) lay paralyzed, unable to speak or move. You'd think that that would be a change worth noting, but no one said a thing. Grace and Richard, dressed as though for Sunday church (and there was something austere and church-like in the hospital, the whiteness and ritual, the solemnity and silence), came to see the old man. Grace would talk about friends, the weather, politics, anything, her voice ringing out with terrible brightness, and Richard's father, supported by pillows, would blink his watery eyes while his mouth hung open.

"Kiss your father goodby," Grace would say when these long

visits finally came to an end, and Richard would dutifully go and kiss the dry, pale cheek and smile and say, "See you later, Dad." He had never called his father "Dad," but he found he liked the sound of it. "Get well, Dad," he would say, and he would leave with Grace.

Richard's father died less than a month after being admitted to the hospital, and Richard went to the funeral with Grace. The funeral was held on a viciously hot day at the end of the summer, and Richard thought he might faint. He thought of the ants, busy in his father's body, and he wanted to throw up. He dreamed a terrible dream that night in which he came down to breakfast to find his father sitting at the breakfast table drinking a cup of coffee. Something wasn't right, Richard knew, but he couldn't remember what. Then he noticed that his father's beard seemed to be moving, and instantly he saw that it wasn't hair at all but a thick, busy horde of black ants. Richard saw a trail of ants coming from his father's mouth.

"You're dead!" Richard screamed, pushing away from the table, knocking his chair over.

His father mumbled something, then repeated it, "Willpower, my boy. I choose not to be dead. A man can do what he pleases if he has the will."

Then Richard's father coughed. The cough ignited a series of coughs, and ants spewed onto the tablecloth. Gouts of ants flew from Parrish Senior's mouth, and, as Richard sat transfixed with horror, his father shrank, deflated like a balloon. One limp, ragged hand, like a flattened glove, reached out to touch Richard's cheek, and the awfulness of it woke Richard, sat him straight up in bed.

3

Grace and Richard continued to live in the big house until all the money was gone. Richard once heard his mother tell their lawyer, "I don't like to think about money. It makes my head ache." And so, she didn't think about it until it was gone, and then she married Paul Baynard.

Grace was frank about it. "I married your stepfather for his money," she told her son. "And a good thing I did too, before some heartless bitch came along. I'll make him happy."

Paul Baynard, Richard's new stepfather, was a decent, unambitious man who had been born into a family which, for generations, had accrued wealth compulsively. The old man, Claude Baynard, was still at the helm, still diversifying and cutting throats with piratical zeal.

Paul Baynard was a quiet, vague man who went to clubs and offices, always goaded by duty, always pursued by an obligation. Richard liked him, and rarely saw him.

Richard did not like high school. It was too noisy and raw. He wasn't interested in sports or the companionship of other boys. He preferred being at home with Grace, going up to his room and writing in his diary. Why bother with other people when he could confide everything to the ever-attentive, secret ear of his diary? The crowd of loud, obscene schoolboys could never understand the adventure that unfolded in his diary, the mystery that was revealed to him. It was exhilarating, a clandestine, private world. He was filled with a sense of daring experimentation.

He had nothing but disdain for the public, sniggering lives of his schoolmates. The girls attracted him, but it was the attraction that interested him, that he took back to his room and studied as though it were a multifaceted jewel, a gift for his diary. He never thought seriously of doing anything about these girls. They were the inspiration for fantasies, but they were not attainable.

Then Vivian Decker entered his life. She was a cheerleader, but no mere shrieking girl bouncing in blind ecstasy for a lot of moronic football gladiators. Vivian ennobled the sport. She was studying ballet, and she had a grace, a way of floating off the ground that was exuberant but dignified. The way the stadium lights winked in her eyes, the way her round, ripe mouth shaped the words, "Push 'em back. Waaaaaay back!" suggested a certain bemused distance, an adult indulging children.

Nonetheless, Richard wouldn't have thought much about her if she hadn't actively pursued him. Later she told him, "At first I thought you might be a fairy or something. Sometimes really good-looking guys are fairies, like this guy Marlene dated. You just didn't seem interested, you know. You were always acting like the whole

76

world was this television show you were watching, some crappy, dull game show or something."

Richard had laughed, embarrassed, a little uncomfortable that anyone could know him well enough to say something like that.

But it was okay, because Richard loved Viv. This love was not unmixed with gratitude. He had thought he was just fine, with his diary and his solitude. He had been ignorant of everything. He had been locked in a dank, airless room, and Viv had saved him from a desolate existence, from a life of growing every day more crooked. It was something he had discussed with his diary. "Sometimes I hate how the world is out there and I am in here," he had written.

Now he had Viv. She had introduced him to sex, untraumatically, in a laughing, roughhouse fashion, and she had chided him out of his crookedness, for she was able to match his inherited disdain for the world at large with her own enthusiasm. "Come on, we're going skating. Come on, we're going dancing. Come on, you fish, we're going bowling with Ralph and Marlene." She made a joke of his reserve, and he gratefully joined in the laughter.

He had taken Viv to meet his parents, and his stepfather had been all graciousness, smiling and listening attentively, genuinely pleased to be meeting Richard's girl. Viv was wearing a baby-blue sweater, a pink skirt, high socks, and she looked sweet. Although she later told Richard she was so nervous she thought she would puke, she told some hilarious stories about going to camp where her father, a high school teacher, was an instructor in the summer.

Richard's mother was not so gracious. Grace's smile was a grimace of genteel revulsion. She sat upright in the plush sofa, and although she said almost nothing, she managed, by the force of her considerable character, to portray a mother who has been deeply wronged by an errant son.

"I know you don't like Vivian, Mother," Richard said that evening, "but I do."

"Well, of course you do," Mrs. Parrish-Baynard said. She then winked, a gesture that really wasn't in her physical vocabulary and failed to convey any kind of bawdy camaraderie, and said, "She's a sweet young thing."

"You think she's trash," Richard said.

"Of course I don't. She's a well-groomed, well-spoken girl. There is no doubt in my mind that her parents are decent, hard-working folks."

Richard turned and started to walk up the stairs to his room.

"It's just that she's common," his mother said. "She's so common."

Richard turned. He was shocked. His mother sat on the sofa, her mouth open, as though she had shocked herself by speaking so bluntly. Then she shrugged. Richard glared at her and turned away.

"Viv." They were lying in bed in her room. It was afternoon and both her parents were at work. Richard loved this room, with its teddy bears and dressing table cluttered with cosmetics.

"Hmmmmm," she said, turning over and smiling out of lazy eyes, then reaching to touch his cheek.

"Let's get married."

"That's my dream, you know," Viv said, drowsy-voiced.

"Well, I mean it, Viv. Why not?"

Vivian Decker woke up and blinked. "Richard! You are serious! Oh, Richard!" She hugged him and covered him with kisses. "Let's get married right away."

"I think we should wait until we've both finished high school. That's not so far away."

Vivian was silent, thinking. "I guess not, Richard. I mean, it seems a million miles away, but I guess it really isn't, and I love you."

They were going to get married as soon as they both graduated from high school. They got married earlier, however. It was an old story. Vivian was pregnant.

Richard had a car by then, a new cream-colored Plymouth, and they drove to a town in South Carolina, got married and then drove home. Richard dropped Viv at her parents and promised to call after breaking the news to Grace and his stepfather.

"You fool!" his mother shrieked. He had never seen her in such a rage. "You fool!" She was having a hard time talking. Anger had robbed her of speech. She waved a hand. "Get."

Her husband, a peacemaker, said, "Grace, the boy—"

"No," she said, waving him away. She walked to the window and looked down on the sweeping backyard, groomed to green perfection, a crystal blue swimming pool, a yellow guest cottage that sparkled in the late afternoon sun.

She turned and looked at Richard, honest confusion drawing her face into an older, almost senile version of herself. He could see her come to some conclusion. She walked over to an end table, picked up her purse and fished through it, frantically pulling out sheaves of bills. She counted the money, her lips working. "Two hundred and fifty dollars," she said. She walked to Richard and thrust the money into his hand. "I want you to have this. Lord knows, you'll need it."

She marched back to the window and Richard was left holding the clump of bills. "Mother?"

She said nothing.

"Mother!"

She whirled around and screamed. "Now get out of here. Paul! Nothing out of you! Don't say a word! This is my son. Get out of here, Richard. That's your wedding present, and that's the last you'll get from us. I mean it. You chose your road without consulting us; you can choose your future in the same manner. Goodby."

"I left. There's no arguing with my mother," Richard told Viv, recounting the story.

"What will we do?" Viv said. She was stunned, sick. She had been feeling rotten recently anyway, but the doctor said that was normal. But it didn't feel normal and the doctor was a man so that "normal" business was pretty goddam glib anyway, and now what was she hearing?

"I don't care," Richard said.

Vivian licked her lips. She didn't want to get upset. "She will change her mind, don't you think?"

Richard laughed. "Grace change her mind? I don't think she can. I think she has a one-way mind, like a minnow trap. An opinion can go in but it can't go out."

Vivian frowned. "This isn't funny. Why didn't you tell me that your mother hated my guts? I thought you said she liked me."

"My mother is an awful woman. I don't care what she thinks of you. I love you."

"Well, this is awful," Vivian said, and she sat down in a kitchen chair.

Richard felt a panicky moment as, arms folded, she scowled. His new bride looked, for a moment, fat, unlovely, and full of wrath.

"I'll get a job," he said. He hadn't had time to think about that, but now, having said it, it seemed a strong, sensible solution, and he leaned forward and put his arm around Viv's shoulders and said, "We'll be all right, you'll see."

Viv began to cry. "What kind of job can you get?" she sobbed. "You don't know anything."

Richard's stepfather, in a fit of renegade bravery—for his wife would have been hard to live with had she known—talked to the president of Coleridge Savings and Loan, and quietly secured a position for Richard. The job was dull, but it allowed Richard and Viv to move into a two-room apartment and buy groceries and pay the more pressing bills.

Richard hated the job, but he also felt a sense of freedom, of living in the real world. He was a genuine participant in his life. Vivian didn't understand the delight Richard felt in self-sufficiency.

One night, right after they moved into the apartment, they celebrated with two bottles of wine, and Vivian had got squeaky drunk, outrageous and toy-doll cute. Richard didn't much like it, and she picked up on his displeasure and glared back at him.

"Little Richie's unhappy," she squeaked. "Too bad. Baby's on the way and the money's all dried up. All dried up." She laughed ruefully, mindlessly. She looked at Richard, and he knew she was going to say something cruel. She did. "It's a laugh, you know. You think I got this baby because it's like the wages of sin or something? You think Jesus sends down angels to put holes in rubbers so bad people, messing around, get caught?"

Richard was a little drunk himself, and he wasn't following this speech although he could feel the anger, like heat from an open oven. "Huh?"

"I wanted this baby. I wanted a rich boy's baby, bounce him on my knee in a big house while his big-shot grandparents chuck him under the chin. Joke's on me. Joke's on you, too, Richie. You didn't tell me your mom hated me. You didn't tell me you were gonna be poor."

"You married me because my parents have money?" It was a thought he truly couldn't comprehend. He would never have married for money.

He loved her.

That was the first time he hit her, one open-palmed blow across her cheek. They made up that night, and in the morning Viv couldn't apologize enough. "I shouldn't drink," she said. "It's not me talking when I drink. It's someone who gets inside me and says awful things." Richard believed this and said he was sorry that he had hit her.

At work, his immediate supervisor suggested he work a few hours in the evening without pay. "You want to get ahead, you have to make sacrifices. You want to learn this business, you have to get cracking, my boy."

Richard began to feel tired all the time. The apartment was shabby and smelled of burnt fish. The next-door neighbors, an obese middle-aged couple with an obese child, fought loudly and incessantly. Often when Richard got home, Viv, bulging with her baby, would already be in bed, watching Perry Mason, eyes goggling, eating crackers. "The little accountant guy did it," she would tell Richard. "What do you want to bet?"

He didn't want to bet anything. Vivian Decker was a stranger who had moved into his life. "I don't know where she came from," he told his diary. "I can hardly remember how she got into my life."

Vivian's parents would sometimes come by and sit for an hour and talk about nothing and pretend that they didn't feel the tension in the room. Her mother had a forced heartiness that would not have fooled an autistic child, and Viv's father rolled on about sports in spite of Richard's obvious indifference. Richard's mother never called, and his stepfather would make rare, check-in calls that were dismally furtive.

Petty arguments began to erupt regularly. They were never resolved, these arguments; they were like a cold that won't go away. Occasionally the arguments would be punctuated by a real fight, like the time Richard came home from a bad day at the office and found Vivian reading his diary. She was lying in bed and jumped when he opened the door, but she brazened it out, went back to reading, saying, "Hot stuff here. I haven't gotten to the sex stuff yet, but..."

He beat her up good that time. She lost a tooth, and her face turned purple on the left side and ballooned out, but he felt no remorse, only a kind of wariness when he studied her. He knew she was vicious, capable of terrible retaliation. They both moved around each other carefully for a couple of days, but when Vivian's face returned to normal, the same weary scrapping began again.

Richard couldn't even remember the final argument of the final battle, except that it took place very early in the morning, when his heart felt like a black penny at the bottom of the ocean at the end of the universe—infinitely alone. They had screamed and shouted, and he had gone off to work where he had fought with his supervisor (who falsely accused Richard of intentionally ignoring an account because it was too much trouble) and Richard had walked out and glumly returned home where he found Vivian burning his diary on the patio. She had shaken the house apart to find it, and she had—hidden inside a hollow volume of Shakespeare's collected works, where Richard felt it was safe from accidental discovery. She had found it easily enough, by tumbling the bookcase over. This was outright, frenzied war.

She hadn't counted on Richard's early return, and he was able to save the book, burning his hands. Later, he had to recopy some of the pages, but he recognized his extraordinary good fortune; he had saved his history, his best friend.

Vivian he almost killed. The fat neighbors heard her screams and ceased their own shouting long enough to call the police. When the police came, Richard was sitting on the sofa in the living room and Vivian was out on the patio on her back in a pool of blood. Her face didn't look human, and she was in shock. The worst thing, described by an officer who ran back into the living room and beat the shit out of Richard Parrish, was the way bloody clumps of the victim's blonde hair skidded in the wind across the patio like red-stained tumbleweeds.

Vivian lived, and her face, reconstructed at great expense, looked remarkably like the old Viv. The baby was lost. The marriage ended, and Richard moved back in with his parents.

Grace had shown up at the jail with several lawyers. She had spoken with Vivian about the incredible costs of competent medical care, money in general, and the follies of youth. Then she took her son home and nursed him back to health, reading to him at night, speaking of pleasant times, refusing to bring up the ugly past. Reconciliation was complete.

"Mother was right about Vivian," Richard told his diary. "We weren't suited for each other."

4

In college, Richard Parrish was possessed of a seriousness that repelled certain women and attracted others as though it were an aphrodisiac. He was a handsome young man. An unhealthy delicacy had melted away, and a sense of purpose gave him a capable, masculine air.

Richard Parrish slept with seven girls during college. He found that he fancied a certain blonde type and he was particularly susceptible to high cheekbones and an imperious air. But these brief liaisons made no lasting impression and, indeed, the girls seemed glad to end the relationships, finding a chilly lack of intimacy in Richard.

"You just don't open up," one girl told him, and Richard thought about that and said, "That's true."

"Why should I?" he could have added. He had his diary, and there he could say anything he pleased.

After his marriage—which, in his diary, he referred to as the "Vivian incident"—his mother made him go to an expensive psychiatrist, Dr. James Ellis, a solemn Freudian whose offices exuded an air of masculine power. Dr. Ellis was a grey-haired man with a round face and shaggy eyebrows that must have been worth a fortune in his profession. He dressed in dark suits and spoke in a voice only fractionally louder than a church whisper.

Ellis was cool, Richard thought. An ice man.

"Maybe I'll become a shrink myself," he told the psychiatrist.

Dr. Ellis, lulled perhaps by the oakwood shadows of the room and the polite murmur of the air conditioning, had missed this remark, for later in these sessions when Richard said that he would be leaving for Duke University in three weeks, Dr. Ellis had raised his substantial eyebrows and said, "Three weeks? We are far from through here, I think."

Richard nonetheless left Dr. Ellis's care to go to college. While he had found nothing healing in the sessions with Ellis, he had discovered a goal. He was going to be a psychiatrist. He was going to be above the dirty, ugly clamor of people, the pettiness and the stink. He was going to sit in a cool, dark room and keep his own counsel, a man of power, a shaman—ice cool.

Richard had an ample allowance and was able to live in an apartment off campus (an apartment furnished much more opulently than the wretched apartment of his Vivian exile). He was a good student, and he had the kind of compulsive mentality that makes for successful scholars and bureaucrats. In graduate school, teachers began to remark on his tenacity, his ability to grind massive amounts of research into something possessing a logical shape. There was more than mere endurance going on here, and his teachers began to think of him as brilliant, certainly a student to enlist in their own pet projects.

In his final year at Duke, Richard's stepfather died. Richard was awakened at three in the morning by a wild, incoherent phone call from his mother. She had been drinking—something she almost never did—and it was only after she finally hung up, with a wail, that he was able to piece together what she had been saying. Poor Paul had died of a heart attack, sliding down behind his desk unobtrusively, at the lunch hour, so that he was not discovered until late in the afternoon. But that event had taken place three days ago, and that was not what had prompted his mother's late-night phone call. What had shaken her decorous grief into tears was a meeting with the Baynard lawyers during which she learned that Paul had been a salaried employee, that old man Baynard still owned the company, and that all the evidences of ample wealth were, for the most part, on loan. Grace was reeling under the blow of this black news when she called her son. Richard, lying in bed, caught his mother's fear and remembered the nightmare apartment of his days with Vivian.

As it turned out, the financial picture wasn't quite that bleak. There was a trust fund, insurance, stocks. The mansion had to go, along with servants, but Mrs. Parrish-Baynard was able to live quite well. Richard, however, felt the purse strings tighten, and the fear of poverty and humiliation didn't leave him. He wrote in his diary: "Without money it is all bullshit." He was pleased at the obviousness of this observation, and aware that it wasn't obvious to many of his fellow students, who didn't understand that so many clients of mental health programs had only one disease: poverty.

Parrish interned at a large general hospital in upstate New York and then returned to the south for a residency at Romner Psychiatric Institute in Newburg, North Carolina. When his residency was over, he was asked to join the hospital staff. He accepted.

At the Institute, he labored to be liked, and he succeeded. He talked to everyone, and made himself available to everyone.

Richard was not naturally charming. He was, he realized, not even particularly likeable. It amused him to try to appear otherwise. And there were those of his colleagues who found Dr. Richard Parrish a bit too solicitous, too lavish in his praise. He had no real warmth, they suspected, and, in conference, he was capable of saying things that suggested an underlying indifference to the fate of patients. He was, his colleagues admitted, an astute observer of human behavior, but he often seemed to be observing it from somewhere beyond Andromeda.

Most people were impressed with young Dr. Parrish, however. He was a tall, strikingly handsome man who spoke slowly and with care, and he was possessed of an earnestness of manner that resembled deepest concern.

Several of the nurses were in love with him. Diane Larson found him attractive, but Saul, her wayward rock guitarist, was her world and, in any event, she didn't quite approve of the ribald jokes and unabashed lust of the nurses. Maybe she was stodgy, a puritan throwback, but nurses, acting like giggly cheerleaders, sighing over doctors, seemed woefully out of line, even in jest. Diane wanted to get on with the business of helping people who were desperately in need of help.

She wanted to help Anna, and Richard Parrish was a man who listened. "I'm really worried about a friend of mine," she told him. "She never had much of a life. Ran away from home when she was a kid.

"Then this guy she was living with died of an overdose, and she got into this religious thing. I mean, it's not just tripping on mysticism with Anna. It's not like Hank or Gretchen, these other folks where I live. It's like people when they do speed, words racing, you know. And her whole manner... not exactly crazy, but not exactly rational either. I've seen schizophrenics, and it's sort of like that. David, her new boyfriend, he says she's fine, but I know he doesn't really think that."

Dr. Parrish, sitting across from her at a table in the hospital cafeteria, nodded his head. "I'd like to talk to her," he said.

"I'll try to get her to come in," Diane said. "I don't know. Anna can be difficult."

They left it at that. Richard had forgotten Anna—indeed, had forgotten Diane—when Diane called him at home and asked if he would admit Anna to the hospital.

He had just come back from dinner with Jane Solomon. The evening had been a success. He was slowly winning her skittish, high-born heart.

Always accommodating, Richard had assured Diane that he would take care of the matter immediately, and he had called the ward and spoken to the night ward clerk.

The next day, Dr. Richard Parrish had the first of many interviews with Anna Shockley.

5

Richard Parrish spoke into the Dictaphone. "Anna Shockley is a young woman, presently exhibiting schizophrenic-like behavior: disassociation, religious fervor, hallucinations. Behavior may be drug-related, but neuroleptic medication seems indicated during an initial two-week evaluation period."

He turned the Dictaphone off. He had just come from talking with the girl. His hands were shaking. The minute he had seen her, that baby mouth in a full pout, those wide night eyes and predatory body, he had known her. She was a creature of sexual motives, all deviousness, like Viv, but far more beautiful, utterly beautiful. She had known that he wanted her, and she had smiled at him, knowing her power, as if to say, "Which of us is crazy, Doctor?" He had been irrationally unnerved by her.

That same night Richard called up Jane Solomon and asked her out to dinner, although he had planned not to see her for at least a week. The dinner went well, and he noted that Jane seemed flattered by his enthusiasm.

His interest was real and unfeigned. He wanted her. More precisely, he wanted to be Dr. Ron Solomon's son-in-law. He wanted that with a passion. Richard looked at Jane Solomon's pale face and languid body and his heart raced. As Dr. Solomon's son-in-law, Richard could rule Romner Psychiatric Institute. He yearned for that.

Bobby Starne

1967

6

Bobby Starne lay out in the field and rain came down hard, trying to get into his body, but he was pure and he laughed out loud, and the rain skittered off his soaking shirt and the wet grass shivered. When he was away from the house, his energy returned and he was okay. But he had to go back soon. This time, when he went back, he would do what he had to do.

He was seventeen years old, and school didn't want him and the army didn't want him, and even Coach Bonner, who had once been all brag about his prize fullback, Bobby Starne, didn't want him and got a troubled, dirty look when Bobby came out to watch practice and holler encouragement.

Bobby Starne knew when things had begun to go wrong, and he knew what the cause was.

Bobby stood up and the rain drummed on his shoulders, and pushed his straight black hair over his ears. He stood tall, and walked toward the house.

His dad—a man everyone, including Bobby, called J.D.—was in the kitchen drinking beer. "You're soaking, boy," J.D. shouted. "I swear, you are shaming me with your craziness. Can't even come out of the rain. I'm putting you down to State if you don't get right. They'll shock you. They got them electric shock treatments that'll set your hair on end."

Bobby would have stopped and talked to J.D., but J.D. didn't listen, especially when he was drinking. Besides, the house was already sapping his strength, as he moved closer to the room where Baby Lisa lay, sending out evil currents, weaving a spiderweb of poisonous rays.

Baby Lisa had blinded everyone else, had fogged their minds, so that they had already forgotten how she had murdered his mother in the hospital.

Baby Lisa meant to kill him, too. She knew he knew about her. The very first time he had seen her, when they had brought her back from the hospital, she had opened her eyes and spoken right into his mind. "Bobby," she had said, "you are next. Say your prayers, because I am going to kill you."

Baby Lisa was two months old now, although, of course, she was really thousands of years old, a demon parasite that wandered through the world, killing and spreading disease and ugliness, growing fat on the blood of innocents.

Bobby walked into the baby's room and peered down into the crib. Bobby's sister, Ellen, looked after Baby Lisa, but Ellen was at the store. This was when he had to do it.

The room had a bad, pink smell, and a chest of drawers that J.D. had painted yellow took up too much of the room. There was a teddy bear in the crib, and Baby Lisa appeared to be sleeping, with her small head squeezed into a pale frown, but she was watching through the button eyes of the toy bear, and she saw him, and she saw his thoughts, and she started to change them, to make them into doubts.

"She's just a helpless little baby," she made him think. "Your mom died in the hospital because sometimes women die having babies, just like they told you."

Bobby knew that he had to act. As always, he was weakening as he stood in the room, his hands growing numb, his strength leaking into the dim light.

"I won't think your thoughts," he whispered. He leaned forward and picked up the pink blanket next to the baby. He balled the blanket up. Baby Lisa knew the game was up, and she came awake screaming. He pushed the blanket into her face and felt her tiny body bounce.

"Don't do it, Bobby!" she shouted in his mind, but he knew better than to listen.

"Quiet!" He screamed. "Quiet, Baby Lisa!"

"Goddam!" J.D. bellowed. He was standing, reeling at the door, and as Bobby turned, J.D. lurched inside. "You crazy son of a bitch!" J.D. roared. He was holding a bottle in his left hand, and he brought it down on Bobby's head, but Bobby ducked, and the bottle slammed painfully against his shoulder. Bobby howled, turned and ran out of the room.

Bobby was sitting on the curb at Waller's Exxon when the car came up and the two policemen got out and asked him to get in. "Is Baby Lisa dead?" he asked them.

Then he saw the look in their eyes, the wicked anger, and he knew that Baby Lisa was alive. She had sent them.

Richard Parrish—Anna

1967

7

Dr. Richard Parrish's eyes kept shifting to the window where a cold November rain had settled in for the long haul. He glanced at his watch. He had another twenty minutes of group, then he was gone for the day. He sat in his chair, hands in his lap, letting the silence grow. The rain hissed in the silence like a blank tape in a tape player turned to maximum volume. Nobody spoke. They all sat mired in the silence. Bobby Starne smoked a cigarette in a methodical, zonked-out manner, his Thorazine-blind eyes watching the smoke with lunatic intensity. Anna fiddled with her long hair. Mrs. Zimmerman looked scared and Al Bowling looked irritated. Most of the other members of the group just looked bored, lost in flat, tranquilized reflection. Jennie Corning, who hated the vacuum of silence, broke it with a rush of words about going back to her brother.

Dr. Parrish let her talk. When she wound down, he asked the others what they thought about Jennie going home.

Bobby Starne, who was brutally big and obviously nuts, said, "I don't want to go home. I'm safe here. Baby Lisa can't get me here."

The other patients had been quick to understand that Bobby was authentically crazy, and they paid no attention to him.

"Anna," Dr. Parrish said, "what do you think Jennie should do?"

Anna looked up from combing her hair and shot Dr. Parrish a quick, angry look. Parrish was surprised at how the brightness of those dark eyes caught him, started some reflexive, unwarranted apology in his mind. "I don't know about Jennie," Anna said. "I don't think people can tell other people how to run their lives."

"No, we can't tell others how to run their lives," Parrish said, "but sometimes we need the help of other people who can see something we can't see because we are standing too close to the

91

problem. It's like standing six inches from an oil painting. It all looks like a confusion of colors, but when you move back, it turns out to be a landscape, a lake, forest, clouds."

Mrs. Zimmerman sighed. "I used to paint," she said. "But I never did like that painty smell, that turpentine and the way it got in your clothes."

"Jesus Christ," Al Bowling said, leaning forward. "We are not talking about fucking paintings, lady."

Dr. Parrish continued. "Do you think Jennie should go back to living with her brother, or should she try to get a place of her own, maybe go to a halfway house?"

"Okay," Anna said. "I think she should go back to her brother."

"Why?" Parrish asked. Jennie, pleased that her problem was the center of a discussion, set her small, thin face in an earnest smile and leaned forward.

"They are karmically involved," Anna said. "They can't escape each other, so they might as well not try. I mean, she can go to a halfway house if she wants to, but it won't work, because he'll draw her back, the magnetism of his aura will reach out. She can run but she can't get away."

Jennie, who insisted that her brother was constantly making sexual advances toward her (an insistence that was entirely delusional) nodded her head.

Anna began speaking more rapidly, breathlessly. "This sort of thing is all arranged, and the test is whether or not you can accept it and go through it in a learning spirit. That's what life is: learning stuff, and you can learn with grace or without grace. Like, you can go to a halfway house and get dragged out of that situation like a snail being ripped out of its shell, or you can accept your role and go on back to your brother to work it through."

Jennie, still nodding her head, was beginning to cry.

Anna, who was sitting next to Jennie, touched the older woman's arm solicitously and said, quietly, "Don't cry." Then, destroying the warmth of the moment, Anna added, "Don't cry. I don't even like you." Jennie didn't appear to hear this. She continued to sob and nod her head.

Parrish leaned back and said, "So Anna, you believe that

everything is already decided. That your fate is already determined."

Anna shot him another hot glance, and again he felt oddly unbalanced. How did she do it? How did she establish an assumption of intimacy between them, a sense of shared knowledge so that, in an instant, he could feel false and unworthy? The bitch. The presumptuous little slut.

"No," Anna said. She opened her mouth to say more, and stopped, pouting. He knew the look. He wasn't going to get any more out of her. He had misinterpreted her, offended her somehow. The damnable thing was that she could make him feel so inadequate. How did she manage it? There was nothing special about her. The world contained a sad surfeit of pretty girls going crazy. Anna Shockley was one of many.

"I don't understand," Parrish said.

"No," Anna agreed, still pouting, "you don't."

Al Bowling, an overweight man in his mid-forties, admitted to the Institute by his family doctor for depression, said, "You are all too serious, if you ask me. When I was your age, I was having a ball."

The hour was over. Parrish dismissed the group and walked back to his office where he dictated a desultory account of a new patient, a young boy who had attempted suicide by stabbing himself in the stomach with a scissors. From his office window, he could see that the storm had, if anything, increased in violence. The parking lot was filled with rivulets of black water.

Still feeling harried by obligations, Parrish called Jane's number. Her voice was tremulous. "Richard. I was hoping you wouldn't get tied up. I really need you today. This weather has made me feel so blue, so worthless."

He had intended to beg off, but this obviously wasn't the day to do it.

Parrish met her at The Retreat, a small, inexpensive restaurant in downtown Newburg. Jane was already seated at a table.

Jane Solomon was an aristocratic beauty, possessed of a nervous angularity, a rueful and general unease that lessened the effect of her fine features and sleek, exercised body. She communicated an unhappiness and desperation that Parrish might have diagnosed as hysteric under clinical conditions. She wore a tan sweater and her dark hair was pulled tightly back.

Jane was the daughter of Dr. Ron Solomon, president of ExcellCare, a vast corporation owning a variety of medical facilities including Romner Psychiatric Institute.

While Jane was undeniably a good-looking woman, her looks weren't the sort that normally attracted Richard. He pursued her because she was the daughter of the fabulous Dr. Solomon. She was, therefore, the end of the rainbow. She was all ambitions realized.

And she was no fool. She knew about fortune hunters. There had been one or two in her past. Parrish was careful not to seem overly eager. He was always interested, always available, but he wasn't in a hurry. He talked about dedication, about striving to help others, about his frustration with the red tape of hospital operations. He was rewarded with Jane's concern. "You work too hard," she told him. "I know you want to help everyone, but you have to take some time for yourself."

From the beginning, Parrish had decided that his best bet was the role of slightly abstracted, unworldly doctor. He had, it seemed, made the right decision. Jane now took pride in having brought him into the wider world, taken him to plays, introduced him to good music, fine food. She had taught him to laugh, to take pleasure in life. She was pleased with herself, for in doing this she had helped create a doctor more in tune with humanity, more capable of sympathizing with the world, more effective with his patients.

Dr. Ron Solomon was harder to read, but Parrish felt that the old man approved of him, at least tentatively. The legendary Dr. Solomon was a Midwesterner with a narrow face and skeptical features. He had extended his hand, on first meeting Parrish, and drawled, "Well, you're the shrink my daughter is so keen on. Pleased to meet you. How do you find Romner?"

Dr. Solomon had then spent the next forty minutes asking questions about Parrish's personal experiences at the hospital, his opinion on various doctors, administrative problems, modes of treatment. It felt like an interview, and Richard didn't object to that. He answered carefully, not wanting to step on any toes but wanting to portray himself—obliquely, of course—as a concerned and dedicated doctor who wanted the best for his patients.

The interview had been terminated by Jane. "Daddy, that's enough! I didn't bring Richard here to have you grill him. He worries too much already. You can ring him up at work if you want to talk about work." Solomon had, good-naturedly, thrown up his hands. "I apologize," he had said. "My daughter is right. In this house, she is generally right."

Now Richard smiled across the table at Jane. He raised his champagne glass and said, "You look lovely today. Just seeing you dispels my gloom." Jane smiled crookedly at his flattery. She was often embarrassed by compliments; they flustered her.

"I like your hair that way," he continued. "You have beautiful bones," he heard himself saying. He was rolling on, trying to quiet joyless voices that were growing in number, muttering that he wasn't happy, that his life was a fraud.

"I'm a nuisance," she said. "I know that. You probably had something else to do. I think I sensed that in your voice when I called, but I wasn't about to let you out of it. Was I right? Did you have something else planned?"

Parrish reached across the table and held her wrist. He narrowed his eyes and turned up the modulation on his voice. "Jane, I don't understand how a beautiful woman like you can have so little self-confidence. There isn't a man in this town who wouldn't give his right arm to be having lunch with you, and I know it. However, you are right. Lunch was not on my mind when you called." Parrish winked. "If your afternoon is free, I thought I might take you back to my apartment."

Jane Solomon blushed and giggled. Then she stopped. "Are you all right?" she asked. Parrish's ribald smile had drifted into blankness.

"Are you all right?" he heard her say. He coughed sharply, and the black, accusatory eyes of Anna Shockley disappeared, retreating to whatever alcove they had been inhabiting until they chose to leap so suddenly into his consciousness.

Why was he thinking of Anna Shockley? Now there was

somebody's millstone, a girl calculated to drag some poor whimpering male into misery. She did have a blatant sort of sexuality that Jane Solomon would never have. Anna did have a kind of brash, heavy-metal eroticism, the volume cranked up all the way. Jane was more subtle. Flutes, maybe.

"I'm fine," he said, when Jane asked, and her startled expression warned him to watch his voice. "I've been overworked," he added. "I apologize."

The steady, relentless rain helped salvage the day. They had rushed from the restaurant to Jane's car, running clumsily under Richard's umbrella, the cold, furious rain outwitted.

At the apartment, Richard poured them glasses of wine and they sat on the sofa, feeling closer and more secure in the warmth. "Sometimes I'm so scared," Jane said. "I don't even know what I'm scared of, but I'm also scared of just living my life in somebody's shadow, Daddy's, even yours. That's why I always tend to withdraw, Richard. You've been so good about it. It's not being coy or anything..."

Richard reached over and held her. "I know," he said. He put his arms around her and held her.

He undid the buttons on her blouse. He expected to be rebuffed, for Jane, although she was twenty-four years old and no virgin, had been chaste the last two years in reaction to a romance that had ended badly. She had traced the bad end to the good sex, addictive, wild, dangerously exhilarating. Richard hadn't followed her reasoning, but he hadn't minded the forced abstinence, indeed, he felt his gentle acquiescence to her unreasonable demands gave him a high card in the game of courtship and guilt. Her reticence was an opportunity to show his understanding, the depth of his caring.

But this afternoon she didn't stop him. She allowed him to undress her without protest. Richard had only intended a token overture, and he was momentarily irritated, awkwardly shifting gears. He carried her into the bedroom. Naked, she was more self-possessed, less predictable. She laughed, catching him and pulling him to her. Lightning turned the room white, scattering shadows. He saw her face and body in the exclamations of the storm, dreamlike, fading in and out of focus.

She was surprisingly vocal in her lovemaking, shouting her delight, and this, in turn, filled him with a sense of his own power. He worked carefully, thoughtfully, cementing this commitment. She wouldn't turn back now. She would marry him. The high value she placed on sex made it the ultimate contract.

In the midst of these thoughts, Jane mewing beneath him, an orgasm overtook and surprised him.

She left at midnight, saying she had to go home and get some sleep and sort things out.

"I'll call you in the morning," she said. "I love you."

"I love you too," he said. And he did.

In the morning the hospital called to tell him that Anna was signing herself out of the hospital, going home. He told them to hold on to her until he talked to her. He would be right there. He dressed hurriedly and drove to the hospital in the darkness. The rain had stopped, but the temperature had plummeted and the roads were icy. The car slipped and shivered through traffic. The day promised perils, misadventure. He tried to remember last night's good fortune, but already it was illusory. He went directly to the restroom and swallowed two Valiums, splashed water in his face, and studied his eyes until some of the dread had left them, squeezed out by hard, mirror-staring effort. Then, feeling in control again, he went to talk to Anna.

They had parked Anna in his office, and she was fidgeting with her hair, looking particularly glum and belligerent.

"I don't want to argue about it," she said. "I can't stay here."

"Why not?" he asked, sitting down at his desk. He picked a pencil out of a drawer and tapped it on the desk top. "Why do you have to leave, Anna?"

Anna shrugged. "I don't want to stay where I'm not wanted."

"Who doesn't want you here?"

Anna narrowed her eyes and leaned forward. "You don't."

"Of course I want you to stay," Parrish said.

"I'm not going to stay," Anna said. "I'm sorry, but I made a big mistake coming here in the first place, and now I feel awful and I just want to get out." She sat down.

Parrish noticed that Anna had dressed for this occasion. Her hair was combed back, and she was even wearing some makeup, unusual for Anna. The makeup was inexpertly applied, but appealing for that very reason, emphasizing her waiflike quality, demanding protection under the rights of innocence.

"Anna," Parrish said, "I want you to stay. I think you need to stay here for awhile because there are some things that you should think about, some decisions that you really have to make. I think that a lot of bad things have happened in your life, and you have adapted to those bad things, developed ways of coping. But some of the ways of getting by have hurt you, and you have to learn new ways. Remember yesterday when you were talking about getting a job? Your friend Diane in vocational rehabilitation was going to help you look for a job, and you were excited about that. What about that?"

Anna pushed her lower lip forward and stared at the desk. She was beginning to look like a child being reprimanded by the principal. Parrish had an urge to lean forward and kiss her—he imagined her eyes growing big with shock, her mouth falling open— but he wrapped his hands together and waited for Anna to say something. When she did speak, he could hardly hear her. She whispered.

Parrish leaned forward. "What's that?"

She looked up. Her eyes were wet with tears. "I'm sorry," she said, her voice coming out in a loud hiccup. She began to cry, and Parrish went to her and hugged her and—no helping it now—found himself patting her head.

"There's nothing to be sorry for," he said. He held her and she cried and hugged him back. He gave her some tissues and she blew her nose, a loud, unfeminine honk, and smiled.

"Okay," Anna said. "I'll stay."

"Good," Parrish said. He nodded his head. "I'm glad. I would miss you if you left." Parrish looked at his watch and raised his eyebrows. "It's almost time for group, and I haven't eaten any breakfast. I've got to run downstairs and beg something from the kitchen. I'll see you in group." Parrish walked her to the door.

Anna was excited now, eyes bright and outlined with wet mascara. She smiled, lowered her eyelids and said, "I'll see you then, Dr. Parrish." They walked out into the hall and Parrish closed his office door. He waved and began walking away from her. She shouted after him. "Thank you, Dr. Parrish," she shouted. "Thank you for everything."

8

Anna got a job as a cashier at Nathan's Drugs. She left Romner and moved back to the Villa where Kalso let her rent her old room. Parrish wasn't happy with Anna's living at the Villa, but he could sense that Anna wasn't negotiating on that point, and he didn't want to scare her off by refusing to compromise. He didn't want to lose her.

Richard Parrish and Jane Solomon were officially engaged in March, and Parrish's mother had flown up, ostensibly on a whim— "Can't a mother miss her only child?"—but, in fact, to meet Jane and her legendary father. Richard had sweated through a long dinner at the Solomon mansion. How Grace had wrested this invitation from the semi-reclusive Dr. Solomon was a mystery, but she had done it, and Richard watched his mother charm skeptical father and reticent daughter with her caricature of a dotty Southern belle. She told delightful stories of her girlhood; of an eccentric father who wrote scathing letters to editors on any and all subjects and whose favorite word was "scandalous," used loosely to describe anything he disapproved of from presidents to toothpaste; of a fearful but loving mother who believed that a parked automobile was like a sleeping bull and might, at any moment, erupt into electric life and rush about maiming and murdering. Richard had never heard these anecdotes, and had rarely seen his mother in this nostalgic and whimsical mood.

At the airport, when she was preparing to leave, she told her son, "Marry that girl. She's money in the bank."

"Mother," he said, frowning at her.

She frowned back. "I'm your mother, Richard. I would just as soon you didn't dissemble. For one thing, you do it so poorly. You fumble so when it comes to faking an emotion. We both like money, and you can *smell* the money in those people." His mother's face possessed a manic eagerness as she talked, and she clasped her hands in an unintentional parody of greed. "She's lovely the way only the rich can be lovely, Richard, and I will kill you if you don't marry her." She kissed him then and marched off for her flight. Watching her small, brittle frame negotiate an escalator, Richard realized that she meant it. He was realizing her deepest dreams.

Anna didn't come to the after-care session, and Richard fretted and had difficulty sleeping. He had rented a house that was sheltered by maples and evergreens, and the cool leaves allowed him to sleep with the windows open, without the distasteful, clammy breath of the air conditioning. But he awoke sweating from a nightmare in which he had been crumbling apart, rotting away. In the dream, he had been sitting at his desk and had felt a loose tooth with his tongue. He had reached up and pulled the tooth out. It had come out with a squishy pop, and he had discovered that the other teeth were as easily removed. He couldn't help himself, he slowly pulled them all out. Then, rubbing the flesh of his cheek, he discovered that it was numb, a rubbery stuff that came off in his fingers. He began to fall apart in other ways, portions of his body dropping off, melting, an eyeball thumping on the desk to stare up at him, unwinking and baleful.

He awoke from this horrible, mortal moult and went downstairs, turning on lights as he went. He sat in a chair and began to write in his diary. Writing in the diary always invigorated him. He wrote, "That little bitch." He put the pen down. She was beginning to infect all things, even this, his refuge. He no longer felt like writing.

When the first faint sunlight illuminated the drawn curtains, he stalked upstairs and sank into grudging sleep.

He couldn't help it. He was elated when she showed up for the next session. "Where were you?" he asked, adopting a mock stern tone.

She told him she had gone to a meeting of the Dancers of the Divine Logic with Hank and Gretchen. Parrish couldn't hide his irritation. "I thought we agreed that you weren't going there for awhile. I thought we agreed that you were going to let that cool off a little, get your life in order and then see how you felt about those folks."

He tried to hide the anger, but Anna was always quick to see such things. "I work all day," she shouted back. "You don't want me to drink or do any drugs. You want me to sit in my room with the lights out, I guess. I've got to have *some* kind of social life."

"I understand that."

Anna folded her arms and looked away, eyes misting. "I don't think you understand anything. How could you? It's different for you."

"I am trying to understand," Parrish said. "I want to. I am genuinely concerned about you."

"Are you genuinely concerned about that debutante you're seeing?" For one weird moment, Richard Parrish felt found out, and Anna's brown eyes seemed to read him with a harsh, effortless cynicism. But he recovered quickly.

"What debutante?"

Anna smiled. "That woman who is always coming to see you. The nervous one with the green eye shadow."

Parrish smiled. "Oh, that one."

"Yeah."

"Maybe it's not your business. Maybe I'm the doctor and you are the patient."

"Maybe."

"That's my girlfriend. We're going to be married, as a matter of fact. I love her. Does that answer your question?"

Anna said nothing. She looked like she had been slapped. Her mouth was slightly open. She slowly narrowed her eyes, enclosing some thought, as though hearing a distant sound that made no sense but might be puzzled out.

She stood up. "That's okay," she said, speaking to a bookcase. "I've got to go—because I've got a life of my own."

Richard Parrish spoke sharply. "Anna, don't just run away. I think we should talk about this. It's not unusual for a patient to feel strongly about her doctor. In fact, it's very common, and it has to do with my role, my authority. This sort of transference doesn't really have anything to do with me."

Anna had one hand on the office doorknob. She still had the look of someone thinking furiously, racing a mental engine in neutral. She suddenly flung the door open, turned and ran out. Parrish raced around his desk and shouted after her as she fled down the hall, her long hair flying, her tennis shoes slapping on the shiny floor.

She banged through the ward doors and out into the lobby and up the exit stairs. Parrish didn't follow, as a nurse stepped out and looked at him. He smiled sadly and shook his head at the nurse and walked back to his office. He locked the door, sat at his desk, and thought, "Well, she's gone. She's someone else's problem now."

He prided himself on the finality of that thought, the offhand way it dispensed with Anna Shockley. His hands were shaking as he rooted through the desk for more Valium.

The next day, Thursday, he went to Nathan's Drugs. "I just wanted to see if you were all right," he told her. She was glad to see him, almost jumping with delight. She was wearing a pink headband and a yellow blouse with small green flowers stitched around its collar, and the effect aimed for was probably old-fashioned innocence. Anna, however, had such an exuberance of body—and the blouse was too small for the full-breasted girl—that the effect was somewhat steamier, making Parrish think of an erotic Victorian novel that he had once discovered in his father's dresser drawer.

"This was great timing," Anna said. "I'm off in ten minutes. We could go get lunch."

Richard Parrish looked at his watch. "It's only one," he said.

"I'm off at one on Thursdays. I told you that. Fridays I have to work until eight and..." She launched into an elaborate explanation of her schedule, which Parrish didn't hear.

Parrish waited for her to get off. It was a day of boldness, and as he waited outside in the heat he rolled up his sleeves and took off his tie.

Anna came out of the drugstore giggling, exuberantly shedding the workaday world. She threw herself into his car when he opened the door, and they drove off.

They decided they would make a picnic of it so they drove out of town. "I know where to go," Anna said. "It's a great place." Parrish found himself falling easily into the role of obliging chauffeur as Anna told him where to turn. "We're almost there," she said when he thought they had driven too far, when the pull of obligations and guilt chastised him. They stopped and bought a bucket of chicken, and giant Cokes, and a glutton-sized bucket of coleslaw. "I love coleslaw," Anna said.

Richard listened to her babble. Anna had raw energy, no doubt about it. She could infect the rest of group therapy with her moods. This seemed to be tied to her illness, this emotional contagiousness she had. Her pathological self-involvement was also her great charm. Paradoxically, she was often radiantly unself-conscious.

They pulled out of the Kentucky Fried Chicken—and it may have been Richard's imagination but the balding counter man seemed to eye them with lewd envy—and Anna directed Parrish down a dirt road. She showed him where to park the car and they climbed down to the Yurman River. They ate the chicken in the shade of an oak tree, blinking out at the sun and water.

"This is one of my favorite places," Anna said. She was lying on the grass, staring up at the willow-lined bank.

"I can see why," Parrish said. "It's beautiful."

"I drive out here a lot," Anna said. "It helps me think."

"You're making progress. I'm proud of you."

Anna smiled and blushed, as she always did when praised. "You did it," she said.

They didn't say anything for a long time, watching a large white heron wading in the shallows. As they watched, its silver neck darted forward and a thin, shivering shard of fish squirmed in its beak. The fish wiggled down the bird's throat.

Parrish felt enchanted, freed. When Anna leaned over him, smiling, a maiden descending from the clouds saying, "Look, a four-leaf clover," he caught her arm and drew her down to him. He kissed her, and there was less of passion in his kiss than of indolence and general well-being. It was the fierceness of her

103

reciprocated kiss that set the alarm clamoring, swept him with hot fears. He lurched to his feet, rudely pushing her back as though she were an incubus, a demon sent to suck his soul from his lips.

"Anna," he said. "Please...." He had been distracted, muddled by the warmth and perfection of the day, and he watched as Anna's eyes caught and then mirrored his confusion.

"I'm sorry," he said, and Anna turned and ran. He ran after her, but she was quick, and she plunged into the shadowy pine trees. The sun began to set swiftly, fogging detail, producing clumps of thorny brambles that bit his hands, muddy hillocks that caught at city shoes. He shouted her name in the woods and stumbled forward. She didn't answer, and anger mixed with his desperation. *Goddam the bitch.*

He hated himself as he climbed the slippery hill back to his car. Sunset filled the river with glorious red, and he felt more the fool amid this last surge of beauty. He opened the car door and sat down. The red sky drained to darkness, and he felt a dull lumbering fatigue enter his body.

Maybe she had fallen, hurt herself. Maybe she had done herself some intentional harm. Maybe she had simply reached a road and hitchhiked out, leaving him to stew. She was capable of that. She was crazy.

He laughed, a cold, cruel knife of mirth, hurled at himself. He was not in the habit of kissing emotionally disturbed girls. His colleagues would not applaud this maneuver, that's for sure (it was, among other things, blatantly unethical). They hated him, envied him and feared the ramifications of his forthcoming marriage to Jane, and they would gloat horribly at his downfall. He had been lulled, by the day, by her powerful sexuality, and he had imagined that he was someone other than who he was, that she was not a patient in his care.

For the first time in a long time, he thought of Vivian. His chest seemed filled with cement. He sobbed.

He sat in the car in complete darkness. He might have been asleep, or near sleep, when the door opened and Anna slid in on her side. He turned and looked at her. "You can take me home," she said.

He turned the key in the ignition and turned the lights on. Tunneling through the darkness, guided by the yellow beams, he drove back to town. He dropped her at the Villa and drove back to his own house. He hadn't said a word, nor had she. He did not know what to say, but he would have liked to say something. He would have been curious to hear his own voice. Would it have been full of apology, this voice? Would it have been serene, the clinical psychologist returned, or would it have resounded with recrimination, the injured lover, the misunderstood friend, the put-upon Samaritan? If he had said something, his voice might have given him some clue as to how he really felt. But he had been silent, and he entered his house and lay on the bed in confusion until sleep overtook him.

So it came as a surprise, the way his heart jumped two weeks later when he answered a knock at the door and found Anna standing there. He felt momentarily dizzy with excitement. She hadn't come to the last two after-care sessions, and he hadn't thought about her much. When he did think about her, his thoughts were so tinged with recriminations that he was glad to let her image fade. He had been busy with an overloaded patient schedule, and Jane had been more demanding of late.

Since they had made love, Jane had assumed a more proprietary air, and Parrish was finding more and more of the stuff of arguments in the atmosphere. But he did not argue. He was unfailingly amenable. He didn't want an argument that might escalate into a force that could blow them apart. He was interested only in marrying her. After they were married, after he was securely settled, there would come a time when he wouldn't have to submit to her every whim. But, for the moment, he was entirely in agreement with his mother's philosophy: the marriage at all costs.

And so he let a number of resentments seethe and smolder under his flesh, and he smiled and gave no clue to their existence. He thought, when he thought at all about his feelings toward Jane, that he didn't like her much, but that he might have liked her more if he had not been so intent on marrying her.

Now Anna stood in his doorway, with the porch light shining down on her smiling face. "Hi," she said.

She was wearing an extremely short pair of dark blue shorts, sandals, and a yellow and green t-shirt. There seemed, as always, a richness to Anna, a dazzle of Anna, a largess of young womanhood. A large green moth, evidently agreeing, ignored the light and swooped at Anna, and she brushed it away and jumped back. "Eek!"

"Better come in," Parrish said, and he stepped back and let her in.

Anna laughed, still brushing invisible moths from her face. She sat down on a sofa and smiled at him. "I know it's late. What time is it, anyway?"

Parrish looked at his watch. "Not late," he said. "Five after eight."

"Anyway," Anna rushed on, "I thought you might like to go for a drive or something. I mean, I could take you out and buy you a beer. And apologize. Okay. I'm sorry."

Parrish noticed then that Anna's smile, despite its brightness, was starched and untrue. Her eyes glittered, and when she had walked past him he had detected the strong odor of beer.

"I'm the one who should apologize," Parrish said.

"Anyway," Anna continued, "the whole thing is really dumb. You're a shrink, and I'm this rehabilitated dropout who works at a drug store, no match in heaven as they say, and I also wanted to come by to tell you that I've been doing a lot of thinking about what I'm going to do with my life and I've decided to move out to The Home. I didn't talk about this stuff because I know how you feel about Father Walker and the Dancers, but he says I'm really spiritual. He says your average person is like a melody played on a clarinet or something, beautiful but all single notes, you know. He says that I have harmonies in my song, like a symphony is how he explains it, and that he can show me how to glorify my soul."

Richard shook his head ruefully. "Why didn't you tell me about this before? I thought you trusted me, but you don't trust me at all."

Anna shrugged her shoulders. "Hank and Gretchen are moving out to the commune. They asked me to come along. I said I'd think about it. I thought about it. You would have just confused me, so I thought about it myself. Without any help, you know. Look, you

106

don't have to worry about me getting weird like before. Father Walker says that happens sometimes, the experience of divinity can be so powerful that it sets up a physical vibration, like an echo. And the echo isn't real, isn't holiness, but a sickness caused by holiness. Once you've gone through it, it can't happen again, like having the measles."

"That man's a fraud!" Parrish shouted, grabbing Anna's shoulders.

Anna jumped up, shaking her head, hair flying. "He isn't. He cares about me more than you do!"

Parrish shoved her back onto the sofa and sat next to her. He spoke very slowly. "Anna, when you came here you were an extremely ill girl. You are much better now. But you are not well. If you go out to The Home, you'll probably get sick again."

Anna glared at Parrish and said nothing. He waited. The silence stretched out, and the room stretched, all the shadows of it lengthening, and Anna's dark eyes continued to transmit a black and virulent anger. Slowly Parrish took his hands off her shoulders. Anna stood up and walked toward the door.

"I shouldn't have come here," Anna said. "I knew you wouldn't be happy for me."

Parrish could hardly see her. The light from the lamp on the end table expired at her feet, and the light from the porch threw her into silhouette. But she seemed more substantial than anything in his past or present. She seemed the promise of his future, moving forever away.

He couldn't let her leave.

"Anna," he said, and his voice seemed fatally small. He wondered if she would be able to hear it across the long room. "I love you."

"Oh," Anna said. It was an exclamation of confusion, a short intake of breath that fell again into the pooled darkness and left them separated, and then she ran to him.

They made love on the sofa.

It was an awkward, fumbling business. Anna cried out when she came, and her body shuddered and she hissed his name in his ear, "Richard." She had never called him Richard, and it made him giddy in the moment, as he raced toward his own climax. Later, as they lay on the sofa, all damp arms and legs, she called him Richard again, and fear bumped and flapped its wings in his chest as though the use of his first name was somehow more irrevocable than the meshing of bodies. Richard, she had said. They were together, this doomed girl and he. They were intertwined in this new familiarity.

"This is wrong," he said. "I shouldn't have."

A hand, smelling faintly of his own semen, touched his lips and she said, "No, it's right. You don't love her. You love me."

"Her?" For a moment, disoriented, he didn't understand this "her" and then he did. Jane. My God, Jane. His future spiralled into a great black chasm. He sat on the sofa in the darkness and Anna wrapped her warm arms around him and murmured—all unaware of the effect—"Richard, Richard, Richard."

9

Two weeks later Richard Parrish sat in his study and wrote in his diary. He was writing in his defense.

"She sought me out," he wrote. "She has a kind of sexual cunning, not to be underestimated. This is not my fault—although I'd get no understanding, no sympathy from my jealous peers. Wouldn't they revel in it? I've got to stop seeing her." Parrish put the pen down. He felt possessed, lunatic. He picked the pen up and continued, "Jane's bound to find out. Just last night, Jane called when Anna was sleeping next to me. I thought, 'She'll hear Anna breathing,' but she didn't. I talked to Jane, told her I'd call her in the morning, and when I hung up the phone, I felt ravenous for Anna, and I woke her and we screwed until we were both slippery with sweat. But it can't last, and then it's goodby Jane, goodby career, hello jail.

"The patient went right back to sleep, and I lay in the dark. I'm coming down with something, the same virus that has half the staff on sick leave, and that's not helping matters any. I've got a fever. Yesterday, I looked into Anna's eyes and saw Vivian. Vivian before things went wrong, the way Vivian's eyes would fill up with me. The situation is intolerable."

Later entries in the diary: "She says she loves me. There is an implied threat in her words. I am not imagining this. She is aware of her status, her power."

"I am not the first person to be overtaken by a sexual obsession. This could happen to anyone. I can wallow in it or get out. It's that simple."

"Now she says she is pregnant. This is the cheapest, most banal of lies, a sad commentary on her desperation."

"Jesus, it's true."

She came to him in his office and told him. She was smiling, radiant. "I went to see Dr. Hamil today," she said. "He says I'm pregnant. We are going to have a child, Richard."

He hadn't believed her. A week later, beginning to have second thoughts, he had called Hamil. He told Hamil that, as Anna's psychiatrist, he needed the information, needed to know the truth of Anna's declaration. "The girl's a compulsive liar," he told Hamil. And Hamil, a cautious man, had said that he would get back with Parrish. Whomever Hamil talked to had confirmed that Anna Shockley was, in fact, Dr. Parrish's patient.

Dr. Hamil returned Richard's call. He confirmed it; Anna was pregnant.

10

"We'll get married," Anna told him. "You won't regret it. You'll see. I'll make a good wife. I can sew and cook."

Parrish thought that the initial sense of unreality would fade, that the problem would come clear, present itself as a problem in the real world with a real solution. But that wasn't happening. The sense of absurdity was growing rather than shrinking. He was sitting in his office listening to a teenage girl tell him she was going to marry him. An old story. Boy gets girl in trouble, marries girl. He had done it himself: Vivian. Now he had done it again, only now it was utterly ludicrous. For one thing, he was marrying Jane Solomon next month. For another thing, he had no intention of destroying his career.

Anna refused to get an abortion. What she said was, "I'm not going to kill our child."

Richard didn't pursue the subject. He saw something ugly and warning in Anna's eyes at the first mention of such a possibility. She was capable of anything, he realized.

He told her that she couldn't say anything to anyone for now, that he had to arrange things. A premature announcement could get him in trouble with the hospital. She seemed to understand this, or at least she appreciated—probably enjoyed—the secrecy.

"Our secret," she said, and leaned over the desk and kissed his cheek.

Sometimes he thought that he could simply ignore her, deny that he had had sexual relations with her. He would not be the first psychiatrist unjustly accused by a female patient. It happened all the time.

This would fail. He was convinced that he would be unable to bluster through the inevitable investigation. And what about Anna herself? He realized that he was afraid of her, that her scorn and fury would be somehow more devastating than an board of inquiry. Absurdly, he didn't want her to think ill of him.

And, if by some miracle he did brazen it through the whole rotten experience, it might cast just enough of a pall on his career to make Jane and her father shy off. A tide of gossip and scandal would wash him into some stagnant backwater where he would live out his days baby-sitting the brain-damaged. The field had a long memory for tainted histories. His desperate job applications would trigger comments like, "Parrish? Oh yeah, isn't he the guy who was screwing that sexy little teenager? They never got him, but he looked guilty as hell, I remember that. And I saw the girl once. I got one look at her, an incredible bombshell in a fuzzy, fuck-me sweater, and I thought, 'Guilty. The poor bastard is guilty.'"

No. He couldn't just deny his way to freedom.

Could he convince Anna that he couldn't marry her, that she

had to go away and have the baby or his career was doomed? Anna might go for the high drama of being noble.

But there were big problems there. For one thing, Richard Parrish intended to marry Jane Solomon, and there were limits to Anna's nobility.

Also, Anna silent was no guarantee of Anna silent forever. The girl's emotional state was erratic and degenerative. Pregnancy would certainly throw new hormonal monkey wrenches into an already malfunctioning psyche. It was only a matter of time before Anna found someone to tell and told.

The only real silence was Anna dead.

That wouldn't be such an extraordinary thing, would it? She was a self-destructive child.

Anna could die of an overdose. She had been admitted to a hospital once for an overdose.

She could just disappear. Again, the possibility of suicide would be the most logical explanation for a vanished Anna.

She could inhale carbon monoxide, shoot herself through the head, leap from a bridge.

Richard Parrish was still enumerating violent demises—his mind having disassociated from the impetus behind the list and entered into the spirit of list making—when he was paged on the intercom. A patient had run amok on Parrish's ward and broken another patient's arm.

"Bobby Starne," the ward clerk said, and the name didn't surprise Parrish. "He's quiet now and James Fiske has already been taken over to Cameron. You'll want to talk to Nurse Cindar. She's writing up the incident report."

There wasn't much to tell. An orderly had noted that morning that Starne seemed extremely upset. He had run his hands up and down his body and complained of an itching sensation. He had told one of the patients, "Baby Lisa is here."

Five patients had been in occupational therapy when Bobby Starne attacked James Fiske, a skinny blond boy, a new arrival who had already expressed a fear of Bobby and asked to be moved to another ward.

111

Starne had screamed and leaped across the room. James Fiske had had his arm broken immediately when he started to push his chair back and Bobby slammed into him. Fiske's left forearm had been caught between two of the chair slats and neatly snapped. Two orderlies got there before Starne could do any additional damage. Bobby was wailing a terrified wail, as loud as the screams of pain that erupted from his victim.

It had been an exhausting day, and Parrish hadn't left the hospital until dark. The phone was ringing when he unlocked the door. It was Jane.

"Where have you been?" she asked.

"The hospital, of course."

"Oh Richard, how could you forget?" The phone magnified a querulous tone in her voice. "It's Daddy's birthday."

"Oh," Richard said.

"It's too late for you to come by and pick me up," Jane said. "I'll just meet you at Nestor's. Get dressed—please, not that awful brown suit—and try to get there before nine. Really. I can't believe—"

"Sweetheart, I'm very tired. I'm sure your father would understand if I didn't come."

The line was silent. Then, in slow, articulated tones: "Are you saying you are too tired to come?"

The argument was inevitable, as was its conclusion. Jane hung up. Richard listened to the dial tone, smiled grimly.

"Fuck you," he said.

Then Anna tapped softly at the door and he let her in. Her hair was still damp from the shower and her eyes contained such oceans of dark adoration that all the Jane Solomons and all the world's dirty money dissolved in the tidal wave of her embrace.

Richard Parrish did not believe in God, but he believed in the significance of random events. Hadn't his life been shaped by rough accidents? Didn't it behoove a man to listen to all the subtle voices of coincidence? The telephone call from Jane, imperious and shrill; the immediate arrival of Anna, gentle and giving...the most insensible of human beings would have to read something into this juxtaposition of Jane's cold voice and Anna's warm presence. A man ignores such omens at his own peril.

The next morning, as he drove to work under bright, cloudless skies that might have been ordered up for such revelations, he decided that he would renounce Romner Psychiatric, that damnable harridan Jane, and her megalomaniac sire. He would seek out love where love flourished, in the arms of Anna Shockley. Let the world reel with outrage. Let his mother wail like a professional mourner. He had lost sight of everything but ambition, and where did ambition lead? It led to a loveless marriage and a servile relationship with a bully of a father-in-law.

Parrish felt saved. Certainly he was no murderer. He could not take another life. He could not possibly hurt Anna, exquisite Anna. He could marry her, cherish her.

It was an elated, invigorated Richard Parrish who drove toward the hospital. But omens were not done with him yet. On the previous day, in the midst of a hundred petty obligations, he had added one more: he had agreed to pick up his colleague, John Swayles, whose car was in the shop.

John was a hearty, thickset man with mutton chop whiskers. "Hope you don't mind," John said, settling himself into the passenger seat. "I'm fetching a patient on the way in. It slipped my mind. I generally pick the boy up, and I thought I'd have my car by now."

Parrish assured Swayles that it was no problem. Parrish had just resolved the terrible tangle of his life, and he followed Swayles's indifferent directions—"whoops, just passed the left we needed"—with good-humored tolerance.

John Swayles counseled troubled children, and it was one such child, a twelve-year-old boy named Sammy Lyons, that they were picking up. He lived with his parents in a mobile home that was as unlovely a dwelling as Richard had ever seen. It was pale green, a squat rectangle with narrow, suspicious windows. The yard was dirt, and as Parrish walked to the house with John, a sour earth smell worked to close his throat. A rusted swing set, bent sideways, looked like a grim sculpture of the apocalypse.

John knocked on the door. A television set could be heard,

113

blaring, rude and banal. A baby was crying. The door was opened and Vivian, a baby in a diaper balanced on her hip, brushed hair from her forehead and blinked at him.

Parrish stumbled backward.

"This is Viv," John Swayles said.

Parrish found himself in the house, felt it close around him before he could run. He was back in that apartment, suddenly mugged by every detail of squalor. Her name wasn't Vivian at all; it was Liz, and that is how John had introduced her. She didn't even look like Viv, not really. The same eyes, maybe. You could see a headache in those pale, grey eyes, and weariness in the hand that brushed a strand of dirty blonde hair from her forehead. She had that cheerleader prettiness, the face just beginning to bloat and blur.

"Excuse the mess," she said, her voice as flat as a highway through desert. "Sammy!" she shouted. "Come on out here now. Dr. Swayles is here." Parrish found his eyes traveling around the room. A hotplate was plugged into the wall, a pan of tomato soup boiling on it. The image on the TV set rolled. Sammy came out—a skinny, boneless boy with a round face—and Liz leaned forward and shook him. "What did I say about cigarettes?" she wanted to know. Sammy looked at the floor and Liz shook him.

"We've got to get going," Swayles said. "Come on, Sammy."

"Your dad will set your bottom on fire," Liz shouted after them as they moved toward the car.

Richard Parrish climbed back into the car and started it up. His heart was beating painfully. He had seen it. He had seen where love would send him. How could he have forgotten?

Back in his office, he locked the door and sat behind his desk. What was he going to do? He couldn't marry Anna. He had just had a glimpse of the reality of living with her. Impossible. She would be unhappy too. They were not equals in the world. She would sense the distance, feel betrayed by it.

Jane was his equal—for all her abrasiveness, she was his equal. And now... was she even speaking to him?

Richard dialed her number.

"Oh Richard," she began, "I'm so sorry about last night. I was dreadful. And Daddy lit into me too. He says if I am going to be a doctor's wife I had better start learning what that means. You were exhausted, and I was such a shrew...I mean, not a thought to how you felt. Will you forgive me?"

Richard assured her that she was forgiven. He felt a rush of gratitude, another outpouring of emotion.

This was exhausting stuff. If only Anna would go away. Life held very little for her, really. If she could see the future as he saw it, she would see the pain, the suffering. She would not wish to go on. If only she could be relieved of the burden.

Thinking this, Richard felt a great wave of compassion, of god-clean love, pour out of him. But the feeling was swiftly followed by despair. What could he do?

He could get on with his day. He was, after all, at work. First on the list was an unpleasant task. An interview with Bobby Starne, star psychopath and arm breaker.

"It was Baby Lisa," Starne told Parrish. "She knows I'm here. I could feel her searching for me all morning. I could feel the light probes."

Parrish was only half listening to Starne. They had upped the boy's medication after the incident, and the drugs made the boy appear even duller, a sleepy-eyed, clay-faced giant in a too-tight t-shirt with a silk-screened palm tree on it.

Parrish was convinced that Bobby Starne should have been relegated to another ward or transferred to State long ago. Starne obviously wasn't in any shape to interact with peers, and Parrish had said as much—several times—and been ignored. Now, this incident would serve to ditch Starne, and that was fine. This interview was just a formality, and Parrish listened distantly, staring at a ghost.

Then Bobby said, "I didn't get her, though. Baby Lisa jumped out of his body when I caught him. I'm sorry I hurt him, because she wasn't even there." The boy's voice suddenly leaped to a reedy whine, and this change in pitch and volume seemed to underline the words, and an instant connection occurred in Richard Parrish's mind, a wild, ecstatic jump of genius.

"Tell me where she's gone," Bobby whined. "Just tell me where she went. If I can catch her, if I can kill her, then everything will be all right." Bobby Starnes's big, brutal body squirmed, and his face looked stony, less human than ever.

Parrish shivered. Oh, such a day of signs and omens. Here was the solution. It may have been the sheer insanity of the boy's voice; it may have been the alien resolve on the boy's features. It may have been Parrish's own voice, when his thoughts locked so effortlessly into *the solution* and he said, "I think I can help you. I think I know where Baby Lisa is."

Wherever it came from, it had arrived: the solution.

11

Richard sat in his study, writing in his diary, waiting for Anna to arrive. A memory of Vivian surfaced and he didn't pull away from it. He had been so young then. He felt a wave of pity and love for the boy of his memory. Love figured much in his thoughts these days. He loved Anna and if he was engineering her death—let us not mince words here—he was doing it as God might do it, letting the great world take her. He would not put his arms around her pale throat and throttle her. He would not touch her. He would set events in motion, and these events, if they so chose, would answer for Anna's fate. He was no assassin, no blood-soaked, demon killer.

There wasn't much time left. He was to marry Jane in a quiet, unpublicized ceremony at her father's mansion on the twenty-eighth of June, a bare two weeks away. Anna was unaware of her lover's upcoming wedding. Parrish had talked Jane out of a lavish wedding, sold her on the romantic notion that their love was too pure for the carnival convention of a fancy wedding.

Still, Anna might find out, somehow, some way. And Jane could stumble onto these midnight visits of Anna's. Risky all around, and Parrish found himself reveling in it.

Anna knocked on the door and he let her in. She had parked farther down the quiet, shady street, and stolen to his door. He knew she did not understand his need for secrecy, but she didn't need to. Something in her responded to secrecy. She liked to sneak.

He lifted her up and carried her into the bedroom.

This was certainly the most foolish aspect of it all, that he continued to make love to her. He told himself that it was his way of reassuring her, of monitoring her, but the truth was he still wanted her, wanted her desperately, and as the time grew shorter she exerted a more powerful erotic force. And he loved her, of course, and could not deny her.

She was lying on top of the sheets on her stomach when he came out of the bathroom. The night light sprayed the room with a thin, silver dust that washed over the sheer lines of her buttocks and shoulders.

Lovely, silky animal, he thought, as he leaned over her and ran his hand down her back. Anna rolled over and smiled. She didn't say anything, but she caught his hand and pulled it to her mouth. She kissed his hand. Then she bit him.

He screamed. Her teeth had plunged into the fleshy palm, bringing blood. He jerked his hand away.

"Goddam it!" he shouted. He clutched his injured hand. "What are you doing?"

Anna frowned back. She was never intimidated by him. She sat up slowly. "I don't want to fool around any more. I want to get married. I don't want any more excuses."

He might have hit her then, beaten her bloody, but the rush of anger that filled him, stretched his skin, and raised the temperature of his bones, frightened him with its magnitude. Moments before he had been confident of his powers, his control. Now this awesome darkness, this violence from nowhere.

He smiled at Anna. "You didn't have to bite me," he said.

"I wanted to get your attention."

"You have it. We'll get married next week. Would Friday suit you?"

She laughed then. "Richard," she said. "Come here."

He took her in a variety of positions that night. He seemed inexhaustible in his need. He memorized the nape of her neck, her breasts, the sweet narrowing of her waist, the way her eyes would open on an invisible panorama of joy, mouth open, tongue poised on the tip of wonder. He marveled at the way she moved, the sleepy kiss of her body when they were both wet and slippery and sated. He wanted to remember everything, for this would be the last time.

Fortunately, the conditioning was complete. The plan could fail, of course, but it wouldn't fail for lack of preparation. He had moved quickly after that first moment of revelation when he had heard Bobby Starne ask where Baby Lisa had gone.

He had realized, then, that he could solve the problem of Anna without raising a hand against her. He would simply speak certain words and cause and effect would do the rest.

"I know where Baby Lisa is," he told Bobby Starne.

When Bobby Starne's fate was being decided among the counselors, Richard Parrish surprised everyone by coming to the troubled boy's defense, arguing that he remain on the ward and receive additional private counseling. Parrish felt strongly on this matter, even offered to work with the boy himself. His colleagues were impressed by this concern and one of them voiced a general sentiment when he said, "I may have been wrong about Parrish. I always thought of him as somewhat cold and aloof, but he's really a very compassionate man."

Behind closed doors, Richard Parrish worked long and hard with Bobby Starne.

"Baby Lisa has taken over Anna Shockley," he warned Bobby. "You must kill her before she destroys everything."

Bobby understood. He recognized the pictures of Anna, remembered her from when she was in group.

Bobby would nod, stolidly, and swear silence (for the spies of Baby Lisa might be anywhere) but Parrish knew this wasn't enough. He had to drive the obsession deep. He talked with Dr. Jenner, who was in charge of medication on the ward but who was generally amenable to whatever a particular doctor recommended for his patient. Parrish convinced Jenner that the Starne boy wasn't going to make any progress unless his dosages were cut down. Jenner had some reservations; the boy was violent and paranoid, but Parrish launched an impassioned speech on the necessity of risk in the practice of psychotherapy, and Jenner quickly demurred.

Parrish warned Bobby that, when the time came, he would have to act quickly, because Baby Lisa would certainly try to kill him. "As soon as you have killed her," Parrish said, "you must take a pill that will prevent Baby Lisa from entering your body, from leaping into your living flesh. I will give you that protection." Parrish smiled to himself, for this was the fail-safe part of the plan, a brilliant touch.

This lurid, outrageous scenario was just right. It was too bizarre to ever be presented in any court as a plan for murder. And yet, Parrish knew, it entered the logic of Bobby Starne's mind with flawless ease.

12

Parrish checked the wires again. He wasn't sure if he had it right, but he certainly didn't want to consult anyone else on this critical part of the conditioning. He could hardly tell someone what he was up to. He could hardly say, "I am trying to drive a crazy person farther around the bend."

Parrish got up and walked out of his office and down the hall to the dayroom. The ward cat, Alice, was sleeping on the sofa, and Parrish reached down and picked her up. He looked at his watch. It was ten-twenty. Group would be out in another ten or fifteen minutes, and he would be seeing Bobby Starne in his office at eleven. Plenty of time.

Whispering in the cat's ear, Parrish walked back to his office. He put the drowsy animal on the chair where Bobby Starne would be sitting. He petted the cat and cooed over it. "Good Alice," he cooed, scratching its ears. The cat purred, stretched, and curled into a tight black ball. Satisfied that the cat wasn't going anywhere, Richard carefully moved away from the animal. He waked over to the light switch near the sofa. He waited a moment, then flicked the switch. The cat leaped into the air, magically levitated, and darted across the room. It ran in small, frenzied circles, mewed piteously at the door, and finally skulked under the sofa. A coppery smell that reminded Parrish of childhood train sets lingered in the room.

Parrish grinned broadly. Not bad for a guy whose electrical

expertise had formerly extended only to the changing of light bulbs, the replacing of frayed electrical cords.

He went over to the closet and took out the movie screen and projector. He took the film canister out of his briefcase and carefully threaded the film into the projector.

He drew the blinds. He sat in the dark and watched a cartoon about a mouse outwitting a cat. The mouse was tiptoeing around a corner with a burning stick of dynamite when suddenly Anna's image appeared on the screen, smiling, laughing. She was reacting to the camera, waving it away with her hand. She laughed. Then her image disappeared, replaced by the cartoon. Now the cat was locking the mouse in a trunk. The trunk, however, had no bottom.

Parrish stopped the projector and rewound the film. He was proud of himself, but not overly confident, not yet.

He hunted the cat down and took it back to the dayroom. Then he returned to his office and waited for Bobby Starne.

"I have a special treat for you today," Richard told Bobby. "I know how you love cartoons. I thought we could watch a cartoon together. What do you say?"

"That would be okay," Bobby said. Since Bobby's medications had been reduced, he was more wary and jittery than ever. He looked weirder too. As one of the ward nurses put it, "He looks like he's going to blow a fuse."

Bobby sat in the chair, but he was restless, and he grunted when the lights were turned off.

"It's okay," Parrish said, and he started the cartoon. Bobby was soon laughing, a heavy, *huh, huh* noise, and gripping the arms of his chair.

Anna's face jumped on the screen, and Parrish flipped the light switch and Bobby jolted out of the chair.

Parrish calmed Bobby down, returned him to the chair, and they continued to watch the movie.

But the third time Anna's face appeared, the third time Bobby Starne felt his body invaded by hissing, electric serpents, there was no calming him down. Parrish turned the projector off and turned on the room lights.

Parrish hugged the boy on the sofa. Bobby Starne was shivering, mumbling.

Parrish smiled and nodded. "Yes, yes, that's right. Baby Lisa. She's getting stronger. I think it's time to do something, don't you? I think we have to kill her quickly, or it will be too late."

When Bobby Starne was taken back to his room, shaking and whining incoherently, Richard told the orderly that Bobby's session had been traumatic, and that he should be isolated from the other patients for the rest of the day while he quieted down. No, he was not to be medicated heavily.

After the orderly left, Parrish locked his office, turned the projector on again and watched Anna's laughing face. The camera moved away from her to reveal her surroundings, the rushing water, the sun-white pines. He remembered the day they had gone to the Yurman River and he had filmed her. That had been a fine, inviolate day. Anna had been flattered by his attention.

He rewound the film and put it back in the canister and replaced the canister in his briefcase. He methodically dismantled his "electric" chair and then he walked to his desk and called Anna at work.

"I want to play hookey," he told her. "I'm sick of work today. I know you get off at one. What do you say I meet you at our river? Around two, okay?"

Anna, delighted, said she would be there, and Parrish hung up with a sense of satisfaction. Events were moving properly toward their conclusion. All that remained was for Bobby Starne to escape.

This was the part of the plan most apt to go awry, the one risky part of the business. Bobby had to "escape" from Romner Psychiatric Institute. Patients did escape occasionally, and Bobby wasn't on a high security ward—although he would have been transferred to such a ward had Dr. Parrish failed to intervene on his behalf after the arm-breaking episode—but some precautions were still observed. Parrish waited until one o'clock when lunch was over and most patients were either downstairs in occupational therapy or in private sessions with assigned counselors. Bobby would have been downstairs with the others if Parrish hadn't requested that he be isolated. This meant that Bobby would be locked in his room for the afternoon.

Parrish pushed through the swinging doors and walked down the middle of the corridor. This ward had the feel of a college dorm, brighter, more hopeful, with dressers, desks, carpet in each room. Bobby's room was 118, and Parrish stopped in front of the door. He looked up and down the hall, and, seeing no one, he quickly bent and unlocked the door. Bobby was sitting on the bed, and he looked up when Parrish entered.

"Hullo, Dr. Parrish," he said.

"Hello, Bobby. You are going to have to be very quiet now. You have to do just what I tell you, okay?"

Bobby nodded his head.

"Good. We don't have much time. We have to kill Baby Lisa today or we will never have another chance. She will jump again, and we will never find her. We won't know where she is until she comes looking for us."

Bobby nodded grimly.

Parrish took the scissors blade out of his inside coat pocket and hacked at the wood around the door latch. It was the sort of latch that could be burgled with a credit card, so no one would be surprised that Bobby had managed to force it. They would wonder how he had managed to conceal the scissors (stolen over a week ago from the nursing station) through two room searches, and they might wonder how it came to be so sharp (for Parrish had lovingly honed it with a stone). They wouldn't wonder for long; they would dismiss the mystery, for, as Parrish had observed, a certain number of inexplicable events occurred weekly at Romner, as though the craziness contained in the place worked its way out of the patients' minds and into the walls, warping natural law.

For the same reason they would quickly cease wondering how the double doors at the end of the hall, the ones facing an expanse of rolling hills and green woods, had come to be open.

Having told Bobby what to do, and having had him repeat it, Richard peered out into the still-empty hallway, quickly slipped into the hall, closed the door behind him, and walked briskly in the direction of the nurses' station. He was prepared to talk to the ward clerk, but as he approached, he saw her turn away to answer a phone. The orderly was slumped in a chair, reading a paperback. He didn't look up as Parrish went by.

In the parking lot, Parrish looked at his watch again. It was one-twenty. He climbed in his car and drove off the lot. He drove slowly down Burnett Avenue and turned into the park at Burnett and Weaver. The park was named Hammet Field Park, and it had fallen into disrepair when the larger community center had been built a quarter of a mile to the south. Today, as usual, it was nearly empty except for a teenage couple sitting on a bench looking disconsolate and a fat woman dragging a small, shaggy dog behind her. The dog's small feet pinwheeled and it leaned against a taut leash. The woman gave it an occasional ill-tempered yank.

Parrish drove past the people and down a residential street and back into the L-shaped end of the park, now scrub vegetation and twisted, tormented trees. He waited.

He waited for fifteen minutes, and the heat of the day sparked perspiration on his forehead. He felt a tickle of panic. The whole plan seemed ludicrous. Bobby had been too crazy to understand, too lost in his convoluted world.

Then Bobby lurched out of the dark woods, his head bobbing oddly, his huge chest heaving. Parrish waited, and Bobby saw him and ran to the car. Parrish reached behind the seat and opened the back door.

"Lie on the floor," he told Bobby. "We can't let her see you."

"Baby Lisa?" Bobby said. Bobby scrambled in and lay down on the backseat. Parrish could hear his heavy, scratchy breathing as the car pulled out of the park and he maneuvered it through residential streets, into the busier, downtown district, then out onto the highway. He rolled down a window and let the hot summer air race in. It felt like freedom.

13

Bobby Starne forgot where he was, lying there in the backseat with the sound of the wheels whirring in his ears, then he thought maybe he was dead, and the sound was a saw, coming to cut him like cord wood, to stack him for the fires of hell. But he couldn't move. He was held down by a fierce magnet that locked his bones to the scratchy, buckled floor.

He lay there for a long time, and then the saw sound stopped and the sunlight flooded in and Dr. Parrish was bending over him saying, "Bobby. We are here. It is time to do what has to be done."

He got out of the car, and he remembered that they were going to kill Baby Lisa, and the thought frightened him, but he didn't want Dr. Parrish to think he was afraid, because Dr. Parrish was counting on him, so he took the special killing blade that Dr. Parrish gave him, and he held it close to his leg, blade pointed down. His hands were wet with sweat, and the sunlight buzzed around him like angry gnats, and there was too much of everything in the air, too much of trees and grass. Dr. Parrish stood too tall against a hissing blue sky, and when Bobby looked down the hill, he could see the river, and it was white and fierce. The river twisted wildly, and he remembered when J.D. had nailed a garter snake to the ground with an ice pick. The snake had whipped and fought in the dirt. The river was like that, trying to free itself. He didn't want to go near the river, but he knew he would have to before Dr. Parrish said anything. Bobby knew this: If you hated a thing, it would call you.

"She mustn't see the blade," Dr. Parrish said. "We don't want her to run away. We have to trick her. If she knows you mean her harm, she will kill you with a look."

Bobby transferred the blade to his back pocket with the blade pointing up. Then he smiled. "Hi," he said, practicing. It wasn't easy, because Dr. Parrish was watching his performance with a scowl. The truth was, Bobby knew he wasn't much of an actor, and Baby Lisa would surely know he had come to kill her, so Baby Lisa would kill him.

But Dr. Parrish reassured him. "She will think you are fooled," he said. Parrish smiled. "She thinks she has us all fooled."

Bobby made a real smile, imagining the joke on Baby Lisa when the killing blade leaped into her heart.

As soon as Bobby Starne entered the trees and began to descend the hill toward the river, Parrish climbed back in the car, threw it in reverse, backed up, and drove away. Whatever happened now was meant to happen. He did not want to watch it happen, did not want to think much about it at all. Oddly enough, he felt no fear of failure. Certainly Bobby Starne's damaged brain was capable of misfiring. The crazy giant might simply march off into the woods, forgetting what he was supposed to do. Anna might not show. Or Anna might show and, seeing Bobby, bolt immediately.

He had set events in motion. He had done what he could, and now he felt that he was relieved of the burden of action, of thought. His part in it was over, and he felt fine. Perhaps he felt a little sad, as God might feel watching His inexorable machinery move.

It was a beautiful day. He had to get out more often, get away from the hospital. He drove past a pond with two cows plunged up to their stomachs in the sweet, dark water. A delicate net of willow trees exhaled a pale, tentative green against the darker green of hills dotted with yellow dandelions. He turned the radio on, buzzed the dial through the obscene rock stations, and landed on a classical station where garbled but majestic Beethoven sang in God's ear.

14

It was five after two when Anna reached the river. She didn't see Richard's car, but she wasn't surprised to find that she had arrived first. You had to be realistic in a relationship with a doctor. The world was filled with emergencies. A doctor couldn't say to his patients, "Hey, forget it. I've got stuff to do this afternoon."

Anna was willing to wait. She felt at peace this afternoon. Yesterday had been a bad day for her. No reason why, but all day she had felt crummy like back when she was doing the heavy drinking. She had tried to sleep her way through yesterday, and it hadn't worked, and she had kept burrowing into the mattress, hearing the muted voices of other Villa residents, and she had finally slept and dreamed of her mother and her mother was saying, "Anna Shockley, you are hell-bound without Jesus," in that flat, hopeless voice that Anna had always hated, hated even before she understood the words.

Anna woke up yesterday and tried to erase the vision of her tight-lipped mother by saying the words Father Walker had given her for her own Dance, and that had helped, but it was a day when her mind kept going back to that ugly little town of her birth, the Jesus-haunted wheat fields, the immensity of sky, the cruel, long highways and flat, child-hating storefronts.

She should have run away from there sooner, that was all she regretted about leaving. She stayed too long, stayed for fifteen long years, and then she heard the voice of that preacher, a fat man with one of those reedy, moist voices that the Lord gives preachers, saying, "Look to your children, my friends. Raise them so that they may know right from wrong. Satan drives up and down this highway, and all our young folks have to do is put out their thumbs and they are gone, flying off into perdition."

The preacher hadn't meant it as advice, but that's how Anna took it, and she eyed that highway with great intensity and confusion, and then, on the edge of the tenth grade, with autumn in the air and a feeling of change that the dying town refused to acknowledge, she stuck her arm out, and if it was Satan who stopped for her, it was a sorry kind of a Satan, a skinny auto mechanic pretending to be a big shot. He was on his way to see some folks in Charlotte, North Carolina, and it was in Charlotte that Anna met Larry in a bar—she had always looked older than her age, what her mother had called "physically mature"—and Larry had impressed her. He was real sure of himself, carried himself like somebody. He had a way of laughing that didn't hold back anything and the world's whitest teeth. The drugs hadn't turned him mean back then, and right off he bought her this silk mini-dress that she admired although the price was way out of line and she wouldn't have let him buy it if she'd known.

Larry had style.

Anna pushed all these thoughts away, because they were beginning to make her feel the way she had felt yesterday, and she didn't need that. She didn't need the past, not any of it, and you couldn't get her to talk about it, because talking about it might draw her back somehow.

Father Walker agreed. He said the past was like a room where all the oxygen had been breathed already. You went back into a room like that, you'd suffocate.

It was too bad that Richard hated Father Walker and the Dancers so much. Richard just refused to listen when she talked about the Dancers. She knew to stop when his eyes narrowed that way. Well, they'd have a lifetime to get that straight. A person's religion was important, and she wasn't going to let it go just because Richard didn't approve.

David hadn't approved either. But she didn't want to think about David either. She had sent him a letter. Maybe he would understand and be happy for her. Some things just happened, like lightning hitting a tree. Anyway, she had never been any good for David.

Anna leaned over the car's backseat and hauled out a frayed orange blanket. She took the suntan lotion out of the glove compartment and got out of the car. Richard would know she was here and join her down on the riverbank.

Bobby Starne crouched under a large, lichen-mottled boulder in the shadow of the trees. He blinked out at the grassy, naked expanse that lay between him and the river. Grasshoppers in the tall grass chittered, mocking him. The white water looked hungry and fierce.

He didn't see Baby Lisa anywhere, and he wanted to turn and run back up through the trees and leap in the car and forget about it. He was afraid, and there wasn't any strength in him. He took the killing blade out of his back pocket and held it in his hand. Sun jumped on the blade, and he put his fingers through the handle, and he felt slightly better.

He looked up, and there was Baby Lisa, coming out of the woods no more than fifty feet to his left. All the goodness and strength that the blade had inspired went out of him, and the terror of Baby Lisa's presence, the rays from her, penetrated his bones. He could feel the rays, like worms, sliding in the hollows of his bones.

Baby Lisa was wearing the body of Anna Shockley, just as Dr. Parrish said. But Bobby would have known that this was Baby Lisa even if Dr. Parrish hadn't warned him. Baby Lisa was smiling wickedly and she was dressed for sin, in tiny jean cutoffs and a tight t-shirt that showed her nipples clearly. Bobby remembered Anna Shockley from group, and that girl would never have dressed this evil way. This was Baby Lisa, looking to snare him any way she could, coming after him now with whore tricks.

Bobby stood up and walked out of the shadows. But the sun was so heavy that it stopped him immediately. He couldn't move. He looked down at his hand and saw that he still held the scissors blade, and he returned it to his back pocket. He looked up again and watched Baby Lisa marching easily through the tall, yellow grass. She hadn't seen him. Maybe he could sneak up on her.

But he knew he couldn't. She would see him. Fire would leap from her eyes, and he would fall to the ground, nothing but bits of ashes that the wind would blow away. He saw the image so clearly that he knew it was true.

Then he remembered the pill. Dr. Parrish had told him to take the pill immediately after killing Baby Lisa so that Baby Lisa could not jump from the husk of Anna Shockley into his own body. Dr. Parrish had also said, "Don't take the pill until you kill Baby Lisa. It is important that you take the pill right *after* you kill her. Not before. Is that clear?"

Bobby had said that he understood.

But it was all Bobby Starne could do to remain standing under the awesome weight of the sun. He felt his kneecaps swell with green pain, felt the bones in his spine scrape together, making a sound louder than the drone of the grasshoppers. With all his will, he fumbled in his pocket, drew out the piece of crumpled aluminum foil and shakily unwrapped it, revealing the plastic capsule, his one hope, his salvation. He popped it in his dry mouth and swallowed. It was tremendously large, but he got it down—and it *worked*. Immediately, strength returned to his limbs. The sun released him, and he was able to march forward.

He felt calm and protected now. He smiled. He felt like a hero. He had almost reached Baby Lisa, who was now sitting on an orange blanket and looking up toward the river. She turned, lifted a hand to her eyes, and squinted at him.

He smiled and waved his hand. He must be very smooth and

cunning. He would trick her. He would let her think that he didn't know who she was. "Hi, Anna," he said.

"What are you doing here?" she asked. Already there was suspicion and anger or fear on her face. Her face was tight and Baby Lisa looked out of it without trying to hide. She had risen up a little on one knee and one of her hands was forward on the blanket, balancing her.

"Hi, Anna," he said again, still walking closer. He would have said something else, but he thought too many thoughts, too fast, and he couldn't slow one down to make it into words.

She stood up. "What do you want?" She was ready to run now, and fear was bobbing in her eyes. Bobby wanted to laugh, but he didn't. She knew he was protected, powerful, and it made him want to laugh.

"I was driving around, and I parked up there, and then I saw you and I thought I would say hi," he said, all in a rush. This was the pill speaking, cunning, giving him words he could not have caught on his own. He wanted to jump up in the air and roar for joy, because he knew that he was a hero.

"Go away," she said. Her voice was quiet, and unless you listened with sharp ears, you might have been fooled and thought it was an angry voice. Really, it was a scared voice. Something moved beyond Anna's image, and Bobby shifted focus and saw two kids—gangly, barefoot boys—across the river. They were too far away to save her now.

"No, Baby Lisa," Bobby hissed. Then, suddenly a hot, crackling fire burst in his stomach, seared his ribs, took the breath from him. He screamed. The scream came out of him at a hundred miles an hour, a long, tortured whistle of sound that pulled chilly fear behind it.

Baby Lisa was killing him! Somehow his protection was gone. There was no time at all now.

"Go away," Anna said. Jesus. Bobby Starne. When she had turned and seen him, looking crazier than ever, like he had just been beamed down from Mrs, her heart had immediately shifted into overdrive. He was so goddam big and so goddam crazy-looking and crazy-acting. She had been relieved when he had been taken out of her group, because he always seemed on the edge of exploding.

Now he was here, sweating waterfalls, birdie eyes goggling, monster-sized and wearing a white dress shirt with the sleeves rolled up and wrinkled chinos.

He must have followed her. He hadn't just accidentally found her here. The word *rape* entered her mind, and her heart went into a high-pitched whine.

He lumbered closer. He said something, but she couldn't catch the words. *Baby? Had he said "baby"?*

Then he screamed and jerked forward, as though someone had drilled a fastball into his stomach. The scream was like nothing Anna had ever heard, inspiring both horror and pity.

The scream took her by surprise, kept her from running.

Bobby Starne stopped screaming and suddenly uncoiled. His huge bulk covered the remaining distance between them in seconds. He grabbed her arm, and she spun around, tried to run. Then she was falling, but he still held her arm, and she regained her balance. She looked back at him in time to see his other hand plummeting, the blade bright. Terror slowed everything, allowed her to form the slow thought, *I'm going to die*, as though the words were printed in some child's primer, laboriously puzzled out by her soul.

The steel pierced her shoulder with a thudding kind of pain that released her from the dreadful, slow-motion panic. She stumbled backwards, already running before she was aware that she was free. She could feel her blood rushing from the throbbing shoulder.

She ran away from him, toward the river. There were two people across the river, and she shouted to them. They were jumping up and down, waving their arms, shouting back. They were just kids, and they were too far away. She would die while they watched.

A cold rush of anger—rage against her own helplessness, the stupidity of her approaching death—propelled her forward. She scrambled over the riverbank rocks. He was right behind her; she could hear his rasping breath, the sound of his feet. She knew, somehow, that turning to look would lose the race; he'd catch her.

So she didn't look. She ran on into the river.

Instantly, the river knocked her sideways. She leaned into the violence of the current, felt the rocky, perilous bottom lash at her bare feet. The water was white ice and roaring. She was immediately wet to the bone. Water crashed against slick boulders and the silver skeletons of felled pines. She could see the opposite bank through a mist of shattered rapids. She was a fair swimmer, but certainly she would drown in the treacherous, frenzied current.

She would rather drown. She pushed forward.

She was surprised by the blow that slammed her face down into the water, then sick as the steel twisting in her back screamed her failure. She twisted underwater, miraculously found her feet and pushed up through the relentless, hurrying current to face her killer.

He stood in the boiling water, rocking back and forth. The knife was bloody—her blood!—and all human semblance had fled his eyes. His mouth was open and he was trying to say something. She could see his tongue working soundlessly, a writhing poisonous worm. She felt weak. The sky shifted, bloomed with new brightness. She couldn't turn and run again, not with the knowledge of that descending blade. She watched as Bobby Starne mumbled silently and moved forward amid the crashing waters.

And then he stopped and stood utterly still as though listening. His alien, astonished eyes bulged and he said, "Ah," and looked down at his chest and coughed once, sharply. He looked up with the same dazed, bewildered expression, and now his white shirt had a great garish bloodstain and blood flecked his lips, and he coughed another bloody cough and slowly began to sink.

Anna watched from the last outpost of her consciousness. She didn't understand what was happening. The brute had fallen to his knees, was sliding under water. There was a moment when just the top of his head showed, like a wet, mossy rock, and then that too was gone. Then there was nothing but the water, jumping, wilder perhaps. Anna stared at the water, expecting Bobby to leap up again, howling. He didn't.

Anna started back to the shore. She pushed upstream first, away from where Bobby Starne had disappeared.

The nightmare was over. She could get to the shore. Richard.

The thought of Richard gave her courage.

Then the sky canted, and she knew that it was too late. A coldness that had to be death—because it was so vastly and unutterably more chilling than the river—filled her. She was numb, paralyzed.

The rushing current tipped her over, and she spun away from the shore, from Richard, from all her desperate dreams.

She bounced against the river bottom, was hurled to the surface again by extravagant forces. She gulped air reflexively, was dragged down into deeper waters where the darkness embraced her. She was through fighting. She returned the embrace.

Part 3
David Livingston
September 1980

1

I knew his voice immediately, but I didn't know who it was. I couldn't make the connection. It had been a long time.

"Kalso," he said. "Robert Kalso. Your old Svengali, remember?"

I had fallen asleep on the sofa watching the six o'clock news. The room was dark now except for an eerie blue light cast by Johnny Carson and Buddy Hackett. I stared out the window. I was living in a high-rise in Alexandria, Virginia, and the lights of the nation's capital glittered balefully on my horizon. I felt sick to my stomach, vaguely frightened. I told Kalso it was great to hear from him, but it wasn't. I hadn't seen or talked to him in years, and the only thing between us now was the past, and I was no big fan of the past.

Kalso was calling from downtown. He was having a photo exhibit at a gallery in Georgetown, and he wanted me to come to the opening on Friday. I didn't want to go. I told him I would certainly be there. I had no intention of going. I was too muddled for an immediate excuse, but I figured I could think one up later on.

"I think you'll like it," Kalso continued. "I've got a surprise for you which is guaranteed to bowl you over." This cemented my desire to avoid the affair. I hate surprises.

I went. I got to feeling guilty, and guilt can always get me going where a nobler impulse would fail. I had dropped Kalso as an agent after I left Newburg. How many years ago was that? Thirteen?

Jesus. We had parted amiably enough. I think he understood my wanting to get away from all those associations. And I hadn't deprived him of a fortune, since my romance with the New York art entrepreneurs languished and died. I found it hard to stir up much enthusiasm for what I was doing. No one was happy with the stuff I was producing. I hasn't happy with myself. And I painted less and less. It got harder to begin a painting. I drank a lot, and one day drinking was more important than painting, and I knew it. I took all the canvases, finished and unfinished, that filled up the apartment—I was living in Florida at the time; I got around a bit after Newburg but it isn't a rousing travelogue—and I piled them in a heap and poured gasoline on them and set them on fire. I felt a sense of immense relief.

Friday came and I drove down to Georgetown, parked at the bottom of Wisconsin Avenue and walked up to the gallery. It was around seven in the evening, a chilly, wet day, and I was already having reservations about going. Georgetown isn't my favorite place on a good day. There are a lot of people in Washington, D.C., with a lot of money—this is the country of the Mercedes Benz—and they come to Georgetown to buy tasteful things. These are successful citizens who appreciate Beauty and are willing to pay for the endorsed, genuine article. This lust for elegance is fierce and depressing.

I found the gallery, a narrow townhouse with a little gold-and-black sign about the size of a license plate. The place was already thick with people, cigarette smoke, noise.

I didn't see Kalso so I started looking at the photographs. I was alone in this pursuit. The other people were drinking wine, laughing. I suppose they had already seen the exhibit or were so intimately connected with the photographer that they didn't feel required to feign interest in his stuff. This wasn't the gawking public; this was the inner circle, knowledgeable, slightly bored.

I started edging along the walls, studying Kalso's photographs. My first impression was that his style hadn't changed much, hadn't flown off in some outrageous direction. Many of the photos were quite small, postcard size or smaller. They were in color, but the colors were muted, fading away. There were landscapes, rural stuff, a photo of some raggedy kids playing baseball on a country road. Evening is coming on, a blond head seems to glow, a baseball bat burns iconlike in the twilight.

I moved down the hall. There were pictures of a group of women in long dresses, holding hands, laughing beneath a blue sky. There was a picture of an old woman in a rocking chair, proudly holding a large box turtle on her lap. There were more landscapes.

There was a photo of Anna, looking directly into the camera with her odd, small smile and her bright eyes. She was wearing a high-collared blouse and a long blue skirt, and her hands were folded primly in her lap. He hair was pulled back from her forehead and she was sitting on a kitchen chair. I could see part of the kitchen sink, cupboards, a window through which white light streamed.

I had never seen this photo before, and I wondered why Kalso had saved it for this exhibit. I stared at it for a long time, skirting the pain, stricken, as always, by the beauty that Anna could radiate. Then I moved along.

There were two other photos of Anna. In one she was pushing hair out of her face, her hands wet with suds from the sink. Obviously this picture was another from the kitchen, same light, same old-fashioned blouse—with the sleeves rolled up now.

The third picture had been taken, apparently, with a self-timer, for Kalso himself appeared in the photo. He was standing next to Anna. Anna was barefoot in a t-shirt and jeans. Kalso was wearing a business suit. They were in the far left of the picture, which was dominated by a green, stagnant pond, a riot of weeds and willow trees. Anna and Kalso were waving enthusiastically at the camera, like tourists in front of the Grand Canyon.

This picture unsettled me more than the other two, and I didn't know why, couldn't figure it out. Anna was almost out of the picture, although it was unmistakably Anna. Kalso was also in shadow.

I went around the room again to see if I had missed any Anna photos. I hadn't. I came back to that third picture and it still troubled me and I didn't know why.

That's when Robert Kalso came up behind me and tapped me on

the shoulder. "David," he said. "My dear David. What do you think of my surprise?"

"How is it being rich?" Kalso asked me. The party had moved from the gallery to a friend's house, a brief, noisy march down tree-lined blocks of townhouses, and I was drinking a cup of coffee while Kalso poured himself a glass of wine.

"I'm not rich," I said.

Kalso raised his eyebrows. "Perhaps I have you confused with another David Livingston, the one who wrote and illustrated *The Fearless Egg, Eddie Albatross*, and *The Summer Troll*."

"That's me," I said. "Maybe I'm a little rich."

Kalso laughed. "You deserve it. You beat the snobs. You didn't even play their game. Now you have more critical respect—honestly earned—than all those frauds at Keely's or Bard's."

"Luck," I said.

Kalso smiled, raised a glass of wine to his lips, winked, and drank deep.

Well, none of it had been planned. When I gave up painting masterpieces in Florida, I figured I had better find some kind of work. I started doing illustrations for several local publications, and I learned a lot about commercial illustration, learned how to use an airbrush, gouache. Then the drinking put an end to that, and I did some other things in other states, and I got married and I got divorced, and I went into a hospital in Austin, Texas, on a shaky, hallucinatory whim. In that hospital's detoxification unit, I watched Father Martin movies about alcoholism, hung out in group therapy with a jittery bunch of fellow alcoholics, and got ferried to AA meetings in a big van. And I wrote and illustrated a children's book called *The Fearless Egg*, a work of occupational therapy, as it were. I worked on it for another year after I left the rehab, worked on it while spending my daylight hours in chaste, clerk-typist disciplines. Then I sent it off and the third publisher liked it enough to publish it, and it did okay and the next book did better and *The Summer Troll* was presently on *The New York Times* best-seller list and had been there for an outrageous sixty-seven weeks.

"The whole business makes me nervous," I told Kalso. "I'm not saying I don't like it. I like it fine. But it does make me nervous. I guess good fortune has a way of emphasizing the arbitrary nature of things, more even than a series of tragic events. All this stuff happening so fast.... It has an accidental, flimsy feel to it. I don't know."

Kalso nodded. He had grown a mustache somewhere in the last thirteen years, and his features had lengthened somehow. He still conveyed the air of knowing more about what he was doing than most of us know (which wasn't false advertising, I'm sure). He looked more than thirteen years older.

I was feeling pretty good, talking to Kalso, bringing him up to date, and I thought I could broach the subject of Anna without getting weird.

I told him I had enjoyed the exhibit and was indeed surprised by the photographs of Anna. I had figured out that they must have been taken up at the commune, the Divine Dancers or whatever they were called, but I had never seen them before, didn't know they existed.

"That's the surprise," Kalso said, and I didn't understand that, and he was leaning forward, clutching my arm. "They aren't old photographs."

I couldn't make out what he was talking about, but I was staring at his features, wilder with age, red hair flying, mustache bristling, and I realized what had bothered me about the photo of Kalso and Anna. Kalso had had a mustache in that photo. The Kalso in that photo was the Kalso in front of me.

That realization was underlined by Kalso's next sentence. "I took those pictures this summer. Out at the commune."

"Anna's alive?"

Kalso nodded, smiled broadly. "Now there's a surprise, right? Bowl you over or what?"

"That's impossible," I said.

"I think so, too," Kalso said. "On general principles, I refused to credit my senses when I first saw her. But it is her. I talked to her. She recognized me too, said, 'Hey Robert, how you doing?' You know Anna, she never paid much attention to time. What's ten or fifteen years to someone like Anna?"

As Kalso talked, I felt an odd babble of voices blowing in my mind. Anna was dead. I had thirteen years of knowing that, waking up at three in the morning to have it reaffirmed. They never found the body. But two kids watched her being stabbed, watched her drown, and they did recover the body of her murderer. She was dead. Thirteen years of being dead.

Kalso told me about his decision to photograph the commune. "It was an inspired idea, really," Kalso said. "I wanted to show a utopia-gone-to-seed, an over-the-hill commune."

But Father Walker and his followers weren't welcoming visitors, and Kalso had been turned away at the gates. It hadn't been difficult to sneak in, however. All he had had to do was walk across a couple of fields and there he was. He had walked up on the porch of the big white farmhouse and knocked on the door, and the door had been answered by his holiness himself, Father Walker.

And Anna Shockley had been hanging on Father Walker's arm, smiling. That's when she asked Kalso how he was doing.

"Okay," he said. "I thought you were dead."

Anna had giggled.

Father Walker invited Kalso in. Now that Kalso was actually there, they didn't seem upset by his presence. Walker told how one of his people had found Anna, bleeding, almost dead, and this person had fetched others and they had taken her back to Father Walker.

"Death didn't want her," Walker told Kalso. "So we kept her. As you can see, the years have been kind to her. She has nothing to complain of."

I was puzzled and interrupted. "Why the secrecy? Why didn't Walker take her to a hospital?"

Kalso shrugged. "Father Walker doesn't function along entirely rational lines. He strikes me as an authentic guru, very spiritual, very crazy. Like he says, he kept her. Maybe I asked him the same question because I do remember him saying he couldn't, morally, return her to the river since it had given her up. He couldn't throw

138

her back."

I couldn't sort all this in my mind. I kept thinking I had it and then I didn't. I was hyperventilating on some credibility level, and I made Kalso keep repeating the story while the party rushed around us, laughing, hooting, cranking up the stereo. What I really didn't understand was how Anna could stay out there all those years without anyone knowing.

Kalso, speaking with uncharacteristic gentleness, said, "Anna didn't loom so large in most folks' universe. Most of the world did not know Anna Shockley. She was no social butterfly."

"What about the police?" I asked. "Shouldn't the police know about this?"

"Why?" Kalso asked. "What purpose will that serve at this late date? Her attacker died at the same time she did—poisoned himself, according to the coroner—so there isn't any wrong to be righted by her coming forward. The press might be interested, but I don't think Anna would appreciate the publicity." Kalso paused, frowned. "I'm not sure she could hold up under the publicity. I was amazed at how unchanged, how young Anna still looked when I saw her, all these years later. But damage occurred, you understand. I don't know how much, and Anna never thought, never lived in the world on quite the same wavelength as the rest of us so it is hard to say the extent to which she was harmed by that experience. But she was harmed."

I knew that. She couldn't go through the sort of experience she had been through without suffering some emotional and mental trauma. A new thought occurred to me.

"Does Diane know that Anna is alive?"

Kalso sighed. "Diane told me you would ask that one. She does. I told her this summer."

"She never said anything to me." Diane was the only one I still kept in touch with in Newburg.

"No. She went out to the commune with me once and talked to Anna. She said Anna was where she should be. She didn't want me to tell you about it either, but I'm stubborn in my own way."

I wasn't angry with Diane. I realized that she was doing what she thought was right. And when it came to Anna, she didn't trust my judgment. History was on her side.

Another question occurred to me. "Why are you telling me? Diane didn't want you to say anything."

Kalso looked surprisingly serious. "I think you are entitled to know, David. I was around when you and Anna were together, and I was touched by those times, the two of you. I was saddened by the tragedy. I think you deserve to know the rest of the story. I believe in free will. I also believe in advice, and I will give you some: Don't go near her. Rejoice that she is alive and well, and stay as far away from her as possible."

2

I spent the next couple of days thinking, or what passed for thinking. I let fevered thoughts loose, and they raced in frenzied circles until they gasped for breath.

I am not usually very good with advice, accepting advice, but I agreed with Kalso. If Anna had wanted to get in touch with me, she would have. And why, in any event, would I want to go back and revive the most destructive relationship of my whole life? Let sleeping obsessions lie.

One thing I had learned (thanks to my drinking career) was that an addiction *always* looks good to the addict. Anna had been an addiction. But now, with the perspective of years, I realized how doomed that relationship had been.

And my life was full now, busy. I was working on several different projects, including another book, and I had acquired a number of good friends, people I could actually talk to, and I didn't feel compelled to run away, fly screaming toward some chimera of child-love that my imagination had enshrined.

I was a grown-up guy now.

Sharon came over on Tuesday, and we went out to a restaurant, and I told her about Anna while she ate vast quantities of lobster. Sharon Kane is a small, pretty woman of twenty-eight with a voracious appetite. She nodded, said, "Oh boy" a lot and dug right into the lobster.

"This is the crazy girl you told me about, right? The one who shot you?" Her eyes were wide, hungry for sensationalism. I found myself growing defensive. This wasn't a story for the *National Enquirer*.

We had planned to go to a movie after the restaurant, but the only thing we could agree on was way the hell down Connecticut Avenue in the district and neither of us felt up to the effort. We went back to my apartment and made love.

Sharon is a fierce lovemaker, too. Indeed, there is something voracious about everything she does. Maybe this has something to do with her exquisite smallness. I learned in biology that the smaller a mammal is, the greater its body surface/volume ratio, the more heat it loses to its environment, and, consequently, the faster its metabolism.

Anyway, Sharon does have a zest for life.

It was about one in the morning, and Sharon was propped up in bed eating an apple. "You are going to see her," she said.

"No," I said. "I don't think so. She's got her own life now."

Sharon laughed, a sharp bark of a laugh, the sort of laugh used to underline disbelief. "Come on. I know about that Anna. She's the fatal, heartbreak one. You even do this funny thing with your voice when you speak her name, like it's carrying more freight than your average two syllables."

"That's not true."

"It is. You say her name the way Baptists say 'Jesus.'"

"A lie," I said, and I crawled under the sheets and dragged her with me.

Still later, she said, "It's okay if you go. I would prefer you got a look at the reality: Anna in the land of the living. That Jesus analogy I said earlier.... Well, it's a damned good analogy now that I think about it. Risen from the dead, hasn't she? Anyway, whatever is in your head is gonna be tougher competition than any flesh-and-blood woman. So, me, I'd just as soon you went. Okay?"

"What is all this?" I asked. "Are you trying to get me out of town? What's the matter, anyway?"

Sharon began to cry. She does that sometimes, and it always throws me off, because it isn't in character. She's generally frugal in her displays of emotion. She blinked at me, owl-like, angry. It was

141

a look I have identified as saying, "How can you be so dense?" I reached out to hold her and she sprang up and huffed off into the other room. When I walked out she was watching a science fiction movie, an old black-and-white flick about a sinister island where a mad doctor and his daughter create giant insects by injecting regular insects with a special yeast.

I had intended to talk to Sharon, to discover the heart of the problem with some gentle probing, but I am a sucker for science fiction movies, no matter how bad, and I had never seen this one before. Sharon went back into the bedroom, dressed, and left before the picture was over.

Sharon called me up the next day and said, "You know what's wrong with us?"

I recognized this as a rhetorical question and waited.

"I'm not mad at you," she said.

"That's what's wrong?"

"Figure it out," she said and hung up. I couldn't figure it out.

But I thought about it. *Maybe we need a break from each other*, I thought. So I decided to drive down to Newburg, see Diane. Yeah, see Anna too.

She was alive. That was great. I would give her a big hug, wish her well in her new life—except, of course, it wasn't new to her, was it? I mean, she had been doing whatever she was doing for a long time now. I felt a twinge of fear, one snaky, cold tendril reaching out from the pit, tweaking my heart. Did I know what I was doing?

As soon as I got in the car and began to drive south through a cold, glittery morning, I knew I was doing the right thing. Speed equals purpose. When I was drinking, I would often put a couple of six-packs in the car and go somewhere. I always felt closest to being a free human person when I was fleeing one shore and not yet run aground on a new one.

I listened to the radio and smiled as the highway hissed under the wheels. Kalso had warned me against going, but he wouldn't have told me about Anna if he hadn't wanted me to see her. I realized that now. He wanted me to go down there. Because he knew I would.

And it wasn't just an addiction, a selfish hunger on my part. I had loved Anna—more intensely than I had ever loved anyone, maybe ever would. That, no doubt, is what Sharon had meant. Sharon and I liked each other, but we didn't possess the passion for authentic lovers' quarrels. Anna and I had had something. I owed it to Anna to see her, to say I had missed her, that I was glad she was alive.

3

So I drove down to Newburg, assaulted by memories. Once, in a bad period during my marriage (perhaps a redundant phrase), I had gone to a shrink named Dedmon. I had talked about my mother's mental collapse and how I had tried to protect her from my older brother and my father, both of whom seem, in my memory, brutal and insensitive. My mother was brilliant, a gifted painter of watercolors, a beautiful but fragile human. I had also told Dedmon about Anna, and he jumped at the obvious: I was in love with vulnerability, with helplessness. I wanted to be the daddy, the one in charge.

I told Dedmon he had never met Anna. Certainly, he didn't do Anna justice. She was a force in her own right. And she had steel in her, a courage and resourcefulness I have never encountered since.

Dedmon told me I talked about Anna more than I talked about my wife. I told him that that's what I thought I was supposed to do, talk about the past. I told him I was no longer in need of his services.

"Good," he said.

Maybe there was some truth in what he said. I found myself remembering a time I had taken Anna to a party at Ray and Holly's place. The party was composed of professors and grad students, very drunk, very erudite. Nobody completed sentences. It would have been bad manners to complete a sentence. To complete a sentence would suggest that your audience was ignorant of its direction. Nothing was uttered that wasn't swathed in disclaimers. There was much eye rolling and eyebrow lifting on the part of both sexes.

I went to the kitchen and talked to Holly for awhile, and when I got back a lot of people were clustered around Anna, and a thin, effete-looking professor of English literature was looking mock serious, leaning forward, nodding his head.

Anna was talking about her favorite romance writers. Aside from Walker's religious diatribes, Anna read nothing but romance novels, read them with the kind of rapt attention that authors of serious novels would kill for. Anna was telling the entire plot of *Love's Long Summer* or some similar title. Anna had got up some steam, I could see. She was saying something like, "And then Darrell, who is acting real weird, disappears, and Lady Berkley is arrested for treason because Thomas has lied to the king..."

I looked at Anna and I looked at the circle of smirking faces exchanging arch, superior glances, and I grabbed her by the arm and yanked her away from that bloodless, thin-lipped lot. Anna didn't know what was going on, but she was used to erratic, violent behavior, having lived the last years with drug-crazed Larry, and, although she could be infuriatingly stubborn when the mood hit her, she would shrug off really bad behavior with stoical indifference. (As time went by, I realized that Anna wasn't oblivious to these wrongs. She totted them up and saved them, kept an account that she balanced against her own outbursts and inevitable guilt.)

I remember getting in the car, smiling at Anna, who hadn't said anything since my peremptory "We gotta go." The night was warm and humid, and I felt prickly, disgusted with Ray's friends, a disgust that reached out to embrace the vast, impenetrable stupidity of the universe. Anna was looking straight ahead, mouth slightly open, street lamps fluttering by, lightly brushing the pure planes of her face, and I was overwhelmed by her innocence, and I pulled the car over to the side of the road and reached for her desperately and kissed her, and told her I loved her.

Maybe that shrink was right. Anna seemed defenseless that night, and I wanted to shield her from the brutal press of the world. I was angry, I remember, more angry than the situation warranted. And I was head-down, heart-howling in love. Maybe that was part of it, this love: hating the opposition, the cold, steam-rolling universe. Only Anna, an oasis from my anger, burned brightly, warm and vulnerable.

I got to Newburg at about two o'clock in the afternoon. I had toyed with the notion of just finding Diane's house and knocking on the door, but I remembered my last shot at surprise entrances. So I called her from a gas station. She was delighted to hear my voice, and she gave me directions to her house, which turned out to be a pretty, freshly-painted wooden house amid maples. There was a child's big-wheels bike in the yard, and a young beagle came banging out from behind the screen door to howl at me. Diane shouted, "Wimpy, behave!" and then ran to me and gave me a hug.

Back in the house, I met her daughter, Becky, who was a shy, skinny girl of seven with her mother's wonderful eyes and something of her mother's unnerving acuteness. I felt myself being inspected by the both of them.

Becky said, "You wrote *The Summer Troll?*" She seemed a little skeptical. Adults have the same problem with me. I don't look in any way exceptional. I like to think that people would describe me as good-looking, but they would have to remember me first, and I am aware that I don't have a memorable face.

I told her that I had written *The Summer Troll*, and she told me that she admired it greatly. It was a formal but heartfelt compliment.

Becky left, and Diane, who had apparently had time to think about my appearance in Newburg, studied me closely.

"Robert told you," she said.

"It's great to see you," I said. "How are you doing? How is Charles? I'm looking forward to meeting him." Diane Larson was now Mrs. Charles Nichols. I assumed that Charles Nichols was an improvement over Saul. A wolverine would have been an improvement over Saul.

"You'll like Charles," Diane said. "You guys are a lot alike. I fall for a certain type—self-involved, immature, but charming and witty."

"I wasn't aware that you ever fell for me," I said.

"Self-involved," Diane said, nodding. "Self-involved."

We chatted along smoothly. Diane was still working three days a week out at Romner and once I got her going on that she was good for awhile. Then I had to tell her how I had been doing, and about the new book. We talked, inevitably, about old times, and so we came back to Anna.

"Yes, Kalso told me," I said. "And he told me that you already knew, but didn't want to tell me. I understand that. I think you are wrong, but I understand. I don't hold it against you."

"That's big of you."

"Uh-oh," I said. "Are we going to have an argument?"

Diane sighed. We had moved out on the porch to drink coffee. Mottled sunlight decorated the grey floorboards. "You would always do anything to avoid an argument," she said. "You have this dread of arguments, David. Why is that?"

I shrugged. "Beats me."

"Anna never shared that dread. She liked a good fight."

"Yeah. Anna was born to fight. A stormy girl."

Diane smiled. She was a good-looking woman, and now she had a self-assurance, an easy elegance that the younger woman had lacked. She was wearing a frayed grey sweatshirt and her hair was tied back in a pony-tail.

"Why should I fight with you? You are here. You are going to do what you came here to do. You are going to see Anna. I hope it works out. I don't want you to get hurt. And I particularly don't want her to get hurt."

That edge was back in her voice. I have always been wary of women who preface anything with "I don't want to fight" and I was right to be wary.

Diane told me that she thought it was a miracle Anna was sane at all after what she had gone through. Diane said that it was her opinion that Anna might not be sane in any other surroundings. Not much mental equilibrium was required out at Walker's commune. They were more tolerant of eccentricity.

I told Diane I understood all that. I just wanted to see Anna. She might, I said, even want to see me.

The argument warmed up. Diane told me that I was hunting a ghost. Yes, Anna was alive, but not the Anna I had come looking for.

146

I asked her how she could know what I was looking for, how she could read my mind.

"I know you, David," she said. Her face had lost some of its control, and she looked older, more formidable. "You write these scenarios in your head. You have a problem with real people, real intimacy. Remember when I asked you to come? You couldn't make it. If you didn't owe it to me, you owed it to Ray and Holly, but you couldn't make it."

I hadn't been expecting that one, and it hurt. In December of 1971, Ray and Holly had been driving to South Carolina to visit Holly's parents for the holidays. A drunken kid in a rented moving van had slammed into them on the highway. Ray and Holly had been killed instantly.

Diane, traditional bearer of bad news, had called me. Diane and Holly had hit it off back when I first introduced them, and the friendship had grown since I left Newburg. She was almost hysterical when she called, and I knew she needed me; I needed to be there.

"I'm sorry," I said. "I was in a bad way then. I was drinking twenty-four hours a day, and the world just looked black, chaos. When you called, I knew I should come, but I couldn't. I was hallucinating, in and out of d.t.'s, suicidally self-involved. I was afraid of going to that funeral. Ray and Holly were just about the only friends I ever had, and their death seemed so...I don't know...hostile, that's not the word. I wasn't in any shape to comfort anyone; I was dangerous to be around. I really am sorry."

"I know." Diane's voice had softened. I think she recognized genuine remorse, the sound of arguments played out to unforgiving walls on solitary nights. "I was sick then too, and I hated you for not coming, but I understand now. I really do. I'm sorry I brought it up. But it's part of the way you are." She leaned forward to make this point, all earnestness, full of terrible revelation. I fidgeted, studied my sneakers.

"David," she said, "you are good with dreams. You write beautifully illustrated children's stories, because you are a child yourself. It's wonderful, really. The world needs dreams, ideals. But sometimes the dream doesn't mesh with reality. The reality can be

147

unpleasant. Then you step back, you get a bee-stung look, you run. You don't mean any harm, but the rest of us, well, the rest of us don't have any place to go, and you've ducked under a rainbow, and maybe we feel a little abandoned. Maybe we feel betrayed."

Diane was right, but I was beginning to feel schoolboy-reprimanded, and I wanted to get out, get moving.

"You understand why I'm telling you all this?" she asked.

I told her I understood. Then I asked her if she would come with me to see Anna.

"No, I don't think so. My stomach isn't what it used to be."

4

Well, I got her to go. What I lack in charm, I make up for in persistence. I have a lot of bad-mannered endurance. I can engage in hours of shameless wheedling. Diane realized this and gave in quickly, sparing us both.

I wanted to go right away, but Diane said she wasn't about to drive out there this late in the day. We drove out the next morning. The day was crystal bright, and an early cold snap had announced autumn in the veins of some unwary maples and poplars. Red and yellow flames dotted the mountainside, and the smoky air was full of change. I was nervous, and the clarity of the landscape, a riot of detail that seemed to offer every roadside weed and windblown leaf to my eye, crowded my mind, inspiring confusion and doubt. Maybe Diane and Kalso were right. Maybe I had no right to come booming back into Anna's life, even if my motives were excellent. And they probably weren't. I had had thirty-four years to acquire some slight self-knowledge, and the one thing I did know about myself was this: I was a master of rationalization.

Diane, slumped down in her seat with her arms across her chest, was no help. She wrapped herself in her green windbreaker and stared out the window, thinking her own thoughts, squinting against the morning glare.

"Everything is going to be fine," I told myself. I waited for Diane to finish talking to the lanky, long-haired boy in a cowboy hat who sat on the gate. I would have smoked a cigarette, but I had given them up six months ago, and now, bereft of vices, I stood by the side of the road smiling a thin, we-come-in-peace smile, hoping I didn't look as crazy as I felt. As I watched, the boy jumped down from the wooden gate and swung the gate backwards. Diane came running back to the car.

"It's okay," she said. "He remembers me from last time." She leaned back as I started the car again. We bumped over the weedy, deep-rutted road. "Anna is living with Walker, up at the main farmhouse. Over there." Diane pointed out the window to my left. "They've got houses for those who have chosen their Dancer for the Life Dance, married couples. Those long wooden buildings are dorms, co-ed, but keep your sexual fantasies to yourself. I'm told the Dancers are a chaste, decorous lot."

"Looks kind of run down," I said.

"Faded glory," Diane said. "Or at least it is supposed to look like faded glory."

"What do you mean?"

"There are about seventy-five true believers ensconced here now. That's nothing compared to what this place was like in its heyday, but that was Walker's decision. Father Walker decided to keep a low profile. I think he noticed a certain change in the weather, a cruel wind from the heartland. You ask me, this place is intentionally seedy. The flock has reached a self-sustaining level, and it doesn't need to advertise loudly. There are chapters of the Dancers of Divine Logic in every state, and a network of grassroots businesses and some not-so-grassroots businesses. There's even computer software for reaching enlightenment. Put a floppy disk in your computer, and a series of questions will allow you to determine whether or not you are Divine Dancer material or not. You want Apple compatible? IBM compatible? Commodore? Of course, this is no easy road to nirvana. The program will tell you whether or not you have what it takes to join up, but it won't get you to heaven. To do that, you have to see a mentor—names and addresses come with the software—and there are more expenses. The One True Path can look a lot like a toll road, but nobody's complaining."

I could see the white farmhouse looming large at the top of the hill, and it was becoming more difficult to follow what Diane was saying. Any minute now I was going to see Anna again.

And then I saw her. There was a pond next to the farmhouse, off to the right, probably the same pond in Kalso's photo. Anna was standing looking out at the water. Her back was to me, but I knew it was her. Her hair was still long and dark, and her back very straight. She had this way of holding her body, attentive, ready to bolt. But I don't think it was any single physical characteristic or combination that made me recognize her. I believe I have always been tuned to the quality of Anna; something in me resounds to her presence.

I stopped the car and was out of it, running across the field. I heard Diane shout something behind me, but I kept running. I shouted "Anna!" and waved my arms like an idiot.

Reality, as Diane had noted the day before, rarely meshed with my dreams. I didn't expect it to.

That moment, however, was absolutely right, all the gods scribbling on my behalf, writing me into that clear, sunny instant of return. My beloved turned and squinted at me, brushed hair from her eyes. She was wearing a long, tan dress, very plain,with a high collar, and she frowned as I shouted her name again. Then she smiled, leaped in the air, shouting my name.

"David! David!" She ran toward me and I caught her up and spun her in the dizzy air and I found her face, her mouth, and kissed her, and moved away to touch her cheek with my hand, to stroke her hair, and she was laughing all the while. She looked no older than that first time I had seen her in the emergency room.

"Oh Anna, you look good," I said.

She couldn't stop laughing. Laughter always suited her, like song in a warbler's throat.

I kissed her again, holding her tightly, inhaling the scent of her hair, remembering the way she moved, her sweet, empathic gestures, her grace and eternal awkwardness.

"Oh David, you came back. I dreamed you would. I told Walker about it, and he said the dream was a lie, but I knew it wasn't. I knew it was true."

And she hugged me again. I kissed her again.

The gods had written the scene, and I was invulnerable within that moment, and I sensed that and hurried nothing.

"Diane's here," I finally said. "I asked Diane to come."

I looked around for Diane, but she was nowhere to be seen, and I felt foolish. "I guess she went on up to the house," I said.

"Diane will be all right," Anna said. "Walker says she has a gift, the gift of forgiveness, which is the greatest of all the gifts. She is a good friend, don't you think? She told me she was in love with you once."

Studying Anna's face, I found it hard to believe that she was thirty-two. Yes, there were some changes, but they were so easily reconciled with my memory of Anna that it might have been the memory that was at fault. She had the same clear, animated features, the same girlish, quirky ways, erotic and elusive, demon and waif.

"I love you," I said.

Anna smiled and pulled me forward and kissed me long and hard. "I love you too," she said.

We sat on the bank of the pond, and the air warmed under the enthusiastic attentions of the sun, and I told Anna how I had learned that she was still alive from Kalso. I asked her why she hadn't let me know she was alive.

She shrugged her shoulders and pouted, staring into the green water. "You know those things or you don't. It's not up to me. It's all figured out a long time ago." Then she turned and smiled gloriously. "But I knew you would come."

I was so glad to see her. I told her how things were with me, told her about my marriage and its failure. "I realize now that I married her because she was so damned attentive, cared so much for me. I really did her a disservice. She was a wonderful person, but I had no business marrying her simply because I couldn't love myself and needed someone for the job. It was a greedy, selfish thing to do."

Anna nodded. "Walker says even Jesus was selfish, and that is okay. Only death is unselfish."

I told her how my drinking had gotten worse, almost killed me, and how I had stopped drinking and was now doing all right. I told her I wrote and illustrated children's books. I promised her I would bring her copies of my books.

I asked her how she was doing, what had been going on in her life. She didn't want to talk about herself. This evasiveness was nothing new. The Anna I had known had always lived amid secrets, borders that couldn't be crossed, subjects that could not be broached. She was getting nervous, however, and stood up quickly. "Let's go in the house," she said.

"Why?" I asked.

Her eyes were brighter and darker, and she looked at the pond. "I think there's someone under the water," she said. "I believe he has been listening."

"Anna," I said, feeling the shadow of the past, armed and murderous, "there's nothing there."

I put my arm around her shoulder. "You know that," I said.

She looked at me and smiled. "Yes, I know that, David. I can't believe you've come back. I'm so glad to see you."

Together we walked arm-in-arm up to the farmhouse. Diane and Walker came out on the porch—they must have been able to see us from a window in the living room. Walker had a beard now, a fuzzy beard that made him look like a dissolute cherub. There was a fine net of lines around his eyes, and he had the manner of a man who has seen much and narrowly avoided cynicism. He seemed tired. But he smiled and said, "David Livingston. Anna has been telling me you would come. I didn't believe her, which was foolish of me, for I have always known that Anna has the Sight. I hope you will come again."

"Thank you. I will."

Driving back, I said, "Anna looks good."

Diane said nothing.

"Do you think she is sleeping with Walker?" I asked.

Diane turned and looked at me sharply. "What business is it of yours what Anna does?"

I studied the road. "I'm just curious," I said.

"Why don't you ask Anna then? I have never been an authority on Anna. I don't know what she does, what she thinks."

5

I had told myself that all I wished for Anna was happiness. If she was happy where she was, then I would leave her there.

She seemed very happy in her life. I drove out to see her every day. She worked in the kitchen, helping with the preparation of meals. She took her duties seriously, and I couldn't get her to play hookey when she had chores to do.

But she did have plenty of free time in the afternoon, and the gentle autumn was designed for long walks and conversation.

Some of my questions were answered. She did, indeed, sleep with Walker.

"But she's not in love with him," I told Diane.

Diane had shaken her head sadly. "Jesus. How can you possibly know that?"

"Her manner isn't that of a lover," I said. "There isn't any passion in the relationship."

"Hmmmmmmm," Diane said. She had little faith in my judgment in such matters.

Anna was happy in her new world, but there was a dark, troubled side. She was subject to paranoid delusions, odd, hallucinatory episodes. I came to recognize a certain waxy, wary expression that signaled the advent of one of these attacks. She would clutch my wrist and whisper urgently in a small, trembly voice, "David!" My heart would sink as I heard her announce that the hill we were picnicking on was hollow. She could hear voices underneath. "Hush." She would listen acutely. I would try to comfort her, reassure her that there were no voices, no menacing creatures. Sometimes reason would prevail. She was aware that these episodes were not real. But sometimes the panic would get rolling, and I couldn't do anything to calm her. I would take her back to the farmhouse, and we would sit on the sofa in the big living room, and I would hold her tightly until, satisfied that she was safe, she would laugh and talk of other things.

"Wow, I'm a baby," she would say.

* * *

153

"I want Anna to see a psychiatrist," I told Walker. I had been coming to the commune every day for fifteen days, and I was standing in Walker's study, still shaky, but now righteously angry. Walker blinked at me, his expression unreadable, has hands folded in front of him on the desk.

"Please sit down," he said. "And tell me why you think Anna will profit from going out in the world again."

I didn't want to be calm. I wasn't calm. This phony avatar had been allowing Anna to grow steadily worse over the course of long years, benignly nodding his head, muttering platitudes about God's will.

Two hours earlier, Anna and I had been hiking. Anna had become convinced that we were being followed. "Dead people are hiding behind the trees," she told me.

I had brought her back down the hill, back to the safety of the farmhouse, but she had gotten worse in the long walk through the woods, and she was babbling incoherently by the time we reached the farmhouse. I was shaken by the force of this delusion. Anna's demons may not have been real, but her terror was, and I had felt helpless, sick with pity. I calmed her down and went looking for Walker in a rage. I wasn't going to let his smooth affability turn me around. I was prepared for a fight.

"Whatever Anna wants to do, that will be done," he said. "Does she want to go?"

"I haven't asked her," I said.

He raised his eyebrows, spread the fingers of both hands. "If she wants to go, she is free to go. She is not a prisoner here."

"She may not listen to me. I was hoping she would listen to you."

Walker laughed. He stood up and came slowly around his desk and put an arm on my shoulder. "Surely you know Anna better than that. What Anna decides to do, she does. You overrate my influence. Go. Ask her what she wants to do."

I had turned away and reached for the door handle when Walker spoke again, a quiet, reflective voice. "There is no good for her in that world. Of that, I am convinced."

I didn't say anything, didn't waste the time. I was preparing my arguments for Anna. I was aware of how stubborn she could be, and I expected a battle.

She agreed to go without argument. "Yes," she said. "I have to go."

"It's your own decision," I said.

"Oh no." She shook her head. "There isn't any decision to it."

"I don't think I understand," I said.

Anna smiled, and her large eyes were bright, the eyes of a shy, nocturnal creature. We sat on the couch in the living room, twilight drawing the light from the room, leaching it of color. "No, you don't understand. And yet, you are the thing that has happened. You are the beginning of it. I knew you would come. And so it will all come. I can't run away. I have to go forward."

I still didn't understand, but I didn't ask for further clarification. I felt a greater darkness shudder over the both of us. Was I wrong in coming here? Was I the adder in her Eden? Then my rational systems kicked in and I told myself that Anna was getting worse, that her hallucinations and phobic attacks could not be comfortably ignored.

I was doing the right thing.

I have told myself this again and again.

I didn't waste any time, since I didn't want either Anna or Walker to have a change of heart. I got Diane to come with me, and we picked Anna up early the next morning and drove her over to Romner Psychiatric Institute. Diane had arranged for a resident, a Dr. Moore, to see her. Anna's old psychiatrist, Parrish, was still at the hospital, but he was now the director, having married the boss's daughter, so he no longer hung around the emergency room chatting up new arrivals.

Anna, who sat in the backseat, regally silent for most of the drive, spoke up when Diane mentioned Parrish.

"He's the one I have to see," she said. I glanced at the rearview mirror and saw her jaw thrust forward and her eyes narrow in the proscribed, Shockley combat face, and I watched her eyes move, reading each word, as Diane explained why Parrish would be unavailable.

"Well, I've got to see him," Anna repeated, and then she turned, hunkered down into leaden silence and pressed her forehead against the car window. Diane looked at me. I smiled a what-are-you-gonna-do-with-the-girl smile, and we shrugged in unison. The day was gloriously bright, autumn-burnished. In contrast, the emergency room lobby was washed in yellow light and had the funky, bad-luck feel of a bus station in the low rent district. I had another stomach-clenching jolt of uncertainty.

Diane knew the admissions clerk and told her that we were there to see Dr. Moore, who was expecting us. Dr. Moore was paged. Handsome, blond-haired and boyish, Dr. Moore arrived and took the ungracious, glowering Anna ("I didn't come to see you") off to talk with him.

He came out later to tell us that he thought it would be best if they admitted Anna for a few days.

I left, disquiet flickering in my heart like a faulty light bulb about to settle into darkness.

6

Richard Parrish watched them shuffle forward with the massive rosewood desk. There were six of them, big men, but they were still having trouble wrestling this shiny status symbol out the door.

"Careful," Parrish said, and a broad face looked up to scowl at him from under a sweat-boiled brow.

"Motherfucker says be careful," the man said. He was a stocky, dark man, sinewy arms netted in a filigree of blue tatoos.

Parrish turned away. No sense in calling the man on that remark. This sullen bravado was all the man had. The poor and the dispossessed have their insolence, and that is all they have.

Anyway, this was supposed to be a good day. Richard was moving his office to the new wing where he would look out over the lake and the trees beyond. The new office was large and airy, and it spoke eloquently of his position.

Too bad his mother had not lived to see it. Grace would have loved the new office. He could see her, moving around the room, taking her shoes off to wade in the deep carpet, beaming, nodding her head, saying, "Yes. Oh, yes."

She had died three years ago and the first year after her death had been bad for him. He hadn't handled her death well at all, and he still didn't like to think about it. He had flown down to see her, and she had scared him badly, lying there in the hospital bed, dying fiercely, a pathetic, terrified monster. He had left, knowing she was dying, and he had flown back home, back to Jane and his hospital, and he had prayed that the phone would ring and a doctor would say she was dead, and he wouldn't have to go see her again, but that hadn't happened. So he waited and stalled. He was busy. As director of Romner, he was a slave to the place. That, at least, is what he told his mother, and he didn't fly down again. But, as the weeks went by and she didn't die, Jane began to wonder aloud how a son couldn't find time for his own mother. He wrote in his diary, "I wish poor Grace would just die. It would be best for everyone."

When he could no longer ignore his wife's disdain, he booked a flight down to Atlanta. He intended to go see his mother, but found that he couldn't. He couldn't confront what was no longer his mother, what was now a tireless narrator of blood counts and drugs. Instead, he drove a rented car through the labyrinth of the city, circled the hospital, checked into a motel, and watched television until he fell asleep. The next morning, he caught an airplane back to Charlotte where Jane picked him up for the drive back to Newburg.

"How is she?" Jane asked.

He had shrugged. "Okay, I guess."

"Aren't you glad you went to see her?"

"Yeah," he said.

There had been a beat then, a dreadful second of silence, and he had turned and looked at his wife, and she had smiled, the coldest smile.

"Your mother called me right before I left for the airport."

He had wanted to kill Jane then. "You don't understand," he had said. Jane had laughed, a sharp bark, derogatory and irrefutable. They had driven home without exchanging another word.

"She thinks I'm weak," he told his diary. "If I were really weak,

I would break her neck, I would smash every bone in her body. She is fortunate I am not weak."

His mother had finally died, three weeks later, and Jane and Richard had flown down for the funeral. The funeral was a rainy, dirty business that filled him with shame. Why couldn't his mother have died earlier? All his life women had sought to humiliate him, to rob him of his self-worth.

He still kept a diary, but recently the effort had become mechanical, joyless. The walls of his privacy now seemed paper thin, and it was only the habit of a lifetime that kept him writing. He felt that he might be unraveling. In continuing the diary, he hoped to prevent a headlong dash toward the edge.

He couldn't pinpoint the source of this recent dissatisfaction. Jane certainly contributed to his sense of oppressiveness and panic, but it was something internal, prowling within him, that was the real problem.

The phone rang, and he had to hunt for it amid the clutter of the dissembled room. He found it behind the wastebasket. It was Jane, calling, ostensibly, to find out if he was going to be home for dinner, calling, in truth, to berate him for last night's failure in the bedroom. She didn't say so, of course, but there was that in her voice, that vulgar triumph in discerning another weakness, this one physical. He had been tired and unable to perform. Oh, she had been all contrived gentleness, all phony solicitude. And he had wanted to shout, "You disgust me!"

They were engaged in a battle, and they both knew it. He fought to gain control of Romner, and she fought to emasculate him, to have him whimpering beneath her heel. But he would win. He had been making great strides toward freedom over the years. Old Solomon had been infuriatingly slow to acknowledge his son-in-law's competence, but Parrish had been unrelenting in his efforts. He had made friends, solidified his position.

There would come a time, in the near future—and this move to the new wing, while insignificant in itself, was part of the new regime—when neither Jane nor her powerful daddy could dislodge him. Old Solomon was a realist. He would see that Romner Psychiatric's future was inextricably linked to Richard Parrish, and even if he took it into his head to divorce Jane, blood wouldn't prove thicker than the financial waters. The next stockholders' meeting would solidify his position. He had been careful, over the years, to pay close attention to the political winds. There wasn't a significant stockholder that he hadn't done at least one favor for.

So he ignored Jane's attempt to humiliate him, pretending to be oblivious to her taunts. He told her that he would be home in time for dinner. He hung up and discovered that the movers had returned and were hauling his leather armchair out the door.

Feeling besieged, he walked out of his office and, with no destination in mind, wandered the hospital corridors. He enjoyed the stir he caused as he moved through the various wards. He was amused by the reactions of the staff. The true, born-to-kiss-ass sycophants would bounce along beside him, head-bobbing, fast-talking, fearing reprisal for some failing they were sure had come to light. Others would appear openly hostile. This group saw Parrish as the professional administrator, the enemy of the worker. Still others accosted him with demands, showed him failing equipment, complained of fellow workers. Every one of them had an axe to grind. This last bunch kept him from touring the hospital more, since he savored the privilege of power but found its obligations distasteful.

Some of the nurses were obviously attracted to him. He could recognize their interest, was flattered by it, but he didn't intend to do anything about it—for the moment. He was aware that he was good-looking. The years had given him a distinguished air, an assurance, the virility of power.

He was joking with a nurse on 3B, a pretty black-haired girl, indelibly Irish, saucy, quick-witted. He was standing at the nurses' station with his back to the hall corridor when he heard his name spoken.

"Richard!" A girl's voice, not loud, but urgent, it stirred a sediment of thoughts, so that, even as he turned, he felt a tremor of unease.

"Anna!" he said. Her name burst out of him, an exclamation. But there was no mistaking her for someone else; she was wearing jeans and a white, starched blouse with lace at the sleeves and neck.

She was standing, as she had stood in front of him so often, with her arms at her sides, waiting for him to do something, her mouth slightly open, her eyes shining with joy. She was leaning forward, gravity dismissed, time sent away. Richard always felt that this waiting posture, this supernatural stillness, was a kind of condemnation. She was waiting for him to fall short of her expectations, waiting for him to fail.

"Hi, Richard," she said. "I guess I had to come. Are you glad to see me?"

She was gone, dead. He had removed her years ago, and he hadn't thought of her since then. She was an incident in his past, and she had been swallowed in his history, his diary, but she was not a presence in his conscience. He had lost no sleep because of her.

Now she was back. His mind crowded with emotions. There were too many emotions, a strange stew of bewilderment, guilt, horror, fear, and a surprisingly shrill note of yearning. He had forgotten how beautiful she was, how striking. No wonder he had loved her.

Panic set in, set the other emotions spinning. He was leaning against the admissions desk, backed against it, trapped. She had come to destroy him.

The nurse was coming around the desk. "Miss Shockley," she was saying, "I'm afraid patients aren't allowed in the halls at this time. I will have to ask you to go back to your room until your session with Dr. Moore at three."

Control was essential. Anna was going to speak again, say something fatal, damning.

"I'll take her back to her room," Parrish said. And he pushed himself forward, caught Anna by the shoulder, and turned her, pointed her back down the hall.

"Hey," Anna said, confused but coming along.

"We can't talk here," Parrish hissed. His voice was an imperious whisper. Amazing how quickly the melodrama resurfaced, he thought. The thought came from a cool, observing portion of his mind and reassured him. He was still in control.

Anna said nothing else until they reached her room. "Here," she said, and he followed her in.

160

There were two beds, two dressers. "Do you have a roommate?" he asked, still speaking urgently.

"No," Anna said. "I'm supposed to get one, though."

Parrish turned. There was no lock on the inside of the door, of course. Crazy people had no privacy. That was a price you paid for walking out on reality.

"You could be happier to see me," Anna said. Her expression was shifting, moving toward resentment, and Parrish realized he had to keep her from anger.

He reached forward, caught her shoulders. "Oh Anna," he said. "I thought you were dead. All these years. Where have you been?"

Anna laughed. "Right here, Richard. Out at The Home, with Walker. I know you never liked Walker, but you don't know him. He's not a fraud. He's a true holy man."

"Why didn't you let me know that you were alive?"

"I've been meaning to. I'm doing it now. Earlier, it would have been harder." Her eyes suddenly filled with tears as a fierce, tidal emotion surged over her, shaking her body. "I lost the baby." She grabbed him, sobbing wildly. "I lost your baby." She began to speak rapidly, words bobbing on a sea of grief, shoulders convulsing. "I thought I was going to die, and then I wasn't, and then it was worse, because I knew the baby was dead and I couldn't look at you and see our dead baby in your eyes, so I stayed away. But I knew I would have to come, and I thought about it a lot, and then the time came, and I realized it was going to be all right."

Parrish held her, and her shaking body threatened him. Her face was blurred with tears and canted sideways. Strands of her hair stuck to a wet cheek. She smelled the same clean, wildflower smell that he remembered.

Her speech began to settle into slower rhythms as she calmed, and Parrish thought furiously. He didn't know what to do, what to feel. She looked up at him, and she held him with her eyes and said, "We can have another, Richard. I've thought about it."

"Another?"

"Yes. A child. I'm still young enough. I'm healthy. I think we have to. There's a lost soul that's waiting. Our love can bring it back."

161

"A child," he said, nodding vacantly. "Yes, we will have to talk about all this." He blinked at her, smiled, and said, "Wait right here, Anna. I have to do something. I'll be right back."

He backed to the door, smiling fixedly. "Don't go anywhere," he said.

He walked quickly down the hall. He nodded at the nurse, wondering what his face looked like. Like wood, like lead, no doubt. He couldn't get anything from the nurse; it would be logged in. He'd take a large order to the pharmacy, walk it through.

He walked to the elevator, pushed the button for the fourth floor, and waited. "Anna," he muttered. She had come back to murder his fortunes. No. Think rationally here. The girl was deranged, not malicious. Still, she had come for him. Goddam her.

He couldn't afford his anger now. Later. He had to think. What was he so damned afraid of? A crazy girl—obviously her schizophrenia had progressed—was not a threat to him. So what if she said she was pregnant by him years ago? Who would believe her?

Jane might, he thought. Jane was willing to believe the worst, to ruin him.

Well, let the bastards believe whatever suited them. That was long ago, there was no proof. There were no other accusations she could make. She had no more idea than anyone else that Bobby Starne had been sent by him.

He got off at the fourth floor and walked down to the pharmacy where a Japanese man in white greeted him with an enormous smile.

In half an hour, he was back on the elevator with a carton of disposable syringes and a variety of drugs and the realization that the arguments he was playing out in his head were unimportant. She had been a threat years ago, and she was a threat now, more so now when he had to move so carefully, had to solidify his position. She was back. She would have to go away again.

He couldn't help feeling some anger, some frustration. He had closed the door on her; she was buried in his diary, in the past. She had crawled out of the grave, like a vampire, to feed on him again. Okay. He would damn well put a stake through her heart this time, the bitch.

He fished a key out of his pocket and inserted it in the emergency keyhole and stopped the elevator between floors. Then he sat down on the floor, popped a syringe out of its sterile wrapper, and rummaged amid the various vials. He lifted up a clear blue vial and jabbed the needle into its membrane mouth and drained the liquid. He hummed tunelessly, smiling. It wasn't as though she was his equal. He would commit no crime against her that nature hadn't committed years ago. He had diagnosed her as borderline schizophrenic back then, a diagnosis that hedged all bets. She was obviously less in touch now, but living out on that freak's farm all these years might warp the soundest mind. It was hard to tell how much of the girl's disorientation was her own private mental decline and how much was a gift from the guru and his tribe.

Parrish stood up. He squinted at the filled syringe. Borderline schizophrenic. Okay. Here was her ticket across the border.

He started the elevator again and rode it down to the basement. He got out, walked down the hall and out to the enclosed parking lot, and put the drugs and syringes in the trunk of his car. Then he went back inside, the filled syringe making a reassuring weight in his coat pocket, and rode the elevator to ward 3B and Anna.

She was sitting on the bed, and she smiled when he entered, an extraordinary, childlike smile. Such trust, such fearless joy was another face of her illness, the siren side that had lured him to begin with. This brightness could turn black in an instant. *No*, he thought, *You don't fool me.*

"I'm sorry I took so long," he said. "I had some errands to attend to."

Anna laughed and reached for him. He sat down on the bed next to her and held her. He looked at his watch. It was two-forty and he remembered the nurse saying something about Anna's having an appointment with Dr. Moore at three.

"Oh Richard," Anna said. "It's good to see you."

"It's good to see you." He kissed her and stroked her cheek. He pushed her unruly hair away from her face and wondered what was in her dark, solemn eyes. Anything a man dreamed, he supposed. And then you'd pay the price. As he had.

"You must be very tired," he said. "The stress of coming here. Hospitals aren't restful, I know." He caught her shoulders and pushed her backwards. "Lie down, Anna. That's right."

"I'm not tired," Anna said, but she obeyed him, swinging her legs up onto the bed, giggling. "I don't think we should do anything here. I mean, even if we are going to be married."

"No," Parrish said. "It would be most unseemly to do anything here." He chuckled.

"Hey, what are you doing?" Anna said. He was rolling her sleeve up.

"I'm going to give you a shot. Just something to relax you. I'm the doctor, remember. Don't you trust me?"

Anna had started to sit up. She lay back down under the gentle pressure of his arms. "I just don't like needles, and I'm fine."

"For me," Parrish said. "Do it for me."

"Okay."

He turned toward the light and held the syringe up, pushing the plunger until a single glistening drop glinted on the needle. He took an alcohol swab from the bedside table, tore it open, and rubbed it on her shoulder.

"Relax," he told her. "Think of something nice that we could do later on, okay?"

"Okay. Ouch!"

"There," Parrish said, smiling. "That wasn't so bad, was it?"

"How come doctors always say that? It was pretty goddam unpleasant, actually. Getting stuck with needles is never entertainment, you know."

"Oh, I know," Parrish said. "I know." He looked at his watch again. He really wasn't sure how long it would take. A minute, two minutes?

Anna began to convulse. Parrish stood up and turned away. He didn't want to watch. He took no satisfaction in what he was doing. She had brought it on herself, reappearing so suddenly, with her crazy notions of children, marriage.

And he wasn't going to kill her. He was just silencing her mind.

He pushed the door open and stepped out into the hall. A nurse was striding toward him, and his heart jumped as Anna screamed behind him.

"Nurse!" he shouted. "The patient is having a seizure."

A Code Blue brought them swarming.

Parrish found himself shaking. He had intended to be gone before interns and orderlies and lab techs bustled around. He worked at calming down. He went into the bathroom, downed two Valiums, and came back out.

"Is she all right?" he asked a wiry, dark-haired resident.

The resident shrugged. "Looks like an epileptic seizure. We are going to order an EEG and a brain scan. Maybe we'll see something. Could be a reaction to her medication. Who is her doctor?"

"Dr. Moore. He should be down here any minute. I heard the nurse say that he had a session with her at three."

The resident shook his head. "She's not going to be having any breakthrough insights today, that's for sure."

Parrish thanked the man and walked back down the hall. He saw Dr. Moore entering the ward, and stopped him to tell him about Anna's seizure.

Moore went to check on Anna, and then returned to where Parrish was waiting at the nurses' station.

"I've been meaning to talk to you about Miss Shockley," Moore said. "When we admitted her, she wanted to see you. I know that you saw her when she came here years ago, and I thought you might talk to her again. Your perspective would naturally be immensely helpful. She may—"

Parrish interrupted the man. "I'll be glad to do what I can, help in any way. I do fear that we may be dealing with something organic and degenerative. She's quite delusional."

Moore lifted a sculpted eyebrow and drew his hands through his blond hair. "She seemed rational when I admitted her. She told me about the hallucinations, but she was aware that they were hallucinations and that she had come here seeking treatment. I was, and still am, optimistic."

Parrish smiled sadly and placed an arm on Dr. Moore's shoulder. "Good doctors are always optimistic," Parrish said.

7

October was rainy and cold, gutters filling up with dead leaves, black birds huddled like refugees in skeletal trees. I loafed around Diane's house and got in a fight with Diane's husband Charlie after Anna had been in the hospital two weeks. Charlie sold real estate, and he was a stocky, affable guy.

I don't know what the fight was about. Yes I do. It was about mental health. Crazy people, Charlie said, were really just lazy, lying on their backs in institutions, watching TV, farting and pissing on the hardworking taxpayer.

I told Charlie that he certainly had the look of a man who had been farted and pissed on, and Charlie huffed up out of his armchair and went and told on me, and I could hear Diane and Charlie hissing in the kitchen. I knew that Diane, bless her loyal soul, would make allowances for me (stress, immaturity, stupidity). But I knew I had to get out of there, so I talked to Diane later that night, and said I was going to get a hotel room. She made all the obligatory nay-saying noises, but I knew she would be glad to have me out from underfoot. I wasn't good company. It had been nice of her to take me in, but she had forgotten just how crazy I was in regards to Anna, how defensive.

I was experiencing black guilt. Bright-eyed Anna had been leading an idyllic existence when I came back into her life and chucked her into a clammy mental ward and watched her slide into darkness. I couldn't forget Walker's warning. "There is no good for her in that world," he had said. He had been right.

I had practiced great restraint that first week, hadn't gone to see her even though Diane's reports had been infuriatingly vague. "How's Anna?" I would ask whenever Diane returned from a day at Romner.

Diane would look evasive. "These things take time," she would say—or something equally ominous. I didn't like the way she said it, but I figured that was just me. Then one day Diane said, "I don't know. I think she is getting worse."

Then I had to go see Anna. A nurse was just unstrapping the restraints when I came into the room. Anna was wearing a hospital gown and her hair was a tangled mess. "We're not going to be naughty girls anymore, are we?" the nurse was saying as she helped Anna sit up. "Look, you have a visitor." A smell of vomit pierced the mist of disinfectant. Anna's eyes drifted over me without recognition and she said, "Wooster. Where's Wooster?"

"I don't know no Wooster," the nurse said.

"Anna, it's me," I said.

Anna blinked at me, flapped her arms. "Woooooster," she moaned.

I hung around for about twenty minutes and that was all I could take. I raced back to Diane. "Why didn't you tell me?" I shouted. "She didn't even know who I was."

"Oh David, I didn't know what to do," Diane said, and then she started crying. Driving back from the hospital, I had felt hollowed-out, dizzy with self-pity, and I had worked myself up into a nasty, lashing-out fervor, but Diane's tears woke the primitive bonds of friendship, and I hugged her and tried not to think of Anna's face, unearthly in its whiteness, the way her mouth had moved, the death of reason in her eyes.

Diane said, "Sometimes, when they start a patient on new medication, there is a period when the patient seems to grow worse, a sort of transitional period. That's what Dr. Parrish said. He's really concerned about Anna, and he has taken over the case himself. That's very unusual, you know. I told him that she seems worse, and he assured me that the phenomenon is quite common." Diane said it with all the conviction she could muster, but neither of us believed it.

After finally going to see Anna, I made myself go see her every day. I hated going. She didn't know who I was. But that wasn't the worst of it. Her eyes were full of fear. She would sleep and be jolted out of sleep by some brutal ghost. I wanted to comfort her, but I seemed a part of her terrors. She would jump away from me, scramble under the sheets, hunch her knees up to her chin and shiver.

Physically, the changes were equally drastic. Her eyes were dull. There were days when she looked like a stranger, a pale, anonymous refugee of institutions, standing in med lines, shuttling from one social worker to the next. I told the nurse I wanted to see Dr. Richard Parrish, but I couldn't get an audience with that lordly personage. I could see in the nurse's face, her bulging, incredulous eyes, that she found such a request wildly presumptuous.

So I loitered around, made a general nuisance of myself, and finally accosted the elusive doctor when he came on the ward to see Anna.

I knew it was him right away. I knew by the deference allotted him, the way the nurses and orderlies scraped and fawned in his presence. I also knew because an obsequious self-important head nurse named Mackey called him Dr. Parrish every second sentence as though the great man's name were a powerful mantra. "Good to see you, Dr. Parrish. Is there anything I can help you with, Dr. Parrish? Yes sir, that's right, Dr. Parrish."

"Dr. Parrish," I said, coming up beside him as he moved on down the hall. "I'm David Livingston. I'm a friend of Anna Shockley. Diane Nichols and I brought Anna here about two weeks ago last Thursday. I wonder if I could talk to you about her?"

He turned and regarded me with a smile that was elegantly noncommittal. "Oh?" he said. "Well, of course." He waited, holding his hands in front of him with the patience adults grant to children. I didn't like him. He looked like someone who had slipped out of an advertisement for an after-dinner wine, leaving behind, no doubt, a thin fashion model with full lips and an expression of woozy eroticism.

I told him that I thought Anna was in worse shape then when we had brought her in, that whatever medication they had her on was having an adverse effect.

I was not expressing myself with my customary tact, but I didn't think much about it until he interrupted. "I beg your pardon. Are you a doctor?"

I told him that I wasn't. I noticed then that his face had stiffened considerably and, while his smile may actually have widened, his eyes had iced up.

"I understand your concern," he said. He looked thoughtful. "Just what relation are you to Miss Shockley?"

"A friend. We go back a long way."

"So do Miss Shockley and I," he said. "I treated her before the tragedy, her disappearance. The poor girl has been through a lot. I'm afraid I didn't catch your name."

"Livingston, David Livingston."

He nodded his head. "Anna has been through a lot, Mr. Livingston, and what you see as a sudden deterioration is nothing of the kind. Indeed, you may be making demands on her... you may have expectations that she cannot, realistically, fulfill. If so, you could—and I feel I must speak bluntly for my patient's sake—you could impede her recovery. Sometimes those people closest to a patient are the people most damaging to real progress."

I told him that I didn't think I was being hysterical, that I felt—and Diane Nichols agreed with me—that Anna was reacting badly to some drug, was out of her mind.

"That may be," Parrish said. "Patients often experience a period of adjustment to the medication."

I had heard this before, but we went on, talking in circles. I was on the doctor's turf, however, so I was destined to lose the argument. He brushed me off with a facile blaze of amenities, said he had to see Anna and appreciated my concern and was sure she would begin to improve dramatically, et cetera. I watched him walk on down the hall and enter her room. I left. I didn't like waiting around on that ward. Anna had been moved to the fifth floor, a ward with no pretense of hope. A waxen, moon-faced girl sat on the floor, leaning against the wall, rhythmically thumping her back against the wall and shouting, "Ho, ho, ho, ho." A fat woman wearing a man's flight jacket and pajama bottoms argued hotly with two nurses: "You keepin' my children from seein' me. I know you got them children. You hidin' them under the desk. You bring them out and I'll kiss them little darlin's." The woman tried to crawl over the counter, and was hauled back by two disgruntled nurses.

The woman's screams decided me. Anna couldn't stay here. I went down to the lobby and found a pay phone. I had to get her out. I called Diane. It was her hospital; she would know what to do. She agreed with me so I was spared an argument. She said she would do what she had to do and call me back.

"Anna is committed for three months," Diane said. She looked worn out, baffled.

"Committed? Nobody committed her. What are you talking about?"

"Hey, I'm on your side," Diane said.

She spoke slowly, but her voice wobbled. There was disbelief in her voice. "Anna's mother signed commitment papers."

I started to say that Anna's mother was far away and long ago, but Diane was plunging ahead, anticipating me. "Dr. Parrish located Anna's mother in Ohio, had a local lawyer take the papers to her for signing. Parrish himself talked to her on the phone, convinced her of the necessity of committing her daughter."

I listened, shaking my head. "Parrish is busy, isn't he? Do directors of hospitals do this sort of thing as a rule?" I asked.

"No, they don't."

"I want to get Anna out of there," I said.

That night Sharon called. She was my first argument of the night. She wanted to know when I was coming back. I told her I didn't know, that Anna was in a hospital.

"I miss you," Sharon said.

"I miss you too," I said. I had, too, now that I thought about it.

We paused. Telephone silences are worse than other silences, because they are all silence and static, naked, no windows to look out of, no cigarettes to smoke or drinks to drink. Sharon started to tell me about an old boyfriend she had run into again, a guy named George Lasker.

"I always liked George," I said.

"Great," Sharon said, and that was the first clue I had that she wasn't entirely happy with me. I had known that I was staying down in Newburg too long, but her phone call had seemed cheery. "Glad to hear you approve of George."

"What's the matter?"

"You are an asshole, that's what's the matter," she said.

"Look Sharon, I have got to stay down here. Anna's in really bad shape."

"What if I'm in bad shape?"

"Is something wrong?"

Sharon turned the volume down. She sounded tired, disgusted. I have that effect on people sometimes. "No, nothing's wrong. I'm hanging up, okay?" And she did.

That was the same night that Charlie Nichols decided to air his views on mental health opportunists and my second argument of the evening ensued.

The next day I moved to a motel.

The motel was called The Rainbow Motel, and it had a neon sign with an arcing rainbow. The sign had seen better days, and the rainbow now winked fitfully red and yellow, more nightmare than enchantment. That first night, I watched it for about an hour, decided its staccato light held no personal or religious significance and fell asleep in a chair. I woke at about two in the morning thinking about one ripe summer day when Anna and I had gone fishing and Anna had caught a fish and been horrified as the fish flopped around in front of her on the grass.

"It's dying!" she screamed. "It's dying. Do something!"

I unhooked the fish, a small bluegill, and tossed it back into the lake. "Haven't you ever been fishing before?" I asked.

Anna pouted, pushed tears from her red, sunburnt face. "No."

"But you know about fishing. Surely you've seen people fishing before?" For some reason, I wanted, that day, to pursue Anna's outburst, corner her with reason. Maybe I thought that a little logic would temper her eccentricity.

"Yeah," Anna said. "I guess I've seen people fishing. So what?"

"So I don't think you have to get so emotional. I mean, what did you expect would happen? A fish can't live on land."

"I know that," Anna said. "Jesus, David, you always act like you're some old fart of a school teacher and I'm a moron. A fish can't live out of water. Okay."

"So why did you throw a fit when you caught that fish?"

Anna glared at me. "I didn't think it through," she said.

I started laughing, and Anna joined in. "You old fart," she shouted, and she leaped at me and we wrestled into the water and we both came up all muck and kissed and crawled out on the scratchy, weed-thick bank. The mud dried grey and crackly on our flesh. "Dinosaur skin," Anna said, touching my muddy cheek. "You are my dinosaur love."

There had been days like that. Sitting in that motel room, as tacky and barren of dreams as any motel room, I remembered that day, and I felt desperate.

I wasted the morning talking to a lawyer who didn't seem eager to go up against the director of Romner Psychiatric. Apparently Parrish had a father-in-law who owned half of Newburg, and while the lawyer did not want to say that he positively would not take my money, he did indicate that he lived in the town while I was just passing through.

I spent the afternoon more profitably. I went out to see Walker.

"I guess you can say you told me so," I said. We were sitting on the porch. Walker was holding a small chow puppy, chucking its ears.

"I told you so," Walker said. He smiled at me and rocked in the rocking chair. "You know," he said, "I am a wise man. Everyone tells me so, and they are my friends. They have no reason to lie. I believe them. Do you know what my wisdom, in large part, consists of?"

I told him that I didn't.

"It consists of believing in good things, the goodness of life, the goodness of love, believing that the unraveling of events is, against every ugly evidence, benign. I am a guru and a wise man because I believe more ardently than others. I believe, for instance, that you wish Anna well, that you want her to live and thrive, that you mean her no harm. I believe this against the evidence."

I stood up, walked to the edge of the porch, turned. "I am in love with Anna," I said. "I was in love with her thirteen years ago, and I am still in love with her."

"Anna is easy to love," Walker said. "Too easy to love, perhaps."

"What do you mean by that?"

Walker put the puppy down on the porch where it barked its toy-dog bark and began chasing its tail.

Walker pushed himself out of the rocking chair and came over to me. Together we regarded the mountains. "Maybe Anna doesn't need your love. Maybe she needs your understanding."

I realized then that I was talking to Anna's present lover.

"What about you?" I said. "Your interest in her doesn't strike me as entirely altruistic."

Walker turned to me. He had a likeable, open face with grey eyes. His smile was mischievous. "I never said my interest in Anna was altruistic. I love her."

"She trusts you," I said. "She thinks of you as a father."

Walker nodded. "And you feel I take advantage of her trust. I sleep with her. An old man like me. Young Anna. And she was younger then. Inexcusable behavior."

"That's right," I said.

"It was Anna's choice. It was not for me to deny her a natural life."

"Big of you."

Walker laughed. "I am not justifying myself. That would be a curious thing to do. You are the intruder here. Anna has been happy here."

"That was changing," I said. "You can't deny that that was changing. She was having schizophrenic episodes, hallucinations."

Walker frowned. "Schizophrenia is an empty word."

I was growing angry now. "What do you know about it?"

"Enough. The Home has two medical doctors, three clinical psychologists, one extremely disillusioned psychiatrist. I was around when the neuroleptic drugs were touted as the answer to so-called schizophrenia. There was some discussion, when Anna first came to us, of medications. I didn't approve. I still don't approve. Some people have souls that roam considerably. Anna has such a soul. I find it distasteful to call this journeying schizophrenia."

Walker was speaking in a quiet, reflective voice, studying the blurred lines of the mountains. It was a chilly day; we were both wearing jackets, and now he rubbed his hands together and said, "Come inside and we'll have a glass of wine."

He picked the puppy up in his arms and I followed him into the house.

"I don't drink alcohol," I told him.

He looked at me and nodded. "Coffee then?"

He fixed the coffee, talking all the while.

"I am something of a connoisseur of wine. An effete vice, but a harmless one." He waved a hand at a wall glittering with wine bottles. "I'm vain about my wine collection."

"I don't have much of a palate myself," I said. "I once drank a bottle of Listerine. It was okay. Actually, under the circumstances, it was just fine."

Smiling, Walker nodded his head. "Yes. Yes. Addiction is the larger commitment, certainly. My own interest is less passionate. Perhaps I am a less passionate man than you."

He told me about himself, about his years as a high school teacher, founding The Home. He smiled, a sly, good-humored smile. "You were right to distrust me then. It was all ego, all grandiosity. I was a fraud."

I was surprised by these confidences. I assumed he was trying to charm me with candor. He was succeeding.

After we finished the coffee, we walked down to my car, and I glanced over at the lake where I had first seen Anna after thirteen years, miraculously unchanged. Walker caught my look and said, "I want you to bring Anna back here. I want you to understand that she is safe here. She would be protected here."

"I know."

"I need her," he said. He looked older. I got in the car and started the ignition. He waved, a small, bearded man in an oversized sweater with baggy trousers that flapped in the wind. I felt a hollow, empathic pain in my chest.

8

Nurse Mackey was in her element. "I'm sorry," she said, smiling, spectacles glittering, "but Dr. Parrish said that no one, absolutely no one is to see Miss Shockley. She needs complete rest, complete isolation."

"I'll only be a minute," I said.

"I'm sorry," she said. Nurse Mackey wore a sweet, bland smile on her bloated features. I noticed that her uniform was sorely in need of washing, splotched with odd yellow stains, and strands of her grey hair had sprung loose from under her cap, giving her a disheveled, maniacal air. I knew immediately that I didn't want to argue with her, that any arguments I embarked on would meet with sanctimonious indifference.

I thought of bolting down the hall, but a hefty black orderly appeared behind Mackey just as this thought surfaced.

"We don't want no trouble," the orderly said, with the air of a man who has spoken to too many deaf ears. "We let one person break a rule, and all hell break loose, everybody wanting to break one rule, and soon all kinds of nastiness occurring what with people pissing in the halls or playing with their privates and I don't know what all."

The subject of rules looked like a rich one, and I didn't stay for it to be mined to exhaustion. I turned and walked toward the door. A thin, red-haired woman wearing a rainhat reached for me from a doorway. I avoided her and she hissed, "You cannot deceive me. I been washed in the blood. I been virginized!"

"Shut up," I told her. She looked shocked and scuttled back into her room. *Crazy people can dish it out, but they can't take it*, I thought.

I left the ward and went looking for Diane. I found her at her desk and rushed her into a corner.

"I need your help," I said.

9

I waited around until I was sure Nurse Mackey was gone for the day. Then I donned the lab coat that Diane had given me. A small patch identified me as an x-ray tech. I grabbed a parked wheelchair and took the elevator to Anna's floor.

I carried a clipboard, and, as the doors slid open, affected the weary arrogance of a longtime hospital minion. A young, pretty nurse was sitting behind the desk watching a cop show on a portable television. She looked up and blinked. The blink was a question.

"I'm here to get Anna Shockley," I said. "They need another chest x-ray. Corman isn't happy with the last one." Diane had told me that Dr. Corman was the radiologist known for re-shooting, the man with the pain-in-the-ass reputation. Every hospital has its share of perfectionists, dreaded and reviled by the nursing population.

"At this hour?" the girl said.

"Want to tell him it isn't convenient?"

She didn't have to think about that. No one wanted to engage in conversations with the difficult Corman unless such conversations were absolutely unavoidable.

"Come on," she said. I followed her starched, quick-stepping body down the corridor to Anna's room. Anna was wearing a hospital gown and sitting cross-legged on the bed. For a brief moment, she seemed the old Anna, caught in a characteristic pensive moment. Then she looked up at us, and I saw the frightened eyes, spooked by shadows, and the open, gawking mouth through which some critical spark had fled, leaving a hollow, broken doll.

The pretty nurse matter-of-factly helped me lift Anna into the wheelchair. "You have to get another x-ray," she told Anna. "This won't take long at all, honey." She patted Anna's shoulder. Anna mumbled. Her hands dropped to her lap and wrestled with each other.

I wheeled Anna into the elevator, punched the button for the first floor, and whispered in her ear. "I'm getting you out of here. We are getting the hell out of here, Anna." The elevator doors opened and I wheeled Anna out and down the corridor to the emergency room.

I was parked near the emergency room. I realized that I stood a better chance of getting Anna out to my car if I took her through the E.R. My own experience of emergency rooms suggested that the folks who worked in them were too busy—and when not busy simply too fatigued and indifferent—to stop or question someone in a lab coat taking a patient out of the hospital. Happened all the time. The main lobby might have felt differently about it.

For a change, I was right. I wheeled Anna through the doors and out into the evening. The parking lot was brightly lit and the temperature had dropped. The cold felt welcoming, full of tangy freedom. I helped Anna get into the passenger's side and closed the door after her. "It's gonna be okay," I told her.

I drove Anna to Walker's. There really wasn't any other place to go. I assumed someone at the hospital would eventually figure out who had taken Anna. If they were interested enough—and I had no idea how interested they might or might not be—it wouldn't be hard to discover where I had been staying. Besides, I realized—bitterly—that I wasn't capable of taking care of Anna; there was no wondrous healing in my love. Walker and The Home were the ticket. I remembered those physicians on his staff.

If anyone came looking for Anna at The Home, Walker would handle them. Walker had had years of protecting his orphaned flock from betrayed parents, spouses, lawyers. He would know what to do. I realized that, despite my ambivalent feelings toward the man, I had great confidence in his abilities.

Anna slept as I drove through the darkness. My thoughts ran in circles of recrimination. Anna's hospital gown rode up over her knees, and I stopped to wrap her in a jacket. She seemed terribly fragile. A blue vein pulsed in her forehead against the white, sheer flesh. I studied her profile, and I felt a great surge of love followed by a second furious swell—of rage. I wanted to kill Dr. Richard Parrish, the arrogant, unfeeling son of a bitch.

I had wanted to kill those glib watchers at my mother's death, those smug dispensers of drugs and platitudes, but I had never been able to fix a face to that complacent tribe. They seemed as large and anonymous as the world. But Parrish—Parrish was a man I had met. In his blindness, his professional callousness, he had smashed Anna, hadn't even seen the damage he was inflicting. And I had brought her to him.

This last thought wasn't good company for a man who had things to do, so I put it away. I drove toward the mountains, toward The Home.

10

Richard Parrish sat in his new office with the door locked. He had given his secretary strict orders that he wasn't to be disturbed.

Not that that meant anything. He was surrounded by incompetence. He had moved swiftly, brilliantly, when Anna had appeared out of nowhere, reeking of scandal, intent on doing him harm. Acting quickly and coolly, he had silenced her, saved his career.

And it had all gone for nothing, that effort. That crazy son of a bitch impersonating an x-ray technician had taken her out of the hospital. It was unsettling. The ward nurse had called Parrish the next morning, and the phone call had filled him with vertiginous fears. He had hardly been able to speak. "I'll get back to you," was all he could manage.

He had sat there in the dark, thinking. He reassured himself. Anna Shockley was no threat. There was nothing anyone could prove. He could have walked away from her when he first saw her standing there in the hospital ward, and he hadn't because . . . well, he'd been unnerved. It had been like seeing a ghost. But she was no threat, certainly not now. He had been jolting her with massive doses of amphetamines followed by equally massive doses of neuroleptics, effecting a condition of acute schizophrenia, exacerbating the girl's already unstable condition. The girl was no longer coherent. *Girl?* He still thought of her as a girl. Anna Shockley was a woman now, not the child of their first encounter. But she still looked so damnably young, a function, perhaps, of her mental disorder, a fountain of youth that sheltered her from the years, kept her a child in body as well as mind.

He had had to shake the image of Anna Shockley from his mind that night. He tried to calm himself by writing in his diary, but that was no solace any more. A full glass of Scotch proved more effective. Then he called the desk back and advised them that he was taking care of the situation, that they were not to mention the incident to any more people, that those already aware of the situation were not to speak of it. A patient disappearing from the hospital wasn't something he wanted to read about in the papers.

"Let's say she has signed out on my cognizance," he said. "I'll come by in the morning and complete the necessary paperwork."

It was going to be okay, he told himself. Yet the fear kept whispering. *Why did he take her? What has she told him?*

David Livingston. That was the name of the man who had spirited Anna away. It took no great deductive powers to fit the description of the bogus x-ray technician with the man who had accosted Parrish in the hall. The man had said he was a friend of the social worker, Diane Nichols. Parrish had lost no time in seeking Nichols out.

The Nichols woman was obviously expecting a visit. She gave him only what she judged he could get elsewhere. Yes, a longtime friend of Anna's had been staying at her house. Together they had taken Anna to the clinic when they became concerned about her deteriorating mental health. The friend's name was David Livingston and he wrote children's books, and he had left to return to Alexandria, Virginia, where he lived. No, Diane Nichols knew nothing about his posing as an x-ray technician and stealing Anna from the hospital.

The woman was a poor liar, and she seemed to know it, not even making a great effort, just stubbornly claiming ignorance. Parrish knew he would learn nothing from her.

David Livingston. The name jogged a memory and Parrish went back to his early notes on Anna and found a David there, someone she had been writing to when she was in Romner the first time. He, David, had been in an army stockade then.

A *criminal mentality*, Parrish thought with disgust. Parrish had no tolerance for lawbreakers.

It had been a week since Anna was spirited from the hospital. Livingston had dragged her off to Virginia, Parrish supposed. Fine. The guy would discover soon enough that Anna would have to be institutionalized. There were always guys like Livingston, caught by some honey-sexed bitch, ready to dedicate their lives to her recovery. A couple of days or weeks down the road, and they would discover that the little darling wasn't about to snap out of it, that the cunt had screaming fits, saw monsters, slashed her wrists in the tub, and took a notion to set her lover's hair on fire with her lighter. The guy would forsake romance, dump pretty Anna in some public mental health program, and slide away, hoping no one had noticed. A few misguided fucks, anybody could make a mistake.

Calm down, Parrish thought. He laughed. *Maybe I'm jealous*, he thought.

There was no reason to panic. Anna was probably already roaming the halls of some understaffed mental ward, babbling and bumming cigarettes from freaked-out teens. She could tell her story about being screwed by her shrink to other weary shrinks. Maybe that wasn't the most common story on the wards. If not, it was the runner-up.

11

I woke early in the morning, shuffled out of bed with a ragged quilt wrapped around me, and wrestled a small gas stove into life. I started coffee, tugged on a pair of jeans and a sweatshirt, then waited for the coffee to perk, studying the battered grey pot with simple-minded intensity: steaming coffee in an earthenware mug the limits of my future.

I got the coffee and walked to the window where I drank it while gazing at the long building that was The Home's infirmary. Anna was in there, still trapped in whatever hostile environment her mind had fashioned.

Nine days had elapsed since I brought Anna to John Walker's, and I didn't see any improvement. Diane had driven out twice, once with Kalso (who was back from the big city looking pale and thin), and once alone. Both Kalso and Diane were determinedly optimistic, but I could see that it was uphill work after they had seen Anna. Anna's condition didn't inspire optimism. She was, by turns, locked in catatonic solitude or lashed by violent winds of terror.

Her doctor was a young, freckled boy with a pale mustache that emphasized his youth. He was deadly serious in compensation for his youth and insisted on calling me Mr. Livingston.

"All we can do right now is see that she is quiet, replenish some trace minerals that seem badly depleted, see that she isn't further traumatized by medications."

"You don't agree with Dr. Parrish's treatment?" I asked.

"I don't understand it at all," he said.

"What do you mean?"

"We did a thorough physical on Anna when she arrived. Blood, urine, x-rays, EKG, EEG, the works. Parrish was medicating her with amphetamines. That doesn't make any sense with the sort of disorientation and schizophrenic-like episodes Anna was exhibiting."

"Why would he medicate her like that?"

"I have no idea."

I didn't either, but I knew that my feelings for Dr. Richard Parrish, never warm, had solidified into a massive, immutable hatred.

I stared out the window at the infirmary. It was a brick building, painted white, set down like a vast houseboat in a sea of yellow grass. The morning sun was burning off an autumn mist, and the mountains were coming into existence against a grey sky.

I found I was looking at Anna. The mist had allowed her to appear, quite suddenly, and my mind, slow and swarming with its own ghosts, hadn't registered her image. Then I saw her, standing in front of the infirmary. She was wearing jeans and a flannel shirt.

I turned away from the window and ran out the door. My first impulse was to shout her name, but I caught myself at the last moment and ran on silently.

She turned and looked at me.

I stopped running and began walking very slowly, as a child might approach a skittish colt.

"Anna."

Her eyes jerked away with a pained surprise that I had come to know, and I expected her to bolt, arms spinning, pursued by demons. But she made an effort—I could see the strain in her shoulders—and turned back.

I walked up to her but didn't touch her. "It's cold out," I said. "Perhaps we should go back inside."

"I don't mind the cold," Anna said.

"Everybody will be worried about you."

Anna sighed. "The baby's dead, David."

I reached out and touched her shoulder and she turned and threw her arms around me, almost knocking me over with the violence of her grief. She began to sob. "I couldn't bring him back. Couldn't. Couldn't do it."

I didn't say anything, but slowly I steered her toward the infirmary as I saw a nurse and an orderly come out of the building and start down the hill.

Anna's trembling reverberated in my chest as I held her. A gusty wind licked at us. Anna's feet were bare—as were my own—and the frosty grass crackled under our feet.

Anna's sobs subsided, and she stopped walking. She turned to me and said, "You always worry about me, don't you, David? As long as I can remember, you have been worrying about me. Maybe it's bad luck. You don't have to do it any more. I'm going to be fine." And she patted my hand, a gesture of reassurance that sent an unidentifiable but wild-eyed emotion pounding in my heart.

"I know you are going to be okay." I felt truth in the words, felt that some psychic fever had broken, that Anna was back again. The orderly and the nurse seemed to sense it too, even at a distance, for they slowed as they approached, and they looked, for a moment, like brother and sister, their faces shaped by the same confusion, the same tentative smiles.

I let them lead her back to her room. "I'll come see you later," I shouted after her, and I went back to the cottage and finished my coffee. Then I walked up to the big house and sought out Walker and asked him about the baby.

He told me. "When we found Anna, on the riverbank, she was dying. You already know that, but Anna didn't choose to tell you that she was pregnant at the time. She was bleeding profusely. The child was lost."

"Who was the father?"

"Anna said that you were the father."

"I couldn't have been," I said.

Walker nodded his head. "I know. You were in a stockade at the time of the child's conception. Anna has never been good at lying, as I am sure you know. She can lie without guilt, which should make her a good liar, but she lacks the attention to detail that is at the heart of really fine lying."

"Who was the father?"

Walker shrugged. "Anna has never chosen to tell me."

I sensed, that morning, that Walker knew more than he chose to tell me. He was abrupt; his gestures suggested irritation, an irritation that included me.

"I am glad Anna is improving," he said. "She has a clean strong spirit, but the demands on it have been great. Now you must excuse me. I have much to do this morning."

I went back to the cottage and tried to work on the new book, but I was too restless to settle into the required frame of mind.

I went out again and walked to the top of Anna's favorite hill and gazed out over a long, rolling expanse of meadow. A single, king-sized oak tree towered in the middle of the field amid a cluster of short, scrubby evergreens. Anna, laughing, had told me one day that the oak tree looked like it was teaching the smaller trees.

"What's he teaching?" I asked.

"Bullshit oak tree stuff," Anna had said, eyes blazing with sudden anger. "Telling them little pines to grow up to be oak trees. Worthless bullshit."

Anna always surprised me. I could anticipate some of the things that she would do or say, but it was the things that I did not anticipate that somehow bound me to her. I was always afraid for her, and it was this unexpected quality within her, this wild thing darting in its cage, that frightened me. It seemed so arbitrary, so willful, so damnably elusive.

I thought about what Walker had said. *Anna never told me she was pregnant,* I thought, and I realized that my hurt and sense of loss was a product of my massive self-involvement. Why should she tell me? I felt a dizzy self-loathing. Clearly I was more concerned with a betrayal of trust—an ancient blow to my ego—than with Anna's suffering.

Perhaps Walker had seen to my atrophied heart and that explained his present disgust.

I had too much time to think that day. If Anna did come out of her darkness, what would I do? My presence in Anna's life had never been very benign. "Bad luck," to quote Anna.

By afternoon, I was back in my cottage watching a businesslike rain obscure the infirmary and thinking self-pitying thoughts.

That evening I called Sharon. I don't know why I called her.

Perhaps I was simply tired of hearing my own thoughts rail like bedridden philosophers.

Sharon told me not to call anymore. I said okay.

"Jesus," she said. "You might sound crushed. A gentleman would sound crushed even if he were delighted to be let off the hook."

I couldn't think of anything to say.

Sharon said, "Hell, it *is* okay. There wasn't anything between us. I can take care of myself. Come to think of it, that's what turns you off, isn't it? I can take care of myself."

"Huh?"

"Forget it. I really don't mean to be nasty. It ain't a broken heart on this end of the line, it's just a shit-on ego. But shit-on egos are meaner, so I'm hanging up before I say anything I'll regret. So long." And she hung up.

I was a long time going to sleep that night. I felt harried, feverish. But when I finally did sleep, I slept soundly, and I didn't waken until late the next morning, and I felt inexplicably refreshed. Anna was getting better. The sun was out again. Yesterday's recriminations seemed foolish. My concerns were with the future, not the past.

I whistled briskly and cooked eggs.

12

Richard Parrish kissed his wife goodby after slamming the BMW's trunk. She would be gone for the weekend, off to New York with girlfriends to see a hot new play and descend on Bloomingdale's like piranhas on a dead cow. On Monday she would return, breathless and gift-laden. She would talk and talk, assuming, he supposed, that sheer volume would cover the lie. She didn't realize that she could, as easily, have told in detail every nuance of the multiple fucks she had received during her spurious New York jaunt.

Parrish wasn't interested. He knew she was sleeping with someone, knew almost exactly when it had begun, two weeks earlier. If anything, he was relieved. It kept her busy fashioning her needless lies, and so she left him alone.

He watched the car drive away and then he walked back into the house. The phone rang. It was Parrish's father-in-law.

As usual, the old man wasted no time coming to the point. "I got a call from a crazy man today," Dr. Solomon said. "This fellow calls up out of the blue, and what do you think he says? He says, 'I want Richard Parrish to resign.'"

Silence while the old man let this statement—in all its absurdity—settle. Parrish felt a stillness in his bones, a wary animal listening.

Solomon continued, "Turns out this fellow is named John Walker, runs some kind of commune out on the edge of town. I checked up on him later on, and the man does have some money, so maybe he can make some noise, hire him some lawyers and raise a stink, but he'll regret it if he does. Likely it's all wind, and we'll never hear from him again. He's shouting malpractice; one of his flock has been brutalized. You ever hear of a Hannah Shockley?"

"Anna."

"What's that?"

"Anna Shockley. Her name is Anna Shockley." Richard found that he was nodding his head. Yes. Yes. This was what he had been waiting for. The ugliness. The scandal. The vultures. You could almost hear the sound of their wings.

"You there, Richard?"

He nodded his head, realized that that wouldn't do, and said, "Yes, I'm here. I was treating Anna Shockley for schizophrenia. She left the hospital with a friend. I have reason to believe she is in Virginia."

"Well, that may be. I got the impression that she was with this Walker fellow, but that's beside the point. The point is, there isn't anything special I should pass on to our legal department in case this Walker follows through with a malpractice suit?"

"There's no basis for such a suit, if that's what you mean." Richard heard the prim righteousness in his voice. It wasn't assumed. It was real; he was genuinely offended.

"Don't get hot, Richard. That's not what I mean, and you know it. I just thought you might be able to anticipate the direction such a suit would take."

"Anna Shockley is a deeply disturbed woman. She is inclined to fixate on bizarre conspiracy theories. No telling what she thinks. I'm surprised that anyone would be taken in by anything she said."

"That is odd. But Walker is the lunatic fringe himself. Maybe he's as gullible as all those aging hippies that worship him."

"Maybe."

"Anyway, I just wanted you to know what's happening in case this unpleasantness escalates. Has Jane left yet?"

"You missed her by about half an hour."

"Give her my love when she gets back."

"I will."

Parrish hung up the phone. Well, there it was. He had expected it. A month had passed since Anna Shockley had left the hospital, and the passing of time hadn't settled his mind. With each passing day he had grown more aware of the danger, the inevitable explosion of her will. She had bit him once. He smiled wryly. Her teeth were still good. The phone call from Solomon had confirmed his intuitive conviction. She meant to destroy him.

He went into the study and unlocked the desk drawer. He took out the latest volume in his diary, but didn't open it. There was no salvation in these black volumes anymore. Upstairs in the attic, dozens of these little black books were stored in a locked trunk. He dreamed of that trunk exploding, pouring forth rotted corpses, ugliness beyond belief, naked things with purple sores and skin like yellowed cheesecloth.

His solitude was violated forever. Something was happening within him, as though subterranean armies were gathering, their shouts filling the air. Now it seemed that everyone else possessed secrets, powerful secrets. Jane had her secret lover, and Anna had her secret protectors.

His own secrecy was no longer a source of power. He had tried to live a decent, self-contained life, but events had refused to let him live an ordered existence.

He poured himself a drink and drank it quickly. He refilled the glass.

"It's not your fault," he said.

186

13

"My favorite book," Anna said, "is *The Summer Troll*. I like the way Troll changes, becomes a better person."

"You just like it because you're in it," I said.

Anna frowned at me, then her features brightened. "I'm Gloria!"

I nodded my head. "You are Gloria, the Princess of Upover and True Dreamer."

Anna beamed. Her eyes widened. "And you are Troll. Poor David. Always changing because Gloria dreams you different every summer."

"Hey, wait a minute. I'm not Troll at all. I don't write autobiographical stuff. You are Gloria, and that's it."

Anna laughed. "Okay. You aren't Troll."

I got up and poked the fire. It coughed sparks, blazed. I looked back at Anna, whose deep eyes celebrated the firelight. I had never seen her so beautiful.

We were sitting by the fire in Walker's study. Anna had decided that she was going to write a children's book of her own—which she would let me illustrate—and she had written portions of plot and odd bits of poetry on sheets of lined paper that were scattered around the room.

Anna's book was going to be about a house in the mountains. The house is filled with laughing, loving people. Something happens, and the people move to the city and abandon the house. The house becomes very lonely and kidnaps a kid who has gotten lost while hiking with his Boy Scout troop. Something like that. It wasn't entirely clear. Anna admitted it needed work.

"Will you marry me?" I asked.

Anna frowned. "Stop it. It isn't funny."

"I wasn't trying to be funny."

Anna glared at the fire. "I could marry you. I could say 'sure' and you'd do it, because you are crazy."

"I love you."

"You don't even know who I am." Anna rolled over on her back and blinked at the ceiling. "My brain feels like someone ran it through a blender. Behave for awhile, okay?"

"Okay." I logged "awhile" in the wide territory of hope.

Anna reached up and drew me to her. "I'm glad you're here," she said, running her fingers through my hair.

"Me, too. I'm glad I'm here."

One day, when I went to the infirmary to visit Anna, I found her in the television room with young Dr. Simms. Anna was laughing and Dr. Simms looked flushed and somewhat confused, like a puppy who has been praised without knowing exactly why.

"We are talking about medicine," Anna told me. "Dr. Simms knows everything."

Dr. Simms, flustered, stood up and locked the medicine cabinet. He was wearing the same smile, but he seemed to be shaking himself out of a daze. Anna did have a mesmerizing quality. I pointed that out to Walker later on, when Walker had occasion to be less than delighted with young Simms.

Anna's recovery was miraculous. She had cast off the terrified, leaden-eyed husk of her hospital stay and emerged with a fierce, butterfly brightness that eclipsed even my nostalgia-powered dreams of her. Walker explained it in spiritual terms that eluded me. Anna's solemn Dr. Simms may have been the victim of infatuation, but who could blame him?

Anna moved out of the infirmary and back into the main house. I waited. Anna was glad I was there. That was as good a reason as any for remaining. I could work on the book here, in the cottage. Christmas was edging toward us; I intended to celebrate it with Anna.

"You are a patient son of a bitch," Diane told me, sitting on the floor drinking coffee.

"Huh? No one has ever accused me of being patient," I said.

"But you are. You are waiting for Anna to leave with you, and you are willing to wait until she comes around."

"Once again, you are making me out to be far more calculating than I am."

Diane put the coffee cup down and stood up. She walked to the window and looked out. "And once again you are trying to appear more innocent than your years warrant. It's snowing."

I joined her at the window and watched the first large, wet flakes float down, slowly, dreamily, barely licked by gravity. The afternoon dimmed. The windowpane caught the first flakes, which instantly melted, running in crooked silver streams.

"I better get back," Diane said. "I hate driving in snow."

I walked her to her car and kissed her goodby. "It probably won't amount to anything," I said.

The snow began to hurtle down. Darkness came, and the snow rushed through the black air with a heavy, purposeful silence.

It had been snowing the last time I saw my mother. That was my freshman year in college, and I was home for the holidays. It had been a meaner snow, with ice in the heart of each flake, and it rattled on the car, clicked against the windshield, clung in glittering chunks to the wipers.

I had come up on the train, spent the day with my father, brother, my brother's several children, in-laws, aunts. The house was festive: a turkey cooking, Christmas carols chiming, toys clacking, football booming on the TV.

The next morning, I borrowed my brother's car and drove out to see my mother alone, not telling anyone where I was going.

Calvert Hospital was celebrating its own Christmas. There was a large Christmas tree in the dayroom.

"That's a beautiful tree, ain't it?" a thin, uniformed woman with a round face said.

I agreed that it was.

"Course, we don't have no glass ornaments on it, as you will observe. We learned our lesson there. You would be amazed the damage an ordinary Christmas ornament can make on mortal flesh if a poor soul takes a notion."

It was a sobering thought.

My mother was in her room, propped up in bed, reading *Pride and Prejudice*. She smiled when I came in. "David, I'm glad you could come," she said. My mother was an extremely formal woman, not because she lacked warmth, but because she loved the ritual of things.

I kissed her on the cheek. "How are you doing?" I asked.

"I am weathering these unfortunate circumstances." She sighed. "Holmes"—my mother persisted in calling her doctor Holmes in wry homage to his deductive powers—"says I can leave in a few weeks, as soon as the medication makes me totally innocuous to all and sundry, I suppose. And how are you getting on?"

I told her that college was just fine, Father seemed just fine, et cetera. Hospital conversations always run down quickly, and this one was no exception. We talked about books, a favorite subject for both of us and one that kept us occupied until a nurse came in to tell me it was time for me to leave.

"Here, I'll walk you to the door," my mother said, and she got out of bed and walked down the hall, an arm on my shoulder.

"Buck doesn't like to come," she said. "I know that. He has always been a robust man, your father, and he has a mortal fear of frailty. I understand. It isn't his fault at all. You do him an injustice—no, you do, I know you do. And you shouldn't. You shouldn't think ill of your father."

I meant to say something, make some denial, perhaps even explain the exact and subtle nature of my dissatisfaction with Buck Livingston, but my mother's face suddenly altered, her eyes narrowed and she leaned forward and said, "Take me with you. Quickly. We'll leave here. Just walk out. They don't have any cameras here, not in the hall. In the rooms, they have hidden cameras, but not here. Now's our chance."

Her hand was clutching my shoulder, squeezing, and her head shook.

"I can't, Mother. You know that."

She didn't say anything, just shook me with her hand on my shoulder. There was an odd swollen cast to her features, a determination that made her seem a stranger. I was frightened.

Then her grip relaxed. Her features shifted to resignation. I saw my mother as I knew and loved her. "No," she said, patting my shoulder. "Of course you can't. I don't know what came over me. Well, off with you." She kissed me on the cheek, turned, and walked quickly back down the hall.

I drove back to the aunts and uncles, back to the festivities. I never saw my mother again. One of Calvert's cleaning staff left a can of drain cleaner in the bathroom. My mother availed herself of the opportunity. She killed herself on the third day of the new year, leaving no note.

The symmetry of my life is great shrink fodder, I suppose. Long ago, Ray had accused me of falling instantly in love with Anna because she was a suicide. If I could save Anna, I might win this time, at least wrestle the ghost of loss to a draw. That had been Ray's theory, wilder than Freud at his woolgathering best (and Freud was no slouch).

If there was any truth in Ray's theory, Anna seemed to be surviving in spite of me. My redemptive efforts stank.

I jerked awake in the coffin darkness of the storm, my heart racing. A sense of impending doom haunted me, made me get up and turn on the light and study the progress of the storm.

I looked out at the main house, through the blur of still-falling snow. I was reassured by the warm light that burned in the second-story window, Anna's room. As I watched, the light went out.

"Good night, Anna," I said.

I looked at my watch and noticed that it was only a little after ten. I put some coffee on and prepared to reread *Titus Groan*, one of the world's great oddball books in that wonderful Mervyn Peake trilogy of the castle Gormenghast.

I heard the truck's engine heave into life, roar as the accelerator was revved. I looked out the window as the truck's lights went on, blazing in a swirl of fine snow. The truck shook as it backed up, snow falling from its sides. The wipers cut small, myopic arcs, and the truck lurched forward again, its tires spewing snow. Sliding faintly to the left, it turned under the porch light.

Anna was at the wheel. I knew it was her without seeing into the frosted cab. A shadow was all I needed. The truck swung down the driveway, fishtailing, picking up speed. I watched the taillights dwindle and suddenly jump into empty night.

I didn't panic. I poured coffee into a thermos, dressed as warmly as I could, and turned off all the lights before I stepped out into the storm, closing the door behind me.

14

Before the snow had begun to fall, Richard Parrish watched his wife leave. He blinked down at her from the upstairs window, assured that she couldn't see him. If she didn't come back in for a last goodby, he wouldn't have to hit her. He didn't want to hit her, because, almost certainly, he would have to keep hitting her, and he didn't want to do that, because he had more important things to do.

He watched her put the suitcases in the trunk. She was wearing a big, black fur coat that made her appear broad-shouldered and ungainly. Goddam skinny broad, not his type, full of thin suffering. A woman should have some flesh on her bones. Like Anna Shockley—the woman he had always loved.

Jane Solomon looked up and Parrish stepped away from the window.

She stopped looking at the window and got in the car and drove away. Parrish watched the car turn a corner, then he went downstairs.

He poured himself a drink and looked up at the ceiling. He gulped down the drink. Time to get on with it. He hauled the trunks down from the attic and carried them out to the backyard. He opened the trunks and spilled the notebooks and black volumes into the crumbling fireplace. He went back into the house, into his study, breathing rapidly, sweating from exertion, and brought the last of the diaries out. He poured kerosene over the books, his hands shaking. He was nervous but resolute. Time to put away childish things. He struck the match and it seemed to leap of its own accord, flames bursting over his past.

His heart was rocked by a blast of panic when, momentarily, the books defied the flames, went untouched by the sheath of fire. Then they began to writhe, to curl and explode, exhaling black, evil smoke.

Parrish watched the smoke roll toward the sky. His wife was

divorcing him, and old Solomon was no longer an ally—the son of a bitch had suggested that Parrish take a leave of absence.

"We can settle this thing out of court," Solomon had said. "I realize that you've done nothing wrong, but they've documented their side of it, blood tests, doctors' affidavits, even someone on the hospital staff. Jenkins says they can make it unpleasant, and in this business, allegations alone can ruin us. The public is a hanging jury."

At the time Solomon had said that, Jane hadn't yet announced her intentions to leave. This new development would simplify matters for her old man. The next phone call from Solomon would, Parrish knew, dispense with tact. It would be an ultimatum.

The son of a bitch never did like me, Parrish thought. Tears filled his eyes, surprising him. He just wanted to be liked; that's all he ever wanted. The sons of bitches.

One thing Parrish knew: Walker wouldn't let up, wouldn't settle out of court. He couldn't. He was under Anna's spell.

"Oh, there is a sorry lot of us," Parrish said. The alcohol had offered him a profound insight. He wasn't Anna's only victim. There were others. Stopping her, putting her down as though she were some sad, maimed wild thing, would rescue others. He loved her, loved her even though she had made a wreck of his life, but there were other considerations. She had violated a natural law, come back from the dead like a monster in a fairy tale.

Now, leaving the past to burn, he walked back into the house. He fixed himself another drink, noticed that his legs were shaking. He felt unmoored, naked, but he knew that the feeling would pass. He was alone. It was a terrible thing to be alone (the curious tears pressed under his eyelids and he clenched his teeth).

He walked down to the basement, then upstairs, roaming the house, confirming his solitude. He had an urge to record his latest insight but he had left the realm of solitary journals and inaction.

He had been in a dream.

Burning the diaries had made him stir in his sleep.

Anna's death would waken him. She would be free from suffering. The malpractice suit would evaporate and Solomon would see that Parrish was not a man to be dismissed so cavalierly.

A single bold, swift stroke and things could be made right. That was the secret of it: Boldness.

Later, Richard walked outside again. The fire had died down, meditating redly over the ashes. Snow was beginning to tumble from the sky—a good sign, cleansing whiteness. The alcohol had wrapped him in warmth. He smiled, poked the ashes with a stick.

He would have to plan carefully. This time his plan would be seamless.

He went back into the house, finished his drink, and refilled the glass. He was not a drinker, but today he felt that alcohol was part of his declaration of freedom. It let his mind roam, allowed him to reflect objectively on the problem of Anna Shockley. Where was she? In Virginia with Livingston? Or, as Solomon thought, right here in Newburg? She would be easy enough to locate.

If she were in Virginia, it would be inconvenient, but he was confident that he could solve the problem.

"Oh, Anna," he said, speaking out loud, "it's all over. You've stayed up too late and you know how cranky that makes you. You were very naughty, staying up so long past bedtime. Time for Daddy to tuck you in." He raised his glass, finished it with a flourish.

He awoke to a dull, thumping sound and squinted through gluey eyelids. The room was dark except for the end table lamp which glowed weakly—Jane had an infuriating pocket of frugality when it came to buying low wattage bulbs—and the furnace had kicked on, throwing a great, suffocating heat into the room.

Someone was at the door. "Be right there," Parrish shouted, pushing himself out of the armchair where he had fallen asleep. *Never should drink,* he thought, rubbing his face, confused and disoriented.

He swung the door open, and a gust of snow spun around him, the cold stinging his face, startling him.

He snapped the porch light on and Anna, wrapped in a full-length coat and clutching a bottle of wine in gloved hands, smiled at him.

"It's me," she said.

15

The man in the tow truck hollered back to his friend, who waved a hand and shouted something that was caught by the furious swirling snow. The tow truck, wheels spinning, hauled me back onto the road.

It was luck that they had come along when they did. I had just decided to walk, having failed to rock the car out of the ditch, but I knew that it was a good three miles to the next gas station, and the sense of peril, of time running out, had increased.

"You was lucky," the service man said. He was a big man, wearing a hat that said Hartman Auto Repair. "We was on a beer run, heading back from Dixie's. Good luck for you."

I agreed.

"You still set on driving to town?" he asked. "This storm is just getting started. There's more ditches on the way, you know. I wouldn't recommend it."

I told him that I had to get to town and asked if I could buy some snow chains.

"They're steep," he said. "This time of year, this particular hour of the evening, these conditions, chains are steep."

He named a price. It was steep, but I told him I would double it if he could have me back on the road in twenty minutes.

He did it. I was impressed. I drove down the middle of the white, winding road. The chains clattered and a loose link whacked against the side of the car, but I didn't stop to correct it. I leaned forward, peering into the storm, looking for Anna's truck on the side of the road. The truck would have no problem with these roads, but Anna's driving might and I thought there was a good possibility I'd find her foundered somewhere along the route. I didn't.

I was locked in a tunnel defined by the beams of the car, the snow, the dense night. I was moving very slowly, but, whenever I pressed on the accelerator, the car would instantly shift sideways and I would have to let up on the pedal.

I turned on the radio and was greeted with static, the snow's sound effect, and an occasional lost voice, half a sentence, a rattle of music. Silence was more reassuring so I turned the radio off and thought about Anna.

I didn't know why she had left in the storm, what had prompted her, but I thought I knew where she was going. And the knowledge made my slow progress more unendurable. I leaned forward and stared out the foggy window and had the strange conviction that I was driving down a steep incline, into an abyss inhabited by demons.

16

She came into the room, covered with snow, holding the bottle of wine in one hand, something white in the other. She was raucously alive, filling the dim living room with her presence. She took her knit cap off and shook out her hair. Parrish, just awakened, sweaty and unsettled, blinked at her and tried to field just one thought from the confusion.

"Is your wife here?" she asked. "If she is, you should ask her to leave. We have to talk privately."

Parrish shook his head. "She left. She's gone."

Anna looked around the room. "I guess your wife is in charge of decorating."

"Yes."

"This is a big house, a mansion, I guess. Are you surprised that I knew where you lived?"

No, Anna, nothing about you surprises me, he thought, but he said nothing, waited.

"Are you going to ask me to sit down or what? You aren't being a terrific host, you know."

"Please," Richard said. "Sit down. Here, on the sofa. I'll be right back."

Parrish went upstairs and urinated and washed his face in the sink. He studied his face in the mirror as he combed his hair. His eyes seemed devoid of intelligence. There was a numbness in his features, the flesh sullen and passive. Anna was downstairs. She had been delivered to him, as though all the fates were roaring in unison, "Here she is. Now what are you going to do about it?"

He had to act. Damn the drinking. He wasn't awake. He opened the medicine cabinet, found the pills, swallowed two with water from the tap. *Speed kills*, he thought. He promised himself it wouldn't become a habit.

As he walked back down the stairs, he imagined he was already feeling the amphetamine sharpening of focus.

She was sitting primly on the sofa. Her wet coat was thrown over the back of the sofa, and melting snow was leaking into the plush fabric. Jane would have fainted. Richard walked over to the coat, picked it up, and said, "I'll just hang this in the kitchen."

Returning from the kitchen, he said, "It's good to see you, Anna. I was worried about you. And I'm sure your friends are worried about you tonight, out alone in this terrible weather."

Anna smiled. "They don't know I'm here. Nobody knows I'm here."

A gift, Richard thought. It was as though, in breaking his chains, in burning his diaries, he had invoked the awesome powers of the gods of action. He had offered a sacrifice, and this was his reward.

But Anna was still talking. "You weren't worried about me, Richard. I know that now. I've had a lot of time to think. If you really loved me, you would have known I wasn't dead all those years. You would have felt it in your soul; you would have heard my heart beating in your ears."

Richard sank into an armchair facing the sofa. He smiled at Anna. She was so beautiful. Anyone might have been led astray. The cold had reddened her cheeks, and her full lips retained the pouty sensuality of a young girl. Her eyes were the brightest thing in the room. He wanted her, felt the need for her warm and waken him.

"The worst thing," Anna continued, "was our baby." Her voice trembled; her thoughts had led her into violent emotions. "You didn't care about our baby. You didn't care that our baby was alone, frightened."

"There is no baby," Parrish said, and he was surprised at the softness in his voice. It angered him, this softness, as though, after all she had done, he would still seek to comfort her.

Anna said, "You don't even know his name, do you?"

"What?" The girl was losing him, talking nonsense.

"The baby's name is David. After a friend, a true friend. The baby can't come over to this side. He's frightened and confused and sometimes I hear him crying at night. He needs us, Richard."

Parrish shook his head. Such a beauty, housing such a ravaged mind. And this girl had once been capable of overturning his career... it was unthinkable, impossible. "You're not well," Parrish said. "Come back to the hospital."

Anna shook her head. "No. The hospital was bad for me. You should have seen that, but you didn't care."

"You need help."

"I love you," Anna said. "It doesn't matter what I think about it, there it is—I love you. That love was created before I was born. It was sewn inside of me by angels. I can't rip it out." She was talking very rapidly now, licking her lips as she spoke, her hands moving around, touching her knees, darting away. "So I came here. They would all be mad if they knew I was here, but that won't matter. Their anger isn't important. I brought this bottle of wine. It is a rare wine, for special occasions. This is a very special occasion, Richard."

"Come here," Parrish said. He still loved her, here at the end of everything. He stood up. "It's been too long," he said. He reached for her, caught her shoulders and pulled her forward. On his knees, he kissed her rich mouth.

She pushed him away. "No, Richard. That is over with us."

Yes, Anna. All over. He yanked her down from the sofa. She hadn't been expecting that. Her head snapped back and he spun her down, falling on top of her. They wrestled on the floor. "Stop it!" she screamed.

But she didn't want him to stop. She liked it rough.

He took her on the living room floor, his mind free and easy and full of effortless power. Secrets bloomed within him. What would his wife think if she were to suddenly return, hot for reconciliation? The thought filled him with passionate laughter.

He came quickly, his breath ragged and magnified in his head. He crouched naked next to her and looked at the room, strewn with her cast-off clothes. They might have been the center of an explosion—a molten, deadly center.

She was looking at him with those large, serious, nocturnal eyes. It was a look of expectancy, that goddam demanding, hero-hungry look that females got. Parrish felt an urge to crush the false softness in her, to hit her until that innocence fled and the true, ruthless self erupted from the softness, showed its gleaming death's head as it came for him. He was a match for the bitch.

He hugged his knees and stared at her. She smiled up at him. She seemed to be floating on the pale sea of her nakedness. He reached down and cupped her breasts.

He lifted her up and carried her up the stairs. He eased her onto the great bed, on top of the sheets, and then he fell upon her, ravenous again. Now they were engaged in a slow dance, something they might have rehearsed, turning in animal agreement, fast, now slow again. Parrish felt alert, aware of the room and the snow at the window, pervaded by a deep, omnipotent calm.

He entered her from behind, gazing beyond the sleek curve of her spine to the cold, steadfast snow, and, with no feeling of incongruity, indeed, with a sense of perfect timing, the way of her death was revealed to him.

Parrish climaxed again, leaned over her and hugged her shoulders.

He went into the bathroom, to the adjoining room. He tiptoed down the stairs and into his study where he quickly found what he wanted. He filled the syringe with a fast-acting sedative and hurried back upstairs. Even as he acted, his mind moved, refined the inspiration. Sedate her. He could pull the truck into the garage, cut up a garden hose. Still later, he could take the truck to some convenient location, drive it into a snowdrift, leave Anna, and walk home, confident that the falling snow would eradicate any traces of a second person.

He paused in the bathroom and put the syringe on the sink beside him. He was thirsty again and he leaned under the tap and gulped water.

He picked the hypodermic up and pushed the bathroom door open. Anna still lay on the bed, on her stomach. He entered the room quietly and walked to the edge of the bed.

"Richard?" she murmured, turning over.

He reached for her.

She spun around, her eyes fixed on the needle in his hand. "No, Richard. No!" she screamed.

She fought with frenzied strength, surprising him. He was forced to drag her off the bed and set the needle on the night table while he subdued her. He was careful not to hit her. Then, with his knees on her chest, he was able to retrieve the needle and plunge it into her left arm. She ceased struggling and glared at him.

He held her tightly. Silently, they stared at each other. Then her eyelids drooped and her body loosened, resigned to unconsciousness. He wondered what she had been thinking. *Probably pissed.* A giggle escaped his lips. He stood up. His arms ached and his legs felt weak and unreliable.

But he had much to do, no time for weakness.

He stood up and staggered downstairs. He gathered his clothes in the living room and dressed quickly. Then he gathered Anna's. He cursed her as he sought a missing sock, finally finding it wedged behind a sofa leg. "Damn it," he muttered. "Goddam you Anna." But he found the sock and admitted that, in all fairness, it wasn't Anna's fault the sock had slid under the sofa. He couldn't blame her for that.

He went back upstairs and dressed her. It was hard work, dressing an unconscious person, and he found himself cursing her again. He apologized. "I know it's not your fault," he said. When he was finished dressing her, he stepped back. She looked sort of unkempt. Well, an evening spent tossing and turning in a truck before finally falling asleep was going to make a girl somewhat disheveled, now wasn't it?

He took the truck keys from her pocket, put on his coat, and went outside. The snow was still coming down, gathering reassuring momentum. The nearest house was two hundred yards away, and while someone might have been able to see him in broad daylight, he was certainly unobserved now.

He pulled the truck into the garage, got out and closed the garage door. Leaving the truck's motor running, he went to fetch Anna.

17

A snowplow humped along Main Street; a blade scraped the street now and again, sending a fountain of sparks in the air. I got out of my car and ran across the street to the telephone booth. Luck was with me; no one had ripped off the phone book. What luck? Parrish wasn't listed.

I called Diane. She answered on the second ring, sounding sleepy.

"Diane, this is David."

"Hi, David."

She didn't sound delighted to hear from me.

I told her that Anna had run away, that I was in a phone booth in downtown Newburg. Her response was a less than enthusiastic "Oh."

"I've got to have Parrish's address," I said. "I think that's where she was going."

There was a long silence, and then Diane said, "David, I'm not giving you that information."

Outside the phone booth, the storm was going wild, as though emphasizing the urgency of the moment.

"Information? I don't want any fucking information. I just want to know where he lives."

"You don't sound reasonable. I don't know what the problem is exactly, but I can guess. And I'm not going to endorse your insanity if you know what I mean."

I lowered my voice. "I don't have time to explain, but I've got to see her."

"Story of your life," Diane said. "I can't be a party—"

A man's voice suddenly boomed on the line, the no-nonsense voice of Charlie. "Livingston," he said. "That you, Livingston?"

I didn't say anything.

"Do you have any idea what time it is?"

I did. It was late and getting later. I hung up the phone and dialed the hospital.

I opened the phone booth door and let the storm howl into the receiver as I spoke.

"Harmon Pharmacy here," I shouted into the phone. "I've been trying to deliver these prescriptions Dr. Parrish ordered, but I can't find the house."

"I beg your pardon," said a voice, timid enough to give me hope.

"The address I've got is one one two seven..." I held the receiver up into the obliging shriek of the wind, then spoke again. "I don't know if I've got the wrong address or what, but I'm lost, and I don't fancy driving around all night in this stuff. Could you read back the proper address?"

"I'm new here," the voice said. I envisioned a white-haired woman—small, very small.

"I am going to have to forget this order if you can't verify the address."

"Just a minute, please." She put the phone down with a thunk, and I heard her rummaging around. Then she came back on the line, her thin voice fat with satisfaction. "Here it is!" she shouted. "Twenty-seven fourteen Windover Street."

"Twenty-seven fourteen!" I shouted. "No wonder I couldn't find it. Look, thanks lady, thanks very much. Goodby."

I got back in the car. I pulled a map of Newburg out of the glove compartment and studied it under the weak overhead light. Windover looked to be fifteen minutes away, just a short run through town and then a couple of lefts amid the stately, mapled streets of the rich.

I had the road to myself. The snowplow had vanished, leaving a wake of frozen waves. The plow had uncovered ice, and the car weaved past mired storefronts, ice-encrusted trees, darkened streetlights. The moment of elation, of having discovered my destination, was brief. The triumph went out of me, leaving nothing but foreboding. I was too late. I had always been too late.

18

It was done. Anna, once again in her long coat, slept peacefully in the truck's cab, slept like a baby full of warm milk. Parrish had run the garden hose from the exhaust to the truck's window and taped it in place, sealing the window airtight. A job well done.

He came back into the living room and sank into the armchair. Later there would be work, a hard, cold business with nerve-racking risks, but for the moment he could relax.

He stretched his arms over his head, smiled ruefully at the wine bottle on the coffee table. Anna's little peace offering—her fancy wine. He picked up the bottle of wine and studied it. He was no connoisseur of wines, and Anna certainly wasn't either. Still, it did have the look of something expensive.

He couldn't pull the cork out with his fingers, but he managed to get a hold of it with his teeth and slowly work it out. Some of the wine spilled on his pants. Hardly elegant. He laughed at himself.

He poured the wine into his glass and held it to the light. It was dark red.

He had loved her. But he was a realist, like his father. Sometimes you had to amputate. Love doesn't solve everything. "No way," Parrish told the empty room.

The wine smelled like flowers, hot and sweet.

He sipped the wine slowly. It had a strange, sensual texture, seemed to move of its own accord, caressing his tongue, exploring his throat, his stomach.

His eyes fell on the white envelope on the table. Of course, it was what Anna had been holding in her hand when she came to the door. He lifted it up. The single word, IMPORTANT, was printed on the envelope.

Amused, Parrish addressed the room again, "Ah, let's just see what's important, shall we?"

There was a single page of ruled paper, and the handwriting was large and executed with care.

Parrish sipped the wine and read:

Dear Friends,

Please do not grieve for us. Richard and I have chosen to be with our baby. We have taken our earthly lives in order to be with him. There is no sin in this. We act with duty and love. I know that our baby, David, will be glad to see us, and I hope...

The letter slipped away from his fingers. The strength fled from his hands. Parrish discovered he could not stand up. It was as though invisible hands gripped his shoulders, dark angels held him down.

Anna—

19

It took three-quarters of an hour to get to twenty-seven fourteen Windover Street. It was a little after three in the morning. I brushed snow off the mailbox to read the numbers. The house was hidden amid plump, snowy evergreens.

The house was dark, unwelcoming. There were faint indentations leading up the walk, footsteps the snow was quickly erasing. I didn't see Anna's truck. Maybe I had been wrong about her destination.

My original sense of urgency had fled. I felt tired, stupid. I was tired of chasing Anna down, of trying to shore up the walls of a dream that I had slapped together out of plasterboard guilts and adolescent yearning. It was no good anymore.

But I had come the distance, propelled by a crazy sense of purpose, and so I put my head down and waded through the snow to the door. I knocked and waited, vaguely wondering what I would say when the door was opened by an irate Dr. Parrish, routed from sleep by a lovesick stranger. He wouldn't be happy.

I knocked again, louder. I waited, snow melting down my collar. I reached down and turned the knob and the door swung open. I entered the room.

"Hello?" I called.

I saw him in the armchair then, and I knew he was dead but the fear that jumped in me had nothing to do with Parrish.

"Anna!" I shouted. "Anna!"

I ran through the house, shouting her name, upstairs, then downstairs again.

I stopped in the living room, holding myself very still, listening, as though some revelation, some inspired thought, would speak in the silence. That's when I heard it: the truck's engine.

I found her in the garage.

Anna was alive. I carried her upstairs, opened a window. She started to come around.

"My head hurts," she said. Her face was grey, almost blue under her eyes.

I lifted her onto the bed and pulled the covers up around her. I said, "I want you to rest for a few minutes. I've got something I have to do. I'll be back soon, okay?"

I went back to the living room. I didn't look at Parrish. I left the house and drove my car back down Windover and parked it on a parallel street. Nobody was apt to remark on a car abandoned in inclement weather. I cut through a yard and discovered that I had gauged the distance pretty well. I came out on Windover about two hundred yards from the house and I was back inside Parrish's fifteen minutes after I'd left.

I looked at Parrish this time. He was pressed back in the armchair, eyes closed, grinning. Some G-force, some acceleration of sudden death, had shoved him back in the chair, straightened his legs. I picked up the sheet of paper in his lap and read it. I read it twice, and then I understood it.

"You met your match," I said to the corpse. "I could have told you. I could have told you about Anna Shockley. But you didn't ask. You shrinks never ask the right questions." I felt something slipping in my mind, some gear failing to engage as I stood in the living room, speaking to a man with a dried snail's trail of blood issuing from one nostril, cheeks mottled with death's purple hickies.

I sighed. The gear engaged. A heaviness that was the last of my sanity descended. "Hey, I've got to get things cleaned up here," I said. I turned away from the corpse and got to work. I put Anna's letter in my pocket. I emptied the wine bottle in the sink and turned the tap water on. I decided to take the empty bottle with me. I cleaned up as well as I could and went back upstairs.

Anna stirred in the passenger seat as we drove back to Walker's. The truck moved with assurance through the snow, which was still falling relentlessly.

"Don't be mad at me," Anna said.

The words alarmed me. I turned and blinked at Anna. I had

almost forgotten she was there, intent on navigating the treacherous night.

I looked at her. She looked very small, a dark mass of troubled hair and those large, surprised eyes peering over her drawn-up knees.

"I was just trying to do the right thing," she said.

I laughed. A single, short laugh, involuntary as a sneeze, but it hooked a vast, absurd chain and the laughter rushed out of me. The truck caught the mood and swooped off the road, and my foot on the brake spun us around and we lurched to a stop facing the way we had come and the laughter wouldn't stop.

Finally, wheezing, feeling the reawakening of boyhood asthma in my aching chest, I stopped laughing. I felt shaken by some cosmic mugger, my pockets turned out, emptied.

Anna looked alarmed. But she didn't say anything.

I caught my breath and said, "Sorry." I turned the truck around and drove on into the storm.

"Why did you laugh?" Anna asked.

I looked at her. She looked wary, maybe offended. I didn't want to offend her.

"I don't know," I said. "I just had a sort of revelation. Everything struck me funny. I realized—this isn't gonna sound like the funniest joke you ever heard—but I just realized I was out of my depth."

"You don't love me anymore," she said.

I looked at her again, and she was actually pouting, lower lip thrust forward in classic, kittenish pique. She looked quite sweet, actually. I didn't have any more laughter in me, however.

"Anna, I love you." I said it sternly, a reprimand, and her lower lip retreated. Resilient Anna, she smiled.

When I reached The Home, all the lights were on in the main building. During the night, a nurse had discovered that the drug cabinet had been broken into. An inventory had revealed the missing, lethal drug—a bedcheck revealed the missing Anna. Dr. Simms had sheepishly admitted to being the recipient of some questions on the matter of doctors and drugs, lethal and otherwise.

Walker had abandoned his customary calm. "A suicidal patient asks her doctor what prescription drugs are lethal, and he tells her?"

It was then that I came to the young man's defense.

"Anna's got a way with her," I said.

Walker looked at me like I was crazy. Being crazy, I didn't take offense.

Walker and his staff were glad to see us.

They put Anna to bed, and I had a chat with Walker. I told him everything. I asked him if he could drive me into Newburg in a couple of days so I could pick up my car. He said he thought he could do that.

Later that night, Anna tried to kill herself. She had made only the most limited progress, sawing on her wrist with a dull scissors, when a nurse discovered her.

I stayed at Walker's on into December. Parrish's death was big news. It was being called a suicide. I felt that a close look would discover some problems with this assessment. I felt a sense of deja vu—Larry all over again. And, again, no hue and cry arose. In Larry's case, no investigation had been initiated because no one gave a damn. In Parrish's case, I suspected a powerful father-in-law might have had something to do with the limited scope of the investigation. Dr. Solomon had a daughter to protect.

20

Kalso came out to visit me. He was carrying a couple of Christmas presents and looking hearty.

"Come on, open your present," he said. "I see you didn't get me anything, but that's all right. You were always a thoughtless boy. Besides, it is better to give than to receive."

I tore the wrapping paper off and discovered a framed photo of Anna—the one that had brought me back to Newburg. There was Anna in Walker's kitchen, her dark eyes firing point-blank out of the light, the kitchen sink, the stacked dishes, the homey detail that surrounded her, fey child-queen in a straight-backed chair.

A sharp pain raced through me. Tears sprang in my eyes.

"Goddam it, Kalso," I said. I got up and walked into the

bathroom.

When I came back, Kalso said, "Time to move, David. Time to haul ass."

"I just felt a little incongruous there for a moment," I said. "Incongruous" was Kalso's own beloved word, used to describe every misstep on life's path.

Kalso nodded, pursed his lips judiciously. "I'm not kidding. Time to bust loose."

"I know I can't stay here."

"I saw Diane last week. She says you are paralyzed. She says, 'David isn't happy with me. I can't say anything to him. But you can, Robert. So go do it.' I love Diane with a love almost heterosexual in its blind mawkishness. So here I am. Do you want to know why that photograph made you cry?"

"No. I'm tired of amateur shrinks."

"Because it is the photograph that you have coveted all these long years. Anna in her place, locked in beauty, cultivated by distant desire. What keeps you here isn't the real Anna. It's guilt. You feel you have to make things right."

"No, it's not that simple," I said.

"Then why are you staying here?"

"I don't know. I have to figure that out."

Kalso sighed. "You are an irritating boy. You are irritating because you make me feel wise by comparison, and wisdom always suggests age, and age suggests the mortal end. So you depress me a little, making me play the doddering old sage. Nonetheless, I will pass on one more piece of hard-won wisdom: Understanding isn't worth shit. Understanding keeps the shrinks busy, distracts us from the great, thundering engines of time. We talk a lot of nonsense, wonder what it all means. But God isn't happy with all this understanding bullshit. He considers it the wildest presumption. It isn't why he put us here."

"I didn't know you were religious," I said.

Kalso ignored me. "We aren't here to figure stuff out. We are here to learn about acceptance. Acceptance, David. Stop holding your breath. Just exhale. You'll feel a lot better."

Kalso left soon after that, left on that heavy, pontifical note.

Christmas came. I gave Anna a framed original illustration from *The Summer Troll*. She gave me a tie. The new year came. Anna didn't try to kill herself again, but she wasn't very happy. "I shouldn't be here," she said. "It isn't right."

Then, one more miraculous time, Anna got well.

She had the volume turned up on the stereo and she was dancing in circles to "Baby, You're a Rich Man" when I came into the living room. It was late afternoon, shadows long in the room. She threw her arms around me.

"David! I'm so happy," she said.

It was news to me, but it appeared to be true. That wild, strong light was in her eyes again.

"I'm glad."

She saw that I was baffled, and she laughed at my confusion.

"You don't know. But I just learned myself."

She told me the good news.

She had had a physical examination that morning. She was pregnant.

"Congratulations, Anna." I could see it was the required thing to say.

"I hope it's a boy," Anna said. "Richard would have wanted a boy."

"Anna..."

"I always loved Richard. He was hard to know, but he was strong. I couldn't help loving him. I don't know if you can understand that."

On the contrary, despite the limited utility of understanding, I understood.

I left that week. I was holding nothing together. I could not tell myself that I was staying for Anna. Anna was happy without me, and one incongruity too many had robbed me of the proper emotional responses. A leafless tree, poking up through muddy ground, might suddenly strike me as tragic. I would want to cry. A beautiful sunset might fill me with rage. My responses were "inappropriate" as the gimlet-eyed professionals are wont to say. I left before anyone threw a net over me.

I telephoned Diane and told her I was leaving. I apologized for bad behavior. "Things aren't going so well with me and Charlie," she said, a confidence from nowhere.

I started missing Diane as soon as I hung up the phone.

I left Newburg early in the morning. I said goodby to Walker before I left. "This is her home," he said.

"Yes."

Newburg seemed anonymous in the morning light, a town that looked like any other town, nailed to the earth with fast food restaurants, gas stations, churches, shopping malls. Then, just as I pulled onto the highway, a great mass of black birds shot out of the trees, wheeling in a windy, rain-grey sky, and I wanted a drink for the first time in five years, and I leaned over the steering wheel and stepped on the gas. The sky seemed heavy, ready to collapse. The first large drops slapped against the windows just after I crossed the Virginia state line. I began to feel better. I stopped wanting a drink.

Epilogue

July 1986

Jennifer kissed me goodby and I waved to her. "See you on Sunday," she said, waving from her car.

The letter had been waiting for me when we got back from the beach, and I hadn't opened it in front of Jennifer. I didn't open it now, either. Instead, I went into the kitchen and started a pot of coffee.

That gave me time to think.

"I'm doing all right," I told the new, gleaming kitchen. New house, new love—amazing, elegant and undemanding Jennifer—and a new book completed, ready to go. I was proud of the book. It was another children's book, a flashlight shining on the underside of childhood, the monster-closet realm of fledgling nightmare, titled *The Curious Thunder.* Danny Brock, the hero of the book, is a kid afraid of thunderstorms who, it turns out, is right to be frightened. I didn't know what my editor was going to think of the book. It wasn't my usual airbrushed, bright-edged glory. But I was confident it would get published. I was proud of it.

Life was good. There wasn't any melodrama in it and that was fine. Jennifer had strong opinions about the eternal adolescent male's penchant for self-dramatization. I was glad I hadn't encountered her in my arm-waving, soul-rending youth. Those days were an embarrassment now.

I recognized the writing on the envelope, that distinctive, concentrated scrawl. I poured myself a cup of coffee and opened the letter while sitting at the kitchen table. Light poured down from a skylight. It was a house of skylights, filled with light's benediction, tolerating no brooding corners. Some mornings I hated it, hated its hearty morning smile.

The letter began, "Dear David—We miss you. It's been a good summer, and—before I forget—Richard is standing here and he says to tell you that he thinks your books are nifty. He is a great fan of yours, really."

211

It was like Anna to break silence as though only a day had elapsed. I hadn't heard from her in years.

I stopped reading the letter to pick up the photograph that had fallen out. Anna, in a man's shirt with the sleeves rolled up, held her wide-eyed son up to the camera, the both of them smiling. They were on the porch, in golden, morning light, and the little boy seemed pleased with the enterprise, his silky hair fluttering in a breeze, his round belly showing beneath a blue t-shirt. Anna looked, of course, angelic, full of unabashed mother-pride. There was a confidence I had never seen before, an authority in her crooked smile, the cant of her hips.

My hands were shaking as I put the photo down on the table. I felt a strange emotion, sitting there in my expensive, sunny home. I felt as light as a soap bubble. I felt weird and fraudulent.

I picked up the letter and continued reading. It was a chatty, easy letter, not an epistle to evoke strong emotion. She sounded happy and sweetly fixated on young Richard. She enclosed, in a postscript, Walker's telephone number in case I wanted to call.

I spent the rest of the day on the edge of calling.

I've never had any luck with phones, though. I feel like I'm talking to someone at the bottom of a well or a ghost on the moon and the end of a phone call always leaves me with a sense of loss and foreboding.

I don't love her anymore, at least not in the old, needy way. The desperation has been replaced by a deep affection and a realization that the bond between us is the immutable past. Memories are made of steel.

So I should leave the past alone. Still, I know that I can't let this letter go unanswered. It means more than its smooth surface would suggest.

And I don't know just what to say.

There's another alternative, of course. I'm done with another book. I was going to take a vacation anyway. I could just pop down there and surprise her. I know she'd be glad to see me.

I can almost see myself driving up that rutted, weedy road, wildflowers blooming in the dust, the mountains looming like the massive knees of god. She might be down by the lake, her child chasing a dragonfly along the reedy bank, laughing.

I could go there. The thought is attractive, a little unsettling.

No harm in it, though.